GRAFFITI CREEK

By
Matt Coleman

Brooklan,
Follow your dream of
being a model!! You're beautiful!!

Thank you

pandamoon
publishing

www.pandamoonpublishing.com

Jacket design and illustrations © Pandamoon Publishing

Art Design and Direction by Matthew Kramer: Pandamoon Publishing
Editing by Zara Kramer, Rachel Schoenbauer, Jessica Reino, and Forrest Driskel: Pandamoon Publishing

Pandamoon Publishing and the portrayal of a panda and a moon are registered trademarks of Pandamoon Publishing.

Library of Congress Cataloging-in-Publication Data is on file at the Library of Congress, Washington, DC

Edition: 1, ver. 1.00
ISBN-13: 978-1-945502-91-0

Foreward

Beyond the Bloodstains

I read a lot of crime fiction. Some of it is great, but the majority is superficial, formulaic, and trite. The book you are holding, Matt Coleman's *Graffiti Creek*, is none of those. This is a book about people caught in situations they don't deserve. This is a book about corruption and evil agendas. This is a thriller about escape and existence on the lam. Yeah, this is all those things, but it's also something much more special: a narrative in which everyone has a story, a background, a reason.

You see, the main problem with contemporary crime fiction is that the tropes that have come to characterize the genre are no longer impactful in most narratives. They have turned into flavorless ingredients thrown passionlessly into a bland broth that writers keep preparing again and again and again. Crime is a commonplace thing, but that doesn't mean a writer should treat their characters as puppets in order to tell a story about guns, violence, bad decisions, and drugs. In *Graffitti Creek*, the narrative revolves around people. These characters are alive. Cary is multilayered. Marlowe is nuanced. Hell, even the supporting characters act and talk like unique entities. This is what the genre should always strive for: memorable people instead of disposable cutouts. The way Coleman writes, characters feel human. Even those in the background are never simply used as props. When you read about homeless people huddled around a trashcan fire, the writing makes you see them as part of the landscape, the inevitable result of a system designed to swallow us and spit us back out as soon as we make a big mistake or a few small ones. They are not criminals. They are not insulted. Coleman is here as chronicler, not judge, and that allows his prose, and his heart, to shine.

Now, are you ready for the beautiful thing? Ready for the thing that pushes this novel into must-read territory? Well, here it is: balance. Yeah, Coleman wrote a novel that shines a light on "bad" people while treating homeless individuals and those from the wrong side of the track with the humanity they deserve, but he also engages fully with every element readers have come to expect from the genre. There is plenty of blood and violence here. There are twists and turns and high-speed chases and screams and curses and guns and a brilliant scene that includes two Hollywood giants about to shoot it out (I'll let you get to that on your own without more details). There are secret agendas and questions and hiding and escaping from a vehicle as the bullets fly. All of that make this a book that, besides having a ton of heart and being superbly written, entertains constantly in that deep, brain-tingling way only great fiction can.

Now that you know what makes this an outstanding read, dig in. Join Coleman and he hides Do Right and Seamus from you. Join him in looking at a dark, seedy, corrupt world from the inside and with authenticity to spare. Dig in and enjoy a novel that could be used to teach a course on the psychogeography of crime. Most importantly, come join a writer in an adventure that will undoubtedly place him on all those lists about authors to watch. Welcome to *Graffiti Creek*. Oh, and keep your eyes peeled because sometimes the stuff on the walls is actually blood, and Coleman is going to whisper in your ear about the stuff that lies beyond it.

— **Gabino Iglesias Author of** ***ZERO SAINTS, HUNGRY DARKNESS,*** **and** ***GUTMOUTH***

Critical Reviews

"*Graffiti Creek* by Matt Coleman is a non-stop thrill ride that may be the best adventure/chase novel you read this year. From the opening pages, the action begins and keeps the reader on the edge of their seat all the way through to the climactic finale. However, Graffiti Creek is more than just an action adventure novel. Mr. Coleman takes particular care in bringing forth a nuanced cast of characters; each with a story to tell, each believable in their actions and motivations. *Graffiti Creek* is also deftly plotted with more twists and turns within the pages than one of Cary Trubody's many pulse-pounding acts of escape. Mr. Coleman has produced a first-rate thriller. And one that screams to be read in one sitting; those with heart conditions exempted, of course." — **Neil A White for Readers' Favorite**

"I dare you to be able put it down with thoughts of coming back to it later. Just make sure you have a few hours free to read it in one go…and not before bed…or you will be running down alleyways, climbing through windows, wading through Graffiti Creek or finding yourself locked in a car trunk all night long! The tension jumps right off the page. With bodies being knifed, shot and brutalized all over the place, this is one intense read." — **Viga Boland for Readers' Favorite**

"A well-written crime novel with elements of mystery, suspense, and action all equally intertwined in one plot. … A lot like a puzzle in that the story could only be solved when all of the puzzle pieces were in their correct places. I truly enjoyed trying to untangle and solve the plot myself throughout the story, even though I never managed to guess correctly what was going on." — **Sefina Hawke for Readers' Favorite**

"Full of tension and apprehension so much that it touches every one of your senses. A superb story from start to the climactic finish. The ending was perfect and not what I was expecting, because the plot constantly led you down one path and then took you in another direction … a perfect story for anyone who likes a good thriller and whodunit." — **Lesley Jones for Readers' Favorite**

"Readers will be hooked from the very start. The prose is smooth and often downright brilliant in its simplicity. ... **9.50 out of 10**." — **The BookLife Prize by *Publishers Weekly***

"If you like books that have cops, mystery, suspense, mistaken identity, some curse words then you may want to give *Graffiti Creek* by Matt Coleman a try." — **Heidi Lynn's Book Reviews**

Dedication

To Sam.

GRAFFITI CREEK

Chapter 1

On a wall of graffiti, blood splatter gets lost. One more color among the others. Dots and splashes of red across a spray of fonts with too many joints. They were all hard to read already. But with two eyes swollen shut and a fresh overlay of his own blood, Dante couldn't make out a single word on the bridge in front of him.

Detective Mark Thompson gripped and regripped a set of brass knuckles on his right hand. Behind him, his partner, Detective Richard Jolly, stood holding a gun like it was his wife's purse and she was trying on shoes.

Dante spit out a tooth. "I ain't got no more copies, man."

Thompson nodded, shrugging with his whole body. His face even shrugged. "I hear you, brother." He pulled a phone out of his pocket and waggled it in Dante's face. "Why don't you tell me how to unlock this little old phone of yours and let me make sure?"

Dante struggled to raise his head to look at it. Snot and blood dripped down his ripped shirt. When he turned, the light coming in through the trees revealed a knuckle-shaped dent in the side of his head. He tried to talk, but it came out as unintelligible wanderings, "I ain't g—got a copy, m—man. I ain't d—done n—nothin'. I ain't m—man m—man."

Thompson guffawed. "My man! My man! There we go! Now we're chatting like a couple of old pals, huh, Dante? My man, Dante."

Jolly sniffed. "I think he's done, Mark."

Dante kept rambling, snuffling, stuttering, sputtering. His hands were starting to tremble.

Thompson knelt down and got right next to his face. He held Dante up by the bicep, steadying him. "All you gotta do is tell me your code, Dante. We can make this all stop. You got that left in you, buddy?" He tapped lightly on Dante's head with the phone. "You got six numbers left in all those scrambled eggs up there?"

Prying open his left eye, Dante managed to stare into Thompson's splotchy pink face. His breath betrayed his propensity for drinking on the job and the cigarettes he couldn't give up even after a minor heart attack. Dante forced a smile. "You're s—such a f—fucking cliché."

Thompson stood back up and looked back at Jolly with a flailing flop of both arms. "This asshole wants to die slowly, Dick."

Jolly laughed. "They always do. Until they don't."

Thompson wheeled back around and placed the heel of a boot onto the hand Dante had been propping himself up with. He pivoted and ground and grated Dante's fingers into the cold concrete. Dante sobbed and collapsed, pawing at Thompson's leg with his free hand. Thompson sucked at his teeth. "What part of this…cliché is good for you, Dante? In fact, correct me if I'm wrong, brother, but my cliché usually leaves your cliché a little worse for wear. Am I right?"

Dante hung his head into his chest and cried. He mumbled, "Fo …fo …tuh…oh…un…fee."

Thompson let up on his hand and took a step back. "Now, you gonna have to speak some English there, boy."

Jolly stepped forward in front of Thompson, casually tossed out, "Four, four, two, zero, one, three. I got it," and shot Dante in the head.

Chapter 2

All the traffic lights pulsed yellow. They interspersed the road like an airport runway. Cary leaned over onto an elbow as she drove, the caution lights tinting her face saffron every twenty seconds or so. Johnna slouched in the passenger seat and drunkenly chastised her in rhythm with the lights.

"You're 'mbarrassed of me," Johnna mumbled into her palm while stifling a hiccup.

Cary rolled her eyes. "I am not embarrassed of you. I took you around my friends, didn't I?"

Johnna shook her head in lazy loops. "You played cards the whole time. Never touched me."

Cary sat up and switched driving hands to reach for Johnna's leg. "I was winning, Johnna. Did you see the table? Three of those guys kept throwing money away trying to impress me with their bravado. I pegged them as eye-raping assholes during the first hand. All it took was a flirty bat of the lashes and they lost all semblance of a poker face. I walked away with $3,000, for Christ's sake."

Johnna jerked away. "They don't even know we're together! You inta-introduced me as your friend." She punctuated the last two slurred words with air quotes and the voice of a teasing child.

"You are my friend." Johnna curled a lip and glared at her, so Cary scrambled to cover. "My best friend. The love of my life. My girlfriend. You're all of those things. I told you: it's a gradual process. It'll be a bit of a shock to some of them. And I refuse to be reduced to a label. If I surprise everyone with it, then I become someone's 'lesbian friend.' I am not going to be a token, or some sort of badge my jackass friends get to iron onto their jean jackets."

Johnna flailed her hands. "'s been two months, Cary Ann! How long would you wait if I was a guy? Huh?"

The argument had distracted Cary from the road. One of those flashing traffic lights she had cruised through had been red. Her brain registered it two seconds too late. She checked her rearview mirror for validation. The red traffic light throbbed at her like an angry eye. And swirling blue and red police lights erupted from an empty bank parking.

"Shit. Shit, shit, shit."

Johnna craned her neck around wildly. "Wha? Wha's happening?"

Cary eyed her hard. "Don't talk. Sit quietly and let me get a ticket or whatever. Please." She noticed Johnna's purse hanging open in the floorboard, a thick wad of bills clearly visible. "Shit. Hand me that money." She snapped a hand up. "In a way that doesn't look like you're passing me a wad of money."

Johnna reached down to pick up her purse with a drunk's deliberation. She passed the roll of hundreds and twenties over to Cary. Although Cary's mother hated anything with *the sartorial stylings of a militant lesbian*, the tawny green field jacket was still a wardrobe staple. Luckily, its inside pockets held car keys, a phone, and huge wads of money with ease.

Cary pulled into an empty restaurant parking lot and turned off her car. She started fishing for her driver's license as the police officer strolled toward them with a flashlight. Cary hit the window button, but she had killed the engine. She laughed at herself and turned the car back on. The policeman put a hand on his gun and shouted, "Ma'am! Turn the car off!"

Cary jumped, startled, calling out, "I'm only trying to roll down the window!"

The officer backed up and yelled back, "Step out of the vehicle! Both of you! No sudden movements! Hands where I can see them!"

Cary turned the car back off. Johnna gasped and stammered, "What the hell?"

Cary snapped at her. "Do what he says. Try to act sober, Johnna."

They both eased out and followed the directions to walk to the back of the car. He guided them to sit on the curb next to where Cary had parked. His flashlight alternated between their faces, sending their hands up into defensive positions and making Johnna groan in annoyance. The cop loomed over them and spoke sharply. "You ladies been drinking tonight?"

Johnna mumbled something, but Cary spoke over her, "My friend has. I haven't. I'm taking her home. I'm sorry about the light. They had all been yellow before that and—"

The cop held a hand out. "Ma'am. That's enough. I didn't ask. If I want to know something, I'll ask about it." He shined a light on the car. "Anything outstanding on you or your vehicle? Any warrants? Anything I need to know about?"

Cary shook her head. "No. No, sir. I—I'm a graphic designer."

Johnna scoffed under her breath. "Friend. You did it again. Did you even realize it?"

The officer shined his light back at Johnna but didn't respond. He looked back at Cary. "I'm going to check on those plates. I'll be back for your license and registration."

He walked back to his car and sat in the driver's seat with the door open. Johnna continued to mumble things about *friend* this and *friend* that. Cary shushed her multiple times while trying to ascertain what the police officer was doing. Over the course of the next few minutes, Johnna slumped over and fell asleep on the ground. And the cop abandoned his radio and took a call on his cell phone. Cary squinted and concentrated, trying her best to read his lips, but all she could make out was a "Yes, sir," right before he disconnected the call.

He sauntered back over. Cary could make out Reynolds or Reynard on his name badge in the streetlight. He stopped about ten feet away from her, glanced at Johnna, then stared at Cary. "What's your name?"

"Cary Ann Trubody. You want my license?"

He shrugged. "Sure."

She fished it out of a pocket and held it up between two fingers. Instead of accepting it, the officer jerked his chin up at her in an aggressive order. "Up. Face the car."

Cary frowned. Watched him hold the buckle of his belt and sneer at her. Her chin quivered, but she rose. She held out the license, but the cop motioned with his head to her car. "Set it on the car." She slowly turned around. Her pulse quickened. His footsteps churned the gravel of the parking lot toward her. She laid the license down on the back of the car. The cop sucked in on his teeth. "Both hands on the car, fingers splayed." Cary did as asked. Her breath shuddered. He came up behind her, almost touching, and reached around to take her license.

The cop stood right behind her. She could feel him breathing. He flicked her license with a thumb. "Cary Ann Trubody. Five-five, huh? Shame they don't put weight on here anymore, Cary Ann. It's a good picture. Looks like you were a bit thinner then."

Cary swallowed a gag.

Before he could say more, two more cars arrived simultaneously. One was a patrol car, lights going. The other was also a police car, but unmarked. They both pulled in to pin in her car at the front. A female officer climbed out of the patrol car, while two pot-bellied detectives in cheap suits rolled out of the unmarked car.

They all three eyed her as they walked past. One of the detectives asked Officer Reynolds/Reynard, "Is it her?"

He said, "Appears to be. Ask Officer Doyle."

The detective barked, "Go on, Doyle."

Cary heard a woman's voice behind her, commanding, but softer. "Turn around where I can see you."

She did as asked and faced the female officer. She was an inch or two shorter than Cary. Her hair was tied back in a tight ponytail. All of her features angled into dark corners and mysterious points except her eyes. They perfectly matched her skin's deep shade of brown. Soft eyes. Sad. They stared at one another for a moment. Officer Doyle squinted, closed her eyes for a beat, swallowing regret, or resignation. She sighed. "It's her."

Cary batted her eyes at everyone there. "Who? I don't know you. I don't know any of you. I was just driving home from a party."

Officer Reynard (she could make it out now) laughed. "Some party. Three o'clock in the morning?"

One of the detectives stepped forward and ordered her to turn back around. "Where do you keep your phone, Miss Trubody?"

Cary stuttered, confused, "It's—it's in my—my back pocket. Why?"

Without hesitation, the detective slipped her phone out of her pocket and walked over to his partner. They huddled together and studied the screen of Cary's phone. The partner scrutinized Cary. "You got a passcode?"

Cary shook her head.

They spent several minutes perusing through her phone, while Cary tried to peer over her shoulder. Officer Reynard growled at her to turn around several times.

Heaving a sigh, the detective who took Cary's phone walked up waving it at her. "Where is it, Miss Trubody?"

She half-turned. "Where…where is what?"

His partner stared at the night sky. "Jesus. Don't do this."

Cary quivered her head back and forth. "I—I don't know what you're talking about. I think you have the wrong—"

The detective cut her off and turned to Reynard. "You got zip ties?"

Reynard nodded and pulled out a black zip tie. The detective took it and patted Cary on the shoulder. "Hands behind your back, fingers interlaced."

She laughed out objections but did as she was told. The detective guided her toward the unmarked car and placed her in the backseat. He glanced back at the other three. "Get her car and follow me. Reynard, you take care of the friend."

Doyle almost raised her hand, then embarrassedly squeaked. "What about me, sir?"

He laughed. "Get the hell out of here, Doyle. We're done."

Cary craned her neck up from the backseat. "What am I being arrested for?"

The detective chuckled. "You aren't arrested, sweetheart. We're just taking a little drive."

Chapter 3

The Hill Street Cafe sat tucked into a row of squat brick shops less than a block from the beginnings of a labyrinthine complex of governmental buildings. It was one of more than fifty restaurants within walking distance of Dollar Hill—a name given to an area populated by lawyers and politicians.

And cops.

There were cops mingled in and around every part of Dollar Hill. Especially the Hill Street Cafe. Despite its shit box appearance, the Hill Street Cafe had earned a reputation as a favorite hangout of cops, city politicians, and high-ranking officials working in Dollar Hill.

Dollar Hill, for all its problems, championed diversity, with local lobbyists and young lawyers coming from every creed, color, and constitution. However, the Hill Street Cafe remained one of the last vestiges of Old Straight White Male America. Which meant looking too brown or gay could make someone stand out a little.

And Sameer Zardari looked exactly like a Pakistani Freddy Mercury.

On his first visit to the Hill Street Cafe, he even wore a denim jacket and black and white vertically-striped shirt with his Converse high-tops and slim-cut jeans. He peered down at himself in contrast to the suits and police uniforms scattered among the booths and sighed. A waitress approached holding a steaming pot of coffee. She eyed him up and down with a smirk. "Is this your first time here, sweetheart?"

"Well, I drove by once. I noticed the name of your establishment. It stood out to me because, as a child I used to watch reruns of *Hill Street Blues*." Sameer chuckled softly to himself. "I was always partial to the episode where Sgt. Belker wore the chicken suit and—" The waitress had added a pair of raised eyebrows to her smirk, so Sameer nodded and mumbled out a "Yes. It is my first time."

Her amusement grew into a full smile. "You can seat yourself." She leaned closer and almost whispered, "There's an empty booth at the back. Kinda out of the way. I'll be with you in a second."

Sameer nodded a thanks and made his way to the back booth. He felt the need to almost cover himself as if he were naked as he walked between booths and tables full of loaded stares.

After a minute or so, the waitress reappeared with a menu and a notepad. Sameer ordered a cup of coffee and refused the menu. The waitress—Juliana, according to her name tag—wrinkled her brow at him. "You don't want to eat?"

Sameer smiled. "I don't eat much breakfast. I find early meals to be disrupting. Not to say—I do not mean they cause me to—in general, breakfast simply makes me feel heavy, like a—"

"Sweetie," Juliana returned the smile, but interrupted. She glanced over her shoulder at the other patrons, who were still steadily throwing glances in Sameer's direction. "I don't mean to pressure you, but it might draw less attention if you ordered a pancake or something."

Sameer followed her gaze to the rest of the cafe. He noticed a couple of pie plates on the bar with pies resting under them. "Is that a chocolate pie?"

Juliana laughed a little. "Yeah. You want chocolate pie?"

"My mother made what she called 'icebox pie.' Her pie had whipped cream. I've found that I prefer meringue as an adult. The slight caramelization of the top of it appeals to—" Sameer pursed his lips and nodded. "I'll take a slice, yes."

Juliana flipped closed her notepad and laughed again. "You got it. I guess that's the advantage of being a grown-ass adult, huh? Nobody's going to say you can't have pie for breakfast."

They shared a smile before Juliana left to get coffee and pie. Sameer leaned back into his booth, slouching down to provide at least some modicum of privacy. The place was cufflink to cufflink with middle-aged and older white men. They all reeked of wealth and their eyes were hardened by animosity. He didn't find any faces he recognized, but, then again, Seamus knew city politics better than Sameer. More importantly though, he didn't see a single friendly face in the room. He couldn't imagine cold approaching any of the stuffed shirts currently eyeing him like he had horns.

Juliana brought a slice of pie and refilled his coffee a few times. Each trip, she smiled and offered some small talk—a comment about traffic, updating him on the recent switch of coffee brands, complimenting his jacket. When it came time to pay, Sameer realized Juliana might be the only agreeable local he was going to find.

He pulled out a twenty and slid it toward her when she started to hand him the bill. Juliana took the twenty and tossed out, "I'll be right back with some change, sweetie."

Sameer sat forward to catch her. "I don't—I don't need change."

Juliana stopped and turned with raised eyebrows. "You sure?"

Sameer nodded. "I would like to maybe speak with you for a moment, however."

Juliana shifted her weight and gave him a sad smile usually followed by some polite mention of a boyfriend back at home. She started with, "What is it you want to talk about?"

Sameer nodded once and placed his hands on the table in front of him. "My husband."

Juliana's countenance flashed a mixture of surprise and the facial calisthenics of trying not to come across as offensively surprised. She shook her head. "Do I know him or something?"

Sameer shrugged. "Possibly. He is missing. I haven't heard from him in days. Which is not like him. But he's an adult, which means not much being done."

Juliana squinted and nodded. "I'm so sorry." She cocked her head. "But I'm not sure—"

Sameer cut her off. "His name is Seamus Fitzgerald." He pulled a photo out of his pocket. The candid shot showed him and Seamus together at a friend's wedding. They were both in suits and smiling broadly. "His work friends sometimes called him Fitz or Fitzy."

Juliana picked up the photo and studied it before smiling. "You look so happy." She handed it back. "What kind of work?"

Sameer took the photo back with a nodded thanks. "He's a reporter. This is the last place he came. That I know of."

Juliana's eyes suddenly jumped around, nervous. She cleared Sameer's cup and plate, leaning closer to him. "Do you smoke?"

"I once had a cigar. I was at an open market in—" Sameer put a hand on his mouth and shook his head, "No."

Juliana used his napkin to wipe at a spot on the table. "You should start. I take my break one building over in a little alley. Five minutes." She stood back up. "I wish I could help you. I'm sorry, sweetie."

Sameer flustered for a beat but recovered. "Th—thank you. No, I appreciate your help. And the pie. Quite delicious. Thank you." He stood to leave, nodded awkwardly to Juliana, and hurried out.

Outside, Sameer snapped his head in both directions. To his right, an intersection of walkways and bike paths zigzagged off into the maze of governmental complexes. The next building was almost a block away. A row of squat buildings stretched out to his left. The closest one resembled a former restaurant itself. It was vacant. He turned left and walked around the vacant restaurant to find a quiet alley.

Midway down he found a table left over from the restaurant. Two metal chairs sat on either side around an old cup full of cigarette butts on the table.

Sameer pulled out one of the chairs, which had old green paint flaking off of it, and sat down. He didn't have to wait long. Within minutes, Juliana came walking up from the back of the building. She lit a cigarette as she approached and took the seat across from Sameer. Holding out a hand, she said from around her cigarette, "Can I see his picture again?"

Sameer fished out the glossy three-by-five and handed it to her. Juliana examined it and, this time, nodded solemnly. "Seamus 'Fitzy' Fitzgerald, huh?" She laughed and handed back the photo. "His name sounds like a reporter's name."

Sameer smiled. "Have you seen him?"

Juliana nodded. "He's been in. Several times. I didn't recognize him from the picture at first. He worked a little harder at blending in than you did." She laughed. "But yeah, I've seen him. When you said he was a reporter, it rang a bell."

Sameer shook his head. "Why?"

Juliana took a drag. "Well, he came in probably seven or eight times. The first five or so? I didn't think a thing of it. But a couple of weeks back, he started asking questions. General stuff. Like, about who's been in. Who eats with who. That type of thing." She shrugged. "At first, I didn't think much of it. We get some recognizable people in here some. So it brings out the occasional star struck question."

Sameer squinted at her. "At first?"

Juliana nodded. "Yeah. So he keeps it up. More and more questions. After a time or two, another one of the waitresses caught sight of him outside with some kid videoing the front of the cafe. Our boss looked into him a little and said he thinks the guy is a reporter."

Sameer shook his head. "Why would it matter?"

Juliana shrugged. "Doesn't. To me. But our customers are private about their lunch conversation. The last time your husband ate lunch here, he barely touched his food. He was too interested in trying to listen in on the conversation at another table."

"Who?"

Juliana cast a glance back over her shoulder. "There's a state senator and a federal court judge who eat here together all the time. Your husband had asked about them before. Freeman and Halter. Not sure about first names, but you should be able to find them easy enough." She smoked nervously, finishing one cigarette and quickly lighting another. "But the other day, when the cops joined them, that's when your husband showed particular interest. And the thing is, after he left—your husband—those cops followed him out. Or, at least I think they did. It looked like they did."

12

Sameer dug a pen out of his pocket and found an old receipt to write on the back of. "The cops, do you know their names?"

Juliana grimaced and shook her head. "No. I'm sorry. I remember seeing them a time or two, but I never waited on them. They're detectives though. I can always tell from the cheap suits."

Chapter 4

Johnna sobered up fast. The back of a squad car has that effect. Some berry-scented air freshener mingled with the scent of dried vomit. Her sister used the same fragrance—Mulberry—to mask the smell of what she had done in the bathroom one time. Johnna and her friends called the aroma "Shitberry." Her sister couldn't shake the nickname until college. She leaned forward in her seat, pushing her forehead against the plexiglass between her and Officer Reynard. "My nose itches. Can we take these zip ties off? I'm not going to try anything."

Officer Reynard drove on stoically. He called back, "Sit back, ma'am. Please. For your own protection."

Johnna did as told but asked, sweetly, "Am I under arrest?"

Officer Reynard met her eyes in the rearview mirror but didn't respond. He was an attractive guy—dark features and wavy hair flipped back onto his neck. He looked like the kind of guy who could grow a full beard in a few days. He carried himself with arrogance of junior college baseball player.

Johnna inwardly began to panic. Cary snagged her a job interview at a local magazine. But if she got arrested for public intoxication, then she might still be locked up by Monday morning. Surely she couldn't be jailed for being a little tipsy in the passenger seat of a car. Or maybe she could. Johnna knew dick about the law. But she did know one thing: junior college baseball players.

Her hands were locked behind her but rolled her shoulders forward enough to create a little extra cleavage. She pouted her lips into the officer's reflection in the mirror. "Thank you for being so concerned about my well-being, officer."

Reynard chuckled.

"You know, I've always been a huge supporter of the police."

He rolled his eyes. "Oh yeah?"

She let her voice go breathy. "Oh, yeah. Huge." She licked her lips.

Reynard let her advances lie for a beat before swallowing and creaking out. "How supportive are you willing to be?"

Johnna swayed her head, in thought. "Oh, I don't know. Will it," she bit her bottom lip, "get me off?"

Reynard pulled back behind a factory building. A clothes manufacturer of some sort. Johnna thought she recognized the name on the sign—cheap jeans, if memory served. *Wonderful,* she thought to herself, *I'm about to get cop-raped in the parking lot of a shitty jeans factory.*

Reynard parked up against the building. The lot loomed empty, with security lights creating glowing circles in a repeating pattern. The cop car nosed into a swath of shadow stretching from a dumpster to a loading dock.

Reynard opened the back door and helped her out. He gently turned her around and ran fingers down her bare arms. Johnna glanced back in a forced flirtation. He breathed in the essence of her hair as he snapped off the zip tie.

She turned and leaned against the car, trying to smile so she wouldn't show her bluff. Her facade was cracking and she realized it. If she wanted this to work, she would have to dive into it. Reckless abandon and all that shit. Johnna started to slide down to her knees, but Reynard caught her by the arms and raised her back up. She frowned and moped, "But don't you want me to show my appreciation?"

Reynard slid his big hands, with the hairy knuckles, up her arms. Onto her collar bones. He grinned and shook his head in puzzlement. The expression of a little kid with a magnifying glass in the sun. Waiting. Wondering how long before the ant catches fire. His hands continued. Onto her neck.

Johnna squirmed and lost all pretense. "What are you—"

The last word choked out into a croak. Johnna scratched at Reynard's arms. His uniform was thick material. One of her nails broke off completely trying to claw through it. Reynard pressed a meaty knee across her thighs, holding her legs against the car. He kept squeezing, his fingers beginning to meet and lock around her throat. Johnna thought about her sister again. And Cary. And then, nothing.

Chapter 5

Cary wrestled with the zip tie around her wrists. She'd never been bound before. It hurt. Settling on a halfway comfortable position, she leaned her face against the cool of the glass. She had started into panic sweats, feeling the tingling burn creep through her face. She waited for the police station to come into view, but it didn't. They were heading out of town.

She tried to compose herself by talking. "*Take a little drive?* Isn't that a bit on the nose? Do they give you a cop stereotype guidebook, or is it more of an oral tradition?"

The detective snorted a little but said nothing.

Cary pushed at the door handle with a knee, trying to wedge the lever up to try the door. "I don't suppose I get to ask for a lawyer in this situation, right? Get my one phone call, maybe?"

The detective eyed her through the rearview mirror. "One phone call's a myth, honey."

Cary raised her eyebrows. "You don't get one phone call?"

The detective smiled. "You get as many as you want, within reason. As long as you're not being an asshole." He stopped smiling. "When you're under arrest. You? You aren't under arrest."

She nodded. "Oh, you're right. I'm going for a drive. With my good friend whose name I don't know and who handcuffed my hands behind my back."

He nodded. "Oh, we can be friends. You tell me where it is, and we'll be best friends. Braid each other's hair and all kinds of shit."

Cary glanced at his balding, pasty, freckled head and laughed a little. "Where what is? What are you talking about?" She wedged her knee under the door and pushed. The child...or prisoner-safety lock kept the door stuck, as she expected.

The detective shrugged. "We can go that route, too. Your choice."

Cary fought back tears of frustration and stared out the window as the scenery grew less and less familiar. The ambient light from buildings and street lamps faded like her eyes were coming into focus and starting to pick out constellations she couldn't name.

Concrete gave way to trees. Lanes narrowed. The straight-line, masculine grids of the city melted into feminine curves of countryside. Everything darkened. Every dirt road snaking out of sight into the woods intimated mysteries in clusters like mosquitos. Cary cringed at the thought she might be about to become another one.

They wound to a stop in front of a little concrete bridge. Underneath, a creek meandered off into the trees and rocks until disappearing into shadowy bends and twinkles of running water over a bed of moony stones. The bridge itself emerged as a vestige of nearby civilization—an altar to the city amidst the half-forgotten hinterlands.

Graffiti coated the length of the bridge. Some caught the eye in artistic expression, with stylized letters and cartoonish figures peeking out from behind them. In other spots, pure watertower scribbling. There were professions of love with dates and names and unintelligible abbreviations.

The detective pulled Cary out of the car, and they stood staring at the graffiti for a quiet minute. Cary leered over at him. "Where are we?"

He pointed with a nod of his head. "They call it Graffiti Creek. Kids drive out here from the city and spray paint shit on this bridge. Try to make sure whenever they evaporate in the city, there's still some record of them somewhere. The world forgets. Graffiti Creek always remembers."

They turned to the sound of a car pulling up behind them. The detective's partner bobbed behind the wheel of Cary's car. He pulled off the road and bounded down around the creek, angling up and pointing the car back up a hill toward the bridge and Cary.

The detective had gone to his trunk and pulled out an old water hose and some duct tape. He met his partner coming up the hill and traded him the hose and tape for a can of spray paint. The partner headed back toward Cary's car, while the detective walked to the bridge, shaking his can. He called back, "Find anything in the phone? Boyfriend?"

The partner answered, "Yeah. Johnny."

The detective stopped and cocked his head at Cary. "Johnny?"

The partner laughed. "That's what it said."

The detective shrugged and let out a *huh*. He scrawled, "I love you, Johnny. I'm so sorry. CAT" on the side of the bridge in neon orange letters. He scowled down the hill at his partner, who taped the hose to Cary's tailpipe. He tossed the can into the creek. "Orange, Dick? Really?"

Dick, the dick, yelled back. "Picked up the first one. Does it matter?"

The detective walked back and grabbed Cary by the arm. "Guess not."

He dragged her to her car and threw her into the driver's seat. The car's engine hummed, window cracked. Cary started into a chorus of: *What are you doing? Why are you doing this? What did I do?* But they shut the door and taped the hose into the window, sending a plume of dirty smoke right into her lap.

The detectives took a jaunty stroll back to their car, where Cary could just make them out as they sat on the hood to wait.

To wait on her to die.

Cary's throat hurt and her lips smacked with streaming tears. She hadn't even registered how loud she had been trying to scream, how frantically she wept and wailed, how terrified she was. The whole ride and even the walk to her car, Cary felt cool, hardened. But in the quiet of the pooling exhaust, she could recognize what her brother used to call "flight brain," some imagined self she created to make her feel safe. Cary's brother, Casey, was a few years older and prone to stages. His most memorable stage had been that of Casey Trubody, Survivalist Trainer. As a pre-teen, Cary had gotten dragged by the ponytails more times than she could count into the woods so Casey could put her through what had always felt like a useless stream of survival drills. And they would drill over and over and over. Because Casey Trubody, Survivalist Trainer, always told her: "In crisis, there's no time to think. Muscle memory, Cary. You need it to be muscle memory."

She had no time to think. The muscle memory exercise taking root in her head was one she had always felt pretty certain her Survivalist Trainer learned from the TV show *Lost*. Cary closed her eyes and counted slowly, letting her fear fill her body. "Lean into the fear," Casey would say. Let it have you. But only for five seconds. "Don't give it one second more," he'd say it while punctuating each word with a sharp tap to Cary's forehead. And at the silent five count, he'd snap. Cary could hear it as clearly as she could smell the poisoned thickness in the air. She started to hack and cough. Maybe her mind sped up the effects of the exhaust, but the windows were clouded over and Cary had no clue how long something like this took. She could barely see.

Which meant they couldn't see her either.

She shot her hands down under her thighs and wriggled until they came up the other side. She reached down and untied both shoes, and then looped a lace through her ziptie. She painstakingly tied one lace to the one on the other shoe. Working her legs like riding a bike, Cary sawed at the ziptie until the plastic popped loose. She moved both wrists in circles, working out the painful ridges cut into them, and allowed herself a smug nod of appreciation. Getting out of zip ties had been Casey Trubody, Survivalist Trainer's third lesson. They made it into a YouTube video. She reached for the door but stopped. If she stepped out, they'd put her right back with better restraints.

A car is a hell of a thing to get out of if the doors are off limits. Casey's most terrifying lesson had been one on escaping a car submerged in water. Pressure builds around the doors so they won't open. And breaking a window is damn near impossible. Cary knew both of these to be true because her borderline insane brother had locked her in an old jalopy and shoved it into a lake. Casey had to dive in to save her. The first time.

Cary pulled the emergency brake and put the car in neutral. She pulled her shoelaces all the way out and tied one end around the emergency brake release lever in the dashboard.

Coughing and panting, one hand over her mouth and nose, Cary squirmed into the backseat and pulled down the middle console. The opening led to the trunk, where a trunk release faced away from Detective Dick and his sidekick, Detective Evil.

She glanced down at her hips and whimpered, "Dammit all, Cary. This. This is why you should have skipped a dessert or two."

Normally, Cary felt curvy. But occasionally, such as while cramming herself through the narrow opening into the trunk, she felt thick—maybe even a touch chunky. She finally tumbled through into the fetal position in the trunk. The air was clearer and she took a couple of deep breaths of stale, but clean air. She brushed herself off and clucked her tongue. "Nope. Still curvy."

She fumbled around until she found the lever to open the trunk from the inside. Holding the trunk to keep it from popping wide open, she pulled the lever and pressed her face to the opening, siphoning in air greedily. She steeled her nerves and yanked the shoelace as hard as she could.

And nothing happened.

The car sat there, still and silent, filling with toxic fumes. Then, very gradually, it started rolling. Rolling. Faster. Too fast. The hill sloped steeper and longer than she had been able to discern in the dark. Cary would end up farther from the Dicks, but she was about to hit the creek bed at a fifteen-mile-per-hour clip.

Cary went ahead and let the trunk fly open and braced herself. A cluster of rocks blossomed to her right. Without hesitating she jumped from out of the trunk, trying to clear the rocks and hit the water in a roll. In the process, she lost a laceless shoe and banged a knee against a rock. But she landed smooth. Wet, but smooth.

Graffiti Creek

The car careened off to the opposite side from where she landed. She rolled into a ball and came up running. The water came only ankle-deep. Cary kicked off her other shoe to regain some balance and worked her way to the bank. She didn't look back, but she gleaned shouting and running.

The rocks were battering her feet, but she didn't dare slow down. She cut off onto a trail into the woods winding up toward the road. If she made it to the road, she may find a car. At the very least the pavement would be easier on her feet to run. Both of the detectives looked out of shape, and fifty-ish—a good twenty years on her. The slight hill kept her oriented toward the road. She weaved through trees, the limbs scratching her neck and whipping her arms.

Stumbling out into the road, Cary paused and searched up and down for any sign of civilization. Looking to her right, she spotted Detective Dick emerging thirty yards away. They eyed each other for a moment before Dick pulled a gun from under his sports coat. Cary ducked and ran for the tree line. Something whizzed past a tree near her head, sending flakes of bark splintering all around her. A second later a pop jolted her heart, like someone popping a plastic bag right next to her.

She ran hard, staying in the tree line and keeping her head down. She stayed close to the road, even though the tree-nicking and proceeding crack happened three more times. As she ran, she picked up a different noise. Distant, but growing. A breathy whistle. The familiar horn of a train. They had crossed tracks shortly before they came to a stop. She picked up her pace. To her left heavy footsteps pounded and panting hissed through the trees. Behind her, feet on the gravel of the road, moving fast. She was being chased and flanked.

Then she saw it. The light. Barreling toward her at an angle. Through a clearing ahead she could make out the tracks. The train screamed in deafening wails now. She wasn't going to make it. If the train cut her off, it would trap her with the two detectives.

Two more close misses and pops. She ducked and tried not to slow down. The train burst through the tree line, fully visible now, less than fifty feet away. She didn't scrutinize the gun. Dick struck her as the revolver type. He fired six shots, right? It was the only chance she had.

She bolted for the road and glanced back. Dick swore and fumbled with bullets. She picked up speed on the road and sprinted for the tracks. The train's whistle blared and shouts brayed on all sides of her. The tracks were right in front of her, and she felt the train's power bearing down. She took one stretched out leap over the tracks.

The wind from the passing train slapped at her legs as she rolled safely to the other side. Looking back, she watched the detectives search for her through the gaps. Cary turned to keep running. She had a head start, not a safe harbor.

Chapter 6

Marlowe last went to a party somewhere between his fifth and sixth years of college. He used to love them. But after eight years, he needed to shore up and finish out his accounting degree. And then he got a real job. And he realized right away he didn't want to stay in entry-level for any longer than necessary. Marlowe signed up for every survey team, every after-hours review of books, and every extra bit of grunt work. Whenever a promotion came up, he wanted to be the one who "put in his time." So parties got replaced by audits, like the one he begged out of when his little brother came up missing.

Missing was nothing new. Marlowe and his baby sister had been hunting down their brother, the middle child, since he hit junior high. Every time, he ended up in a place like this. Some run-down house in a neighborhood where people didn't file noise complaints. Marlowe forgot how the music felt somatic. Every part of him sensed it. The tips of his fingers even buzzed with it. Each thump gave him this feeling in his heart and stomach, like the nervousness of kissing a girl for the first time. Walking around in a party did something to him—almost too much—made him want to close his eyes and drift up into the social ether.

Marlowe waded through clouds of smoke, trying to keep from breathing too much of it in. He talked to women. As dangerous as approaching women at a party could be, they were always more receptive. A trio of them hung against a wall and held red plastic cups out in front of them like vacancy signs. They brightened when he approached, sizing him up and enjoying what they found. He flashed a smile. "You ladies seen a guy who look like me? Almost identical, but not as attractive. A little shorter. Go by 'Do Right.'"

The girl in the middle clucked her tongue. "Yeah, I know Do Right. I haven't seen him though. Not in a few days."

Marlowe nodded solemnly and thanked them.

"Wait, sugar. Where you going?"

Marlowe laughed and waved politely, still retreating. "To find my brother. You ladies enjoy your evening."

An answer like that meant he needed to try the next party. On his way out to his Civic, Marlowe checked his phone to search for another posting and found a message from his sister.

As an older brother, Marlowe grew up cursed by this juggling act. They all three shared a mom and a dad. People guessed differently, because Marlowe and Do Right resembled so much, while Shelley stood a foot shorter, gleamed several shades darker, and looked at least ten times more beautiful.

They all three grew up as good-looking kids, but Shelley golfed at a different handicap. While the two boys relied on mischievous eyes and boyish grins, Shelley grew up looking like a more compact, shade darker Iman. Having a younger sister with supermodel looks and a younger brother with a propensity to find trouble meant Marlowe took plenty of late night phone calls.

The dad they shared died in a car accident when Shelley was only a few months old. He nodded off on his way to night classes. A few more months and he would have finished an engineering degree—a Willy Wonka Golden Ticket out of the projects. But instead, their mother spent the next decade and a half working two or three jobs.

She found some rich family's address to use in order to put Shelley in better schools than the ones Marlowe and Do Right suffered. Marlowe took up the mantle of "man of the house" with a curled lip and determined gaze. He wore it like a badge of honor. Do Right and Shelley were more responsibilities than they were siblings. And the shoes Marlowe tried to fill grew bigger every year. His father faded from the flesh-and-bones hospital janitor to the legend of a perfect dad—the windmill Marlowe could never conquer.

He worked his way out of a pastiche of puzzle-parked cars and called Shelley from the road. "Shells. What's up?"

"Did you find him?"

"No. Total bust. Found a girl who knew him. But nobody has seen him."

Marlowe listened to Shelley's breathing through the phone. Heavy. Nervous.

"Shelley. What's the matter?"

"I need a favor, Marlowe. A big one."

Marlowe's lip took on its familiar curl. He sniffed once. Resolved. "Yeah. Yeah, of course. Anything."

"Do you know where Graffiti Creek is?"

Chapter 7

After his back-alley meeting with Juliana the waitress, Sameer had two hours to kill before meeting Seamus' editor for lunch. Seamus worked for a news magazine, which provided a little more flexibility than a newspaper. The editor, Margaret, didn't offer much help over the phone. She claimed the magazine tried not to keep too tight of a leash on their writers, so Seamus did not have to keep her abreast of his latest projects. Sameer, however, after ten minutes, convinced her to meet with him while she ate lunch. She would be in a little park next to a falafel truck in Dollar Hill, only about a hundred yards or so from the Hill Street Cafe.

Sameer spent his spare time walking the bike trails and sidewalks of Dollar Hill. There were several small parks dotted about between law offices and government buildings. He didn't stand out as badly as in the Cafe, as there were all kinds of people coming and going. Though most wore business attire.

Seamus didn't talk much about his work, other than to share a story with Sameer once he finished writing it. But Sameer knew one thing about the process. Seamus loved to use homeless people as sources. As he wandered the grounds of Dollar Hill, Sameer came across numerous homeless people, mostly men, lying on benches or leafing through trash bins. He planned for this. His inside jacket pocket brimmed with dollar bills. He would approach each person as if he were trying to pet a strange dog. He would offer up the dollar and the photo of Seamus. But by a quarter to noon, no one admitted having seen or spoken to Seamus. An information void which cost Sameer eighteen dollars.

Having given up on the homeless population, Sameer made certain to be sitting on the concrete ledge around a fountain directly across from the falafel truck by 11:55. As promised, Margaret appeared out of a throng of workers breaking for lunch at straight-up noon.

She was an older woman with the haggard look of a journalistic veteran. Glasses hung around her neck and another pair sat shoved into her tangle of brown hair. She wore a pantsuit neither in fashion nor outdated. She carried a small purse and looked to be a shade healthier than first impressions indicated. She projected a persona of the perfect person to blend in, sneak in, or push in. Sameer got the distinct impression she broke her fair share of stories. Seamus spoke reverently of her. He didn't necessarily like her, but sure as hell tried to learn from her.

"Sameer? Margaret Golding." She held her hand out in a greeting. "You can call me Meg. Never let your husband, but you don't work for me so have at it."

Sameer stood and shook her hand. "Thank you for meeting me."

"Of course. Anything to help. We're all worried sick." As they both took a seat at the fountain, Meg patted Sameer on the knee. "I'm pretty sure we met at last year's holiday party, right?"

Sameer smiled and nodded. "Yes, ma'am. We did."

Meg grimaced. "I was afraid of that. I get drunker than your boozy uncle at holiday parties. I apologize for not remembering sooner."

"Yes. You were very intoxicated. If I remember correctly, you called me Sammy Atari." Sameer winced and hung his head. "I mean, no worries." He looked back up at Meg. "So you can't remember anything Seamus might be working on?"

Meg cocked her head. "Nothing specific, no. Truth of the matter is, I should be calling him on the carpet for not producing. His last piece came in a while back."

Sameer frowned. "I don't understand. He works constantly."

"I agree." She nodded. "Fitzy works hard. But the product's not there. He got lost down a rabbit hole. Happens to all of us at some point or other."

"I had an aunt whose every saying related in one way or another to donkeys. Everything was about a donkey. But never rabbits. She did have one about a donkey hole, but I feel as if it might be very different." Sameer shook his head. "I'm not familiar with the phrasing."

"A wild goose chase of sorts." She smiled wistfully. "Every journalist finds a story that piques your curiosity to a point of obsession. You get lost in it. But some of those stories never actually yield stories. You can't tie up the loose ends enough to write a piece. Nobody will go on record. None of the leads pan out. It happens."

"And what was Seamus' rabbit hole?"

"Fitzy got sucked up in a cold case. Back in the 80s, a reporter named Carnie—not his real name. You know how we have to nickname everybody. But anyway, Carnie went and got himself killed. He got shot while visiting a prostitute. It got written off as solicitation gone wrong or maybe a hook and crook. But never solved. Funny thing though, Carnie took his daughter with him."

Meg frowned at the thought and continued, "What kind of guy takes his daughter to see a whore? I knew Carnie a little. Good guy. I never bought it." She shrugged. "Neither did Fitzy. He started looking into the old story and found out Carnie stood on the banks of some deep shit. He'd been digging around into police corruption and crooked politicians. Hookers and drugs and murder. Nasty stuff. Stuff which, according to your husband, continues right up to this day."

Sameer raised his eyebrows. "Is he right?"

Meg shrugged again. "I think so, yeah. I mean, we've all picked up rumors. But nobody can get a story. Fitzy didn't fare any better. He chased and he chased. He even claimed a friend on the force helping him dig. But in the end, I told him to drop it. At least back burner it. I needed print."

"But he still didn't bring in stories." Sameer shook his head. "So was he still working on the same case?"

"I suspected. But the most recent notes I found were about a little sub community of filmmakers in town. Bunch of urban kids making documentaries and art films. I kept waiting on a story about it, but I never got one."

Sameer sat up straighter. "Do you have those notes?"

Meg nodded and fished a folded stack of papers out of her purse. "I photocopied everything on his desk for you." She gave Sameer the stack, a haphazard array of scribbled notes, many on Post-its or torn scraps of paper, all Xeroxed onto white copy paper. Meg laughed. "Sorry. Bit of a mess. I'm afraid it is our way. We journalists," she tapped her temple, "we've got it all organized up here, but everywhere else? Bit of a mess." She placed a hand on Sameer's shoulder. "Anything else we can do to help, please don't hesitate to ask."

"Yes. Thank you. I will." Nodding to her repeatedly, Sameer clutched the papers to his chest. "And thank you for meeting me and bringing me these. I'm sure they will help." He glanced at the line forming at the falafel truck. "Don't let me keep you."

Meg pointed toward the truck with her head. "Let me buy you lunch?"

Sameer cocked his head. "Oh. The last time I had falafel, I was subsequently bamboozled out of eighty-seven dollars by a street urchin." He shook a finger. "Now, mind you, it was no fault of the falafel. However, any time I am to eat it now, I am reminded of—" Sameer smiled. "No. Thank you. I ate pie."

"Well, good for you, kid."

The two parted ways with Meg getting in line for lunch and Sameer walking back toward where he parked his car, near the Hill Street Cafe. Almost to his car, at the edge of Dollar Hill, a voice called out to him. "Hey! You the one looking for the reporter?"

Sameer spun around to find a homeless man huddled up on a bus stop bench. He almost trotted making his way toward the man. "Yes. Yes, I am. Do you know something? Did you see him? I can show you a picture."

The man waved off Sameer's efforts to retrieve the picture from his pocket. "I don't need a picture. I seen him. How many of those dollars you got left?"

Sameer fumbled around in his pockets and came up with twenty-one dollars in fives and ones. "Here. It's all I have left."

The man eagerly accepted the wad of cash and counted the bills as he spoke. "Yeah, the guy you want to see is named Booker. He's down and out. Like me. But he's a friendly type. Always running to help out and shit. Word has it Booker helped out a young lady some years back." He jerked a thumb back toward the tangle of government buildings. "And some of those types didn't much like it."

Sameer shook his head. "Why not?"

The man shrugged. "Ask Booker. The young lady worked as a—I believe the preferred term is a sex worker. And, if I ain't mistaken, she was sex working for one of those suits. Booker got her out of a tight spot and your fella damn sure wanted to hear all about it."

"Where can I find Booker?"

"There's this group of guys who make movies. They hang out in a coffee shop, I think. Somewhere in Harper's Village. In Midtown. But they're always down here shooting footage. Booker let them put him in some shots sometimes. He wouldn't try to milk them like the rest of us, so they grew to like him. One of those guys helped the reporter find Booker. Must've been where he heard about the story. Those guys might know where Booker's been hanging his hat these days. I ain't seen him down here in a few weeks."

Chapter 8

Cary stuck to the road. Beat the cold pavement with her bare feet. The backwoods farm road curved around bends in two-lanes, but at least the county paved this side of the tracks. The internal clock on the backs of Cary's eyelids read almost four in the morning. No one would be picking up hitchhikers. In fact, the only car she might encounter would be the Ford Taurus that carried her out to the bridge. Dick and Dicker would have surely gone back to it. The thought made her pick up her pace. Going back into the rough ground of the woods would be murder. She sensed the slick warmth of blood on the soles of her feet.

Cary couldn't decide which she'd rather have: shoes or her phone. Or a bottle of water. Maybe whiskey. As she rounded a corner, she saw salvation. Other than the whiskey, she could find everything she needed. The big golden sign with beautiful green letters: Dollar General. Cheap shoes, water, bandages, and a prepaid phone. Halle-fucking-lujah. Because Cary did have three thousand dollars in cash in her jacket pocket.

Approaching the Dollar General, she counted two cars. Good sign. Even if closed, someone in there would open up for a hundred spot. A beat-up truck sat parked over to one side in what looked like an employee spot. In the other car—a Civic—a single driver carried on an animated phone conversation.

Cary doubted the DG allowed bare feet. She hoped the clerk would be too tired to notice. She tried to stroll in as casually as possible, making a beeline for a row of shoes and socks. They had some knock-off Converse and a two-pack of socks with cats on them. She hugged them to her chest and wound her way to the first aid aisle, snagging a box of Scooby-Doo bandaids and some hydrogen peroxide. She added a bottle of orange Gatorade from a nearby cooler on her way to the counter. The sleepy-eyed clerk rang her up. Cary had fished out a twenty to keep from raising any eyebrows.

Taking her change, Cary asked sweetly, "Can I use your restroom?"

He didn't speak but pointed back toward a corner of the store where Cary spotted the familiar male and female silhouettes. She thanked him and started back, only to stop at a display of cell phones.

"Are these pre-paid?"

He nodded. "Yep."

She grabbed a phone and a card promising sixty minutes of "airtime." Another couple of twenties later she padded off to the bathroom to bandage her feet and try to remember anyone's phone number.

In the bathroom, she guzzled the Gatorade and perched on the sink to doctor her feet. They were a mash of cuts and raspberries. Cary dabbed peroxide onto them with a paper towel and slapped on a patchwork of bandaids. She eased on the socks and shoes and whimpered at the ceiling.

The silence of a Dollar General at four in the morning has few rivals. There are many noisier libraries. It's the stillness of an antique store mid-morning. Or a car ride after an argument. So when voices started up at the counter, Cary clearly made out the gruff snarls of her detective friends. She scanned the bathroom for windows, found none, and whispered a curse into the mirror.

Cary shoved her phone and the "airtime" card in her pocket and crouched down to open the door a crack. She peeked out and noticed the trail of bloody footprints leading right to her. "Balls," she muttered. In a duck walk, she made her way along the back wall of the store until she came to an emergency exit. In college, Cary had worked in a little store like this one where she had learned to use the curved mirrors in the corners to catch shoplifters. She found the two men at the counter, and she watched as the dweeby clerk pointed back toward the bathroom. Her time was up.

One hard shove into the emergency door and an alarm blared throughout the store. Cary ducked around a counter and slouched into a sitting position where she could monitor the mirrors. Dick bolted for the back of the store and didn't slow down before exploding out the back exit. But the lead detective stayed. He worked his way down an aisle in a sweep of the store.

During Casey Trubody, Survivalist Trainer's lesson entitled "Evading Capture," Cary's brother claimed "hiding is never about finding somewhere they won't look; it's about making them look somewhere you aren't."

Cary scanned her aisle, full of cookout and camping supplies, and found a fire starter log and a box of long matches. She leaped up and grabbed one of each and moved to an aisle farther away from the detective. Crouching and watching the mirrors, she worked her way from aisle to aisle until she came to a shelf of aerosol

30

bug sprays. She ripped open the log, placing it on the shelf beneath the sprays, and lit match after match until she had a good flame going.

The detective worked his way down an aisle, coming to the back of the store before starting back up the next. He had just rounded the corner when the first can went. The dull thud spun and knocked cans off into the floor. The racket drew his attention with a jolt. The detective jogged along the back of the store toward the noise. Cary took the opportunity to sprint for the front doors.

She stumbled into the parking lot rooting for any escape. The Civic owner still chatted on his phone. Her choices were pretty limited at this point, so she ran for the car, whipped open the passenger side door, and slunk down into the floorboard of the Civic.

The driver jumped and spun with his back against his door and one hand outstretched toward Cary. He fumbled with his phone but managed to catch it and stutter out, "I gotta call you back." He stared Cary down as she begged him with her eyes. After a long twenty seconds of shared silence, he asked, "You gonna tell me what the hell it is you're doing?"

Cary shrunk into the floor but put up both hands beseechingly. "I know. I know. This appears crazy, and I'm sorry. But please, please listen. Give me one minute. Please."

He frowned but nodded once.

Cary nodded rapidly and stammered. "Th—there are two men. Cops. They th—think I'm somebody else or something. I don't know. But they're trying to kill me. I swear. I just need a ride to anywhere but here. If I get out of this car, they'll kill me."

The driver glanced toward the store, swallowed hard, and flashed a quick look back at Cary. "Cops, huh?"

Cary nodded.

"And they tried to kill you?"

"Yes. They shot at me."

The driver glowered at her. "And your answer to how to keep your ass safe from some killer cops was to climb into a car with a black man at four in the morning?"

Cary grimaced. "I am beginning to acknowledge the flaws in it as a plan."

The driver shook his head and thrashed around. "Girl, you gonna get me killed."

"Wait, wait, wait. Please," Cary pleaded. "One time-once, my—my brother," she stammered, "my brother, he told me if I need help there are certain types of people to look for. He said I would know them because their heads would be on swivels and their startled posture would be protective. He said to look for a mom, a cop, a soldier, or an older sibling. I don't know if you're one of those, but

31

when I jumped in the car you reached out, you know, like you were reaching out in a protective manner. Or maybe you were about to punch me. I don't know for sure. But all I can do in this moment is to trust my brother. You see, he used to take me out into the woods and train me to survive in extreme circumstances such as a bear attack or a raging forest fire." Cary was nodding rapidly and begging with her eyes.

The driver glanced back over his shoulder. "There ain't a bear out there, is there?"

Cary shook her head.

He nodded slowly.

Cary winced. "Are you—are you…one of those people? A soldier, maybe, or a—"

The driver sighed and put the car in drive. "Yeah. Yeah, I'm one of those people." He stopped short of pulling out. Frozen, he stared toward the store.

Cary kept folding herself into the floorboard. "What? What is it?"

The man spoke without moving his lips. "One 'uh 'em's 'alkin' o'er here."

"Shit."

The driver rolled his window down. "Morning, detective. Can I help you?"

Cary recognized a familiar voice. "You see a girl run out of here?"

"Yes, sir. I did. Went in right before you all. Left in a hurry. Running up the road toward the tracks."

Everything stalled out for a moment. Gravel crunched and rolled beneath the detective's feet. The driver's Adam's apple worked up and down as he tried to swallow. More gravel churned. Steps. Steps. Steps. The detective crept closer. A flashlight clicked to life. The beam swept into the car, past the driver, wild. He hadn't reached the window yet. She lunged for the door handle.

Police sirens wailed, droning in from a short distance away. The driver instinctively peered over his shoulder. The detective mumbled, "Jesus." The gravel sounds coughed quickly, moving away.

The driver eased forward, looking down at Cary. "What kind of cop runs from the sound of sirens?"

Chapter 9

Johnna couldn't tell when her eyes were open or shut. Her throat felt like a pinched straw. She couldn't swallow and breathing took effort. Consciousness danced around her and left, toying with her, playing Hokey-Pokey, she thought. Her mind was a jar of dirt, with thoughts wiggling to the surface like worms every now and then, only to disappear again into the mush. Her mom brushing her hair in the mornings. The way her grandmother used to talk about Johnna's childhood dance class. Hearing about the job interview. The excitement in Cary's eyes—the look of someone who believed in her.

Officer Reynard had crammed Johnna into this dark space—turned her into the ventriloquist dummy folded into a suitcase. Combing around stung like digging in a tub of ice for a cold drink. Her fingers tingled numb and everything floated off, foreign and dreamy. Her hair was a skein of ribbons cascading over her face. Her breasts swollen lumps. The floor puffed up like the hair of her first boyfriend. Long before she came out. They were middle school sweethearts.

Johnna shook off the memory and tried again to focus. Carpet. All around, carpet. Dark, cramped. Movement. She sensed movement. It wasn't merely the rushing woosh-woosh-woosh in her head. She was in a car. A trunk.

She initially found nothing around her. Even if there had been, her eyes didn't work and her fingers were balloon animals. Sleep kept sneaking up on her. Dreams. Dreams of falling—of Cary—of snakes—of Reynard choking, choking, choking. She woke with a start and groped around again until her hand hit something metal. Slender. Plastic handle. A screwdriver. She could work with that.

She gripped and re-gripped the screwdriver. Practiced poking and stabbing and slicing. On a slice, she scraped the metal of the roof of the trunk. It woke something inside her and she went back to the roof, scratching and chiseling at the roof until she got dizzy. *Save it, Johnna*, she thought, almost aloud. Maybe aloud. Maybe loud. Too loud. She brandished the screwdriver in front of her, ready to stab up and out. Her eyes fluttered. There Cary stood again and her childhood dog ran up and her mother smiled and the dreams reclaimed her.

When she woke up, voices swirled outside. Male and angry. The trunk lay open and light attacked her like bees. The screwdriver had slumped down into her lap, and she moved to hold it with stealthy-steady hands.

One voice was Reynard. The voice she would never forget. He said, "I got here as fast as I could. They're all up at the Dollar General. Nobody's nosing around here."

The other voice was heavier, more authoritative. "Well, they will, won't they, Reytard? Now, pull the bitch out of the trunk."

Johnna tensed. A familiar, calloused, hairy hand clutched her and tugged. She tumbled out onto the dirt and rocks face first, smashing her nose and mouth. Consciousness toyed with her again. Blood pooled up and trailed off in a stream through the dirt.

A third voice coughed out. "What the fuck?"

Reynard whined, "What? Afraid I'll damage the merchandise?"

The authoritative voice barked, "No, you moron. Dead girls don't bleed."

Reynard's tone changed. "What?"

"You didn't kill her, you idiot."

Johnna fought to let the alarm bells of their conversation wake her up. The screwdriver. She had to come up hard with the screwdriver. Loafered feet made their way toward her. The third voice said, "Get out of my way."

She came up hard and made it just above his knee. The screwdriver went in deep—to the handle. And he bellowed. The pained cry of a full-grown man. Johnna scrambled to her feet. Turning, she hit a man in a suit. The material smelled like mothballs and his protruding stomach did not give. The impact sent her rolling back to the loafers. She sprawled out on her back, looking up at the man as he pulled the length of the screwdriver from his leg. He glowered at Johnna as he did it—his eyes steeled against the pain. He held the bloody tool there, dripping onto her face.

Johnna tried to croak out, "Please. No." But no sound made it to the air.

The man came straight down with the screwdriver and drove into Johnna's chest.

Pain erupted through to her back. Adrenaline pulsed to each end of her body. Before realizing what had happened, Johnna vaulted to her feet, rushing past the guy in the cheap suit toward a bridge. The screwdriver bounced and dangled out of her chest. She gasped and sucked for air. Tripping over her heels, she kept on, running. In her mind. But not really. She stumbled in a slow zombie walk.

Johnna kept moving toward the bridge, with its blurry mesh of colors. She pulled at the screwdriver until it came loose and something warm coated her stomach and her crotch. She stopped and fell to her knees, looking down, embarrassed, thinking she had urinated. One of her shoes had fallen off. She picked up her strappy heel and put the screwdriver inside it and threw them both toward the bridge. The momentum took her all the way to the ground, laid prostrate on her side.

The men laughed behind her. Their voices sounded muffled, like they were talking with marshmallows in their mouth—a game she used to play with her sister. One of them said, "She ain't getting up." Johnna opened her mouth to correct him. She always hated that word: *ain't*. Another said, "Let's make sure. What do you say?" And he put a meaty knee over Johnna's throat and chin. The last thing she ever saw. Some cheap-ass pants.

Chapter 10

The little Civic passed about four cop cars, lighting up the front seat with a disco of red and blue lights. Cary climbed up off of the floorboard, but she kept her head down as they passed. When she relaxed a bit she said, "I'm Cary."

The driver gave her an incredulous look. "I don't want to know your name. I don't want to know anything."

Cary closed her eyes and nodded. "I understand."

After a beat, he relented. "Marlowe."

Cary grinned at him. "Well, thank you, Marlowe."

He grunted.

Cary pulled the burner phone out of her pocket, along with the minutes card. She waggled them at Marlowe. "Do you know how to activate this?"

Marlowe clucked his tongue. "What? Because I'm black, I know how to activate a prepaid phone, huh?"

Cary stammered and stuttered out an incoherent response.

"Yeah, okay. I know how to activate a prepaid phone. All right? And it ain't cause I deal drugs or some shit, either. My cousin cheated on his girl. So we got him a second phone. Which is a perfectly white reason to know how to do that."

Cary nodded. "Very white."

Marlowe sniffed. "Don't patronize me." He walked her through setting up the phone as he drove back into the city via a windy path. When the phone's tinny speaker sang out its little activation song, Marlowe eyed Cary. "You have any numbers?"

Cary stared at the phone, and then at him. "What?"

He shrugged. "Nobody knows numbers anymore. Got 'em all programmed in. Do you have anybody's number to call?"

Cary looked back at the phone and hung her head back, staring at the ceiling. "No." Her eyes welled with tears. "I can't even remember Johnna's number. Does that make me a horrible person?"

Marlowe shrugged. "Maybe. I don't know who Johnna is."

Cary flailed her arms out. "Ten numbers. The most important person in my life doesn't merit me remembering ten numbers?" She shook the phone, glaring at it. "We all feel so connected, but it's a fallacy. We've built ourselves a digital security blanket! I can't even reach out to the one person I care about because I've let the world make me cold and broken and—"

Marlowe laughed until Cary swore at him. He ducked and held a hand up in defense. "All right, all right. It's not funny." He forced a more solemn countenance. "I don't mean to laugh. You just," he trailed off, "you remind me a little of my brother, is all. Why don't you tell me what happened? From the beginning."

As Marlowe continued to drive in a looping circle through the city, Cary recounted everything: the traffic stop, the taking of her phone, the attempted staged suicide, the bullet-filled chase through the woods. Before finishing, tears pushed at the edges of Cary's eyes.

Marlowe cleared his throat and spoke before those tears manifested. "So what now? I don't guess you got another car, huh?"

Cary chuckled. "No." She shoved the phone back in her pocket and brightened. "I have another set of keys, though. At my house." Her hand came back from her pocket with the stack of cash. "I can pay you. Please."

Marlowe cocked his head, eyeing the money. "All right, okay." He frowned. "Put your money away, girl. I guess there's a chance we beat them to your house." He sucked at his teeth. "Less of a chance they left your car sitting out there unguarded."

"Turn left at the light." Cary started directing him toward her house. "Not many options yet. I have to try. Unless you want me riding around with you all day."

"Didn't look like you had that much money."

Cary smirked. "I thought you said put it away?"

Marlowe nodded. "I said put it away. I didn't say I wasn't gonna take it."

Cary led Marlowe to an elementary school and told him to park out front in the visitor lot. He scanned the empty lot and scrunched his face up at her. "You live at a school?"

"Turn off your headlights." Cary leaned forward and stared out across the playground. She pointed, "No. I live over there."

Marlowe nodded. "Of course you do. Where the cop car is sitting?"

Cary nodded. "Yep."

38

She started out of the car, and Marlowe grabbed her arm. "What the hell are you doing?"

"I'm going to try to sneak in and find my other keys."

Marlowe locked the doors. "The fuck you are. Are you crazy?"

Cary unlocked the doors. "No. I'm desperate. I need to get my car back. I'm not asking you to go with me."

Marlowe locked the doors back. "Good. Because there ain't no way I'm going in there. And there ain't no way you're going in there. If you get caught, I get caught."

Cary unlocked the doors again and shook her head. "Not true. All you have to do is watch through the playground. If you see me get caught, drive away. If I make it back, drive me one more place and this is all over for you."

Marlowe locked the doors. "No. All I *have* to do is nothing. I picked you up outta Dollar General parking lot. I should be dropping you off at a Walmart and calling it an upgrade for your lifestyle."

Cary unlocked the doors and pulled out the stack of money and set it on the dashboard. "Here. All of it. If I get caught, you can have it all."

Marlowe locked the doors back. "Holy shit. How much money do you have?"

Cary nodded at the stack, unlocking the doors again. "Three thousand. If I make it back, I can give you a hundred dollars. Two hundred. Three. I need one last thing. Please." She locked the doors.

Marlowe hit the button once more, unlocking the doors. "I don't need your money, girl. I got money. But I can't leave your ass either. Because I'm too goddamn nice."

Cary hopped out of the car and leaned back in. "Thanks, Marlowe. This means a lot."

Marlowe frowned back and forth between his door lock button and Cary. The door puffed shut and he side-eyed Cary slinking off across the darkened playground. He called out, "Five hundred!" And slid down in his seat to patrol.

Cary slipped through an opening in the fence into the playground, bending over into a duck walk. She kept to the fence line and crouched behind the cover of monkey bars and slides and park benches. She knew a gate opened up to the street about a block from her house.

The police cruiser sat in front of her rental house facing away from her. If she crossed the street, she could wind her away around to the back of the house and use a spare key under a flowerpot.

Darkness enveloped the street, but Cary couldn't cross at any point without risking the cop catching sight of her in his rearview mirror. After a minute of coming up blank, she caught a break. A car approached and would pass her before, a couple of seconds later, passing the police officer.

She knelt into a crouch—a runner's stance. Her only chance would come right as the car passed the cruiser. The cop would have to look closely, watching for Cary to drive by to check on her house. In that moment, she would have a brief window to cross the street.

She waited for the car to pass, watching the street like a living game of Frogger. When it finally passed, her window of opportunity turned into a door slamming onto her thumb. The car turned out to be another police cruiser.

Cary slid down into the shadow of a bush. "Balls." She craned her neck to view the new cruiser passing the first cop. Instead, it pulled up alongside, and the two spoke through lowered windows. She just made out their mumbling voices from where she sat, hidden. She still caught a window. If they were talking to each other, they wouldn't be watching their rearview mirrors. She muttered again to herself, "Balls." After three quick breaths, she rolled to her feet and darted across the street.

Once on the other side, she slid onto the far side of a neighbor's porch that kept her hidden. After a beat of listening for any change, Cary reasoned with herself not to wait around now. She ran for the side of the house and started down the backyards of her neighbors. There were no dogs or tricky spots—all short fences and clear paths.

She cleared three houses and cut through a back gate, taking the alley over the last two until she reached her own house. Privacy fencing ran along the front of most houses. She rarely noticed any of her neighbors milling around in their backyards. She only needed to worry about making too much noise or casting a shadow through a window once she was inside.

The key lay under the flower pot where she hid it. Cary eased open her back door as quietly as possible. The urge to instinctively hit the light switch almost overwhelmed her. She entered through the kitchen, keeping to almost a crawl.

Cary rented a small two-bedroom, two-story house. And what Cary needed sat shoved in an upstairs closet. In her closet were two things: a bowl with a spare set of car keys and an abandoned day planner. She got the planner for Christmas, and before casting it aside, she filled it with a handful of phone numbers. If she could retrieve those two things without being spotted, she would bolt out the back and run full-out back to the Civic.

The kitchen opened up into a foyer and entryway leading in one direction to a frosted glass door and snaking around the other way to the stairs. Cary continued to stay low and tried to avoid being backlit against any windows. She eased around the corner and up the stairs. They were old and creaky. Every step sounded like a scream to her. When her feet found carpet, she sped up across her bedroom to the closet.

She almost tripped over the contents of a drawer splayed out across the floor. Someone searched her house for whatever they thought she stole or took. The keys were under a pile of jewelry and loose change. The planner sat pushed to the back of a shelf, but easily retrieved. It wouldn't fit in a jacket pocket, so she leafed through until she found the pages with contacts. On one page, she found several numbers, including Johnna's. She tore out the page and tossed the planner on her nightstand on her way to the door.

The lamp never crossed her mind. She pulled the old lamp from her grandmother's estate sale. She always liked that lamp. It sat in the guest room where she slept as a child when she visited her grandmother. Her grandmother used the quirky little lamp, with its dusty looking bronze finish, to read to Cary before bed. Cary would sip hot cocoa, curled up in a horrid blanket her grandmother kept hiding in the closet. And her grandmother would curse the glitchy lamp for always switching on or off every time she dropped the book they were reading next to it.

Which is exactly what the damn thing did when Cary flopped the day planner next to it. The room burst to life with the too-bright bulb Cary had stupidly forced into it. She panicked and froze, staring at the window like it might admonish her. She snapped alert and lunged for the lamp's cord, pulling until it popped from the wall and everything went dark again. Her eyes crawled with electric gnats and she pushed her back against the side of her bed and listened. At first, nothing. The faint rumblings of a train drifted in from somewhere. But then, bump. And again, bump. Car doors.

Cary struggled to her feet and hurried for the stairs. Her mind turned into a wasp's nest of nasty thoughts. Like the one about how the two cops could split up and block both exits from the house. But when she hit the stairs, two flashlight beams twinkled through the frosted glass. Her first step sounded especially loud, moaning and cracking like alarm bells. The flashlight beams froze. She heard whispered voices. And the door—unlocked from when they came in the first time—opened. Cary backpedaled into her bedroom and whipped her head around wildly. Their footsteps crept in cautiously downstairs.

Only one window overlooked the back of Cary's house from upstairs. It opened from her bedroom onto a slanted roof sloping to the point of almost colliding with a decrepit storage shed out back. Her only shot at making it out of the house would be to roll off the shed and in a row of bushes underneath.

She ran for the window and jerked it open. The screen stuck in one corner when she pushed, but it opened enough to fit through. Cary kicked out with both feet and let herself slide onto the roof before she could pause to think too much. This time she thanked empty calories for the extra padding on her ass. She hit the storage shed and rolled. Its shingles flaked and shifted with her weight, and the whole building sounded like it might not make it through the ordeal. But Cary managed to go careening off and into the bushes, which felt like landing in pile of elbows and cat claws. Her hands caught the worst. Tiny branches sliced through her palms. But she got to her feet and started to shake off the loss of equilibrium when she heard a voice yell, "Out back!"

Again she froze, unsure of which direction to go, or, rather, not go. She studied the sides of the house. Simultaneously, from both sides, flashlight beams cut the darkness. They split up. Either way she went would involve a cop and gun.

Cary looked up and discovered the back door still open from when she came in. She didn't hesitate. She covered the backyard and porch in four steps. On her way through the kitchen, she spied silhouettes out windows on both sides of the house. They left the front door standing open, so she never broke stride.

Cary ran straight out, past the empty police cars. She burst through a gate into the playground across from the corner of her front yard. A stitch burned in her side by the time she reached the Civic, but she made it. Marlowe pulled out before she even shut the car door.

Chapter 11

Cary writhed in the seat, holding her side. Marlowe sped down side streets and swiveled back and forth, rattling incoherently, "Shit. Shit, girl. You got shot, didn't you? I didn't hear a shot. He shot you? What do I do?"

Cary tried to catch her breath enough to interrupt him. "No. Not shot," she panted. "Just out of shape."

Marlowe almost collapsed behind the wheel. "Jesus in a clown mask. I thought you'd been shot. You need to join a gym or something, girl."

"Am I being fat shamed during a car chase?"

He rolled his eyes. "Girl, you know I like 'em thick. I'm only shaming the fact that you can't run across a playground without looking like you about to die." He laughed but darted his eyes around behind him. "Wait, what? Are we in a car chase?"

Cary sat up and buckled her seat belt. "No. I don't think so. I'm hoping they didn't see which way I went."

"Damn, girl. Stop scaring me. Shit."

Cary laughed. "Sorry." She jangled her keys out of her pocket. "But you're almost rid of me. If you can take me back out to my car, I'll be on my way to live a life on the run or something."

Marlowe raised his eyebrows at her. "Right now?"

Cary shrugged. "Yeah. I guess. Why not? Kind of the whole point of this shit, right?"

Marlowe shook his head. "No. I mean, you can't. Not right now. I pointed them back toward where you came from. Like you had doubled back. They'll be watching your car for a while, at least. We gotta let the heat die down a bit."

"So, what? Where do we go?"

He cocked his head. "I don't know. I was thinking we'd grab breakfast."

Cary laughed loudly. "Breakfast? Are you shitting me?"

"What? You get chased around and all the sudden you don't eat no more?"

"No. I eat. Obviously. But I don't think stopping for breakfast is the smartest move while becoming a fugitive from the law."

Marlowe clucked his tongue. "'Fugitive from the law.' Jesus. I don't think you're all that quite yet."

"I got shot at!"

"I know! And you deserve some pancakes for that shit!"

Cary started something but stopped. "I do like pancakes."

Marlowe smiled and nodded. "See? Breakfast helps you think. There's this place on St. Ives and Cumberland on the way out of town. *On the way*, girl!" He smacked his lips. "Damn, girl. Can't you at least buy me breakfast? I might still get killed over this shit."

Cary frowned. "So why draw it out? Take me to my car and be done with it."

He snorted out a laugh. "Cary, your brother knew how to survive bears and woods. I know how to survive some city cops. We need to let the shit die down a little. And we might as well have some bacon while we do that. Sound good?"

Cary still frowned but nodded in agreement.

Netta's was a little diner in a converted strip mall. It advertised soul food and looked about as greasy as a greasy spoon was supposed to. At 6:00, the place was empty. Cary wasn't sure if empty was a positive or a negative. There was no crowd to hide in, but, at the same time, there was no one around to notice them. Besides, once they stepped inside, the smell of bacon and coffee overpowered every other thought in her head.

Marlowe had let her wear an L.A. Dodgers cap he had in his backseat, and she pulled it low with the collar of her jacket popped up around her neck. They found a booth in a back corner, and Cary slunk down in her seat with a menu in front of her face. Marlowe shook his head at her. "You want me to run to the store and pick you up some of those Groucho Marx glasses with the mustache?"

Cary peered over her menu. "What?"

"*What?* You look ridiculous."

"I do not."

"Like a damn fool. Relax. Act like you're a goddamn normal person."

She gawked around and sat up straighter. "What am I acting like?"

Marlowe chuckled, "Like somebody running from the cops."

His advice brought her up to a straighter posture, and she even relaxed enough to order a coffee and a short stack of pancakes with bacon. Marlowe ordered the same, but with sausage. And they sat in silence for a moment waiting for each other to talk.

Marlowe poked his chin out at her. "You from here?"

Cary nodded. "Yeah. I left. For college. I stayed gone for seven or eight years. I moved back about a year ago. I had to help my mom after my dad died."

Marlowe squinted. "Sorry."

She shrugged. "What about you?"

He raised his eyebrows and nodded. "Born and raised. Never left. Went to college here. Dropped out. Went back. Dropped out again." He laughed. "But I managed to finish about a year ago. Got me a decent job and everything."

Cary nodded along as she spun her pre-paid phone on the table. "I understand. I was an English major. Did me no good in the job world. But I've managed. I do graphic design work for several places in town. It pays the bills."

Marlowe pointed with his forehead at the phone. "Why ain't you called nobody yet? You don't even know your mom's number?"

She shook her head. "My mom. She—well, she struggles. With reality, sometimes. Something like this," she rolled her neck around, "it would send her over the edge."

"What about your survivalist brother?"

Cary laughed. "He's currently on some kind of walkabout in Australia."

Marlowe nodded. "Of course he is. That's about the least surprising thing you've said yet. But you gotta have somebody."

She nodded. "I do. I have a friend." She smiled. "A girlfriend. She's my girlfriend. As soon as I get my car, I'm going to find her. She was with me when I got picked up, but they let her go."

Marlowe grinned. "Right on."

Cary rolled her eyes. "Shut up."

He threw his hands up. "What? That was all progressive and accepting and shit."

"Not if you call it progressive and accepting."

Their food came, and they ate like a couple of people who had ridden an hour-long adrenaline rush. Between bites, Marlowe asked, "So why you?"

"Why me what?"

"Why you? You said they got the wrong person or something, right? I ain't doubting. I'm only asking. Why you?"

She sighed and shook her head. "I have no clue. The first cop—the one who pulled me over—he checked my license. I figure there must be someone with the same name. Somewhere out there has to be a Cary Trubody who could make some sick sense out of all this."

"So is that what you do? Find her?"

"I feel like it might be my only option. Either find her or find a cop who isn't dirty. They can't all be assholes, right?"

Marlowe cocked his head at her. "Did you just ask a black dude if all cops are assholes?"

She laughed. "Touché."

"Ahhh." He wobbled his head. "Nah. They aren't all assholes. Tons of good cops. The struggle is gonna be knowing who to trust. I mean, unless you go all the way to the top, you got no way to make sure which ones are in on it and which ones ain't."

Cary sipped her coffee. "Yeah. I mean, it's not like I can blindly trust any cop who walks through the door."

As she said it, two police officers entered Netta's and sat at a table beside Cary and Marlowe. The two cops were engrossed in conversation and paid little to no attention to Cary and Marlowe. As did the next pair who came in. And the next.

Cary held her coffee cup in front of her mouth and spoke through her teeth. "Did you bring me to eat at a goddamn cop hangout?"

Marlowe whispered from behind a smile. "I didn't realize it was a cop hangout."

The waitress seemed to recognize all the officers in the place. They totaled nine when it was all said and done. It must have been shift change. None of the nine paid Cary or Marlowe any attention though. Unfortunately, neither did the waitress. The problem did not lie in the nine cops sitting on all sides of them. The problem was the tenth who came strolling through the door. Officer Reynard.

He met Cary's eyes on his first steps through the door. And there was no question he recognized her. His whole body tensed. Cary made one quick motion to run, but Marlowe stopped her with his foot and whispered, "Wait."

Reynard strolled over to a table and exchanged greetings with other cops in the room. The only time he took his eyes off Cary was to type out a message on his phone. When he finished it, he leered up at Cary and gave her a knowing smile.

Cary muttered, "Did you see that?"

Marlowe nodded. "Yeah. But he ain't doing nothing. Because of these other cops. Whatever they want you for, they can't do it in front of other cops. The two at the Dollar General, they ran from those sirens. And this guy, he's not making a move in here."

Cary swallowed. "Yeah. But he's also not letting me out of here. Not without a—" She paused and raised an eyebrow at Marlowe. "What did I say I'd pay you before?"

Marlowe narrowed his eyes at her. "Two hundred."

"I said one hundred."

"Why you ask if you knew?"

"I'll make it three if you'll go along with what I'm about to do."

"I would say to make it four, but I have the feeling I ain't got a choice."

Cary picked up her silverware and slammed it down on the table hard. Then she said, far too loud, "I cannot fucking believe this."

Everyone stopped talking and watched her.

Marlowe muttered, "Yeah, we better make it four."

Cary continued, undeterred. "Every goddamn time. You want to go out, go out, go out. But you never have any fucking money. Are you seriously going to try to make me pay again?"

Marlowe reached out for her hand and said, "But baby, I always get you back."

Cary jerked away. "Oh no. Don't give me this bullshit again. I'm not going to do it this time. You'll have to wash dishes."

The waitress was coming over with a concerned scowl. A couple of cops had moved to stand at her back. When she reached them, she folder her hands in front of her and asked, "Is there a problem, hon?"

Cary flailed her arms. "Yeah there's a problem. I'm dating a motherfucking cheapskate."

A police officer leaned in and set, "Why don't we tone down the language, ma'am."

Marlowe cocked his head. "Man, my girl will talk any way she fucking wants to."

Cary pushed her empty plate across into his chest. "I don't need you to fucking come to my rescue. I can take up for myself."

A second cop stepped forward and held a hand out to Cary. "Ma'am, why don't you let me escort you to your car. I think it's time to go."

Cary stood up in a huff. "Oh, I do, too. I think it's time to go home and pack."

Marlowe stood up and reached for her. "Baby, don't be like that."

Cary stormed for the door, with a cop at her back. Another cop ushered Marlowe behind them. Once outside, the first cop said, "You two need to take this conversation somewhere more private."

Officer Reynard stood in the window, watching, smiling.

Cary and Marlowe both broke character and said, in unison, "Yes, Officer."

Chapter 12

"I can't believe it worked."

"Stop looking at me! Watch back there!" Marlowe took a corner fast enough to make his Civic fishtail.

"But I was pretty clever, huh?"

"Brilliant. Now tell me what you see." Marlowe wove up and down residential streets, slinging Cary around in her seat.

But Cary bounced with pride. "I mean, it worked so perfectly." She stopped and leaned over her seat to stare out the back window. "Shit."

Marlowe craned his neck. "Don't say 'shit.' That makes me think—"

They said together: "Somebody's following us."

Marlowe banged on the steering wheel and sped up. He burst out of a residential neighborhood onto a main thoroughfare—a four lane street with a middle turning lane. He wove in and out of traffic as Cary kept watch out the back. After splitting two delivery trucks, Marlowe used the turning lane to pass a string of three SUVs. He stayed in the turning lane and told Cary, "Tell me if he gets in the turning lane behind me."

After a few seconds, Cary shouted, "He is."

Marlowe had created enough distance between the Civic and the next closest car, so he took a sharp right across both lanes and squealed onto a side street. Cary hugged the headrest of her seat and cursed. The Civic jumped a curb and righted itself before careening into a parked car. Marlowe slowed a bit down the quiet neighborhood street, but he flailed a finger behind him. "Did it work? Did it work?"

Cary worked a pain out of her neck. "Yes. I shit myself."

"You know what I mean."

Cary strained to look back. "Yeah. He missed the turn."

Marlowe made another sharp right. "He'll catch the next one."

After three more zigzagging turns, Cary caught sight of the unmarked, dark sedan trailing them and pointed.

Marlowe nodded. "I see it." He slowed down, allowing the sedan to make its way toward them down a connecting street.

Cary shifted in her seat. "What are you doing?"

"Calm down. I want him to catch up."

"Why?!"

"Because I know this neighborhood. He don't."

Marlowe pulled into a driveway and stopped.

Cary panicked. She hit his arm and watching the sedan creep closer and closer. "Go! What are you doing?!"

Marlowe checked his side view mirror. "Wait. Just wait. I told you, I know this neighborhood. This is my cousin's house."

"What difference does that make?"

The Civic eased forward. "Because I know this driveway," he curved right around the back of the house and eased left around a detached garage, "connects to alleyway."

Marlowe punched the gas, and the little car spun out around the garage, cutting back left down a gravel alley. The alley spit out into a road which connected back to the same four-lane they had been on before. He sped up to around sixty and found a ramp to merge onto a freeway.

Cary sat back and smiled. "That was sort of badass."

Marlowe shrugged. "I have moments."

"Well, we have to get my car now. We can't stay in this Civic."

Marlowe smacked. "Man. You got me all in this shit now."

Cary hung her head. "I know. I am so sorry. I never meant for this—"

"I know. Shut up. I ain't mad at you. I'm mad at my brother."

Cary shook her head. "Your brother?"

Marlowe nodded. "Soldiers, cops, and older siblings, right? Well, my brother is the one who put my damn head on a swivel a long time ago. The reason I can't just walk away from shit like this when I damn well know I should."

They made their way toward the edges of town, taking an exit for the lonely highway winding out toward Cary's car. The drive took almost half an hour, so Cary used the time to try Johnna multiple times, with no luck.

Marlowe peered around at the woods he drove into. "Girl, you realize you're leading me into, like, the whitest part of this city, right? This is a black person horror movie set-up right now."

Cary curled her lip. "Technically not the city, but…"

He looked at her out of the corner of his eye. "Your girl ain't answering?"

Cary shook her head. "I figured they just left her out there to call a cab or something."

Marlowe grimaced. "Yeah. Yeah, I'm sure she's sleeping it off. You said she was pretty lit, right?"

Cary nodded. And tried again. And again.

When they passed the railroad tracks, Marlowe slowed considerably. They hadn't seen any sign of cars, but coming up on Graffiti Creek meant curling around a bend. If someone waited there, they wouldn't see them until too late. About a hundred yards before the curve in the road, Cary spotted a dirt tributary snaking off into the woods. She pointed, and Marlowe needed no explanation. He pulled off and parked far enough off the main road to be hidden by shadows. They got out and stared at each other across the hood of the car for a moment.

The sounds of the stream trickled up from out of sight down an incline. Cary motioned toward the sound with her head. "I followed this creek before. I think if we make our way through the woods and keep the sound of water to our right we'll come up on the car without being spotted."

Marlowe raised his eyebrows. "We?"

Cary swallowed. "If—if there's someone by my car, then I'll—I'll need a distraction to get to it."

He laughed and nodded. "So you want me to lure a dirty cop to chase me through the damn woods while you—"

"Three thousand dollars. All of it."

Marlowe paused and stared.

Cary nodded. "Walk with me through the woods up to my car. If no one is there, we part ways and I'll pay you five hundred—"

He closed one eye.

Cary smiled. "A thousand." She raised her eyebrows and Marlowe nodded slightly. "If someone is watching the car, all you have to do is come back here and honk the horn or something to get their attention. And if we have to do that, then I'll give you all three thousand before you start back."

Marlowe nodded and waved his hands out for her to lead the way. Cary turned on the flashlight on her phone but kept it low. They steadied one another multiple times laboring down the trailless path. Once inside the oil dark pit of trees, everything smelled like mud and rain. Up ahead, the shadows were cut with swirling lights. Red and blue lights. Faint voices drifted through the trees. Marlowe reached out to slow Cary. The rise off the creek drifted up to a cluster of trees which looked out over the base of the bridge. Cary pointed to them, and they gingerly worked their way to them and crouched in behind a jumble of wild bushes.

They were much closer to the scene than they had realized. Maybe twenty or thirty feet separated them from a meandering horde of police buzzing around Cary's abandoned car. Cary whispered, "What are they doing?"

Marlowe swallowed and bit at his lip. "Not sure, but if we hear anybody say 'Search the area,' we run."

There were no uniformed officers. Only a few plain-clothed detective types and several people in CSI gear—white bodysuits and little blue booties. The attention centered around the car's open trunk.

Marlowe leaned close. "What was in your trunk?"

Cary shook her head. "Nothing."

"That don't look like something you do for nothing."

A woman detective appeared to be in charge. She was tall and attractive—thin with a no-nonsense look about her. She looked like a high school principal or a future district attorney. She had tossed out a few orders to different people around the scene. She pointed several times at something in the trunk, and now she stood back from the car to clear a path for one of the CSIs. He stepped back to a kit of some sort to grab something, leaving the view of the trunk wide open for the first time.

Cary stood as much as she dared to manage a peek. Marlowe hissed at her and pulled her to squat back down, but she strained against him and spied over the bushes.

The trunk was not empty. The spindly limbs of a person filled it from one end to the other. The shape started with a tangle of blonde hair splayed across a face. The dress stretched tight and bordered on skimpy, showing off a long pair of legs folded in odd angles like a broken doll. The legs ended in strappy heels. One hung halfway off and the other disappeared behind the lip of the trunk, or altogether. But Cary recognized them. She helped pick them out.

She collapsed back down and fought a scream. Marlowe started to question but stopped. He put a hand on Cary's back. "Your girl?"

She nodded, with her hands gripped over her mouth and tears and snot beginning to bubble up over her knuckles.

Marlowe held her with both hands, almost shaking her. "Hold it. Hold it together. You make a sound and we'll be joining her."

Cary nodded in short, hiccuping jerks.

The CSI finally retrieved what the detective wanted. Marlowe watched as he pulled a phone out of the trunk and handed it to the detective, who had put on one blue glove to handle evidence. She examined the mobile phone for a moment, pushing a couple of buttons and reading. Marlowe looked at the sobbing Cary. Looked at the phone resting by her leg.

The detective hit a button on the phone and held it out in front of her. Other police gathered around to look. Marlowe heard one faint ring coming from the speaker phone in the detective's open palm. A second later, to his right, the phone on the ground chirped loudly, echoing through the trees. Marlowe jerked his head around and saw every cop swivel up to look in their direction. Cary sobered with a sharp shake of her head and fumbled with the phone. She managed to hit decline and make the chirping stop. Marlowe reached for Cary's phone and they both pawed at it. He whispered, "How do you silence it?"

Cary continued shaking her head as the entire police unit took tentative steps in their direction and the detective hit the button again. Cary whispered through tears, "I don't know."

Marlowe heard the faint ring from the speaker phone again. He grabbed the phone from Cary's hand and threw it behind them and farther up the embankment toward the road. The chirp exploded again and continued as the phone bounced and came to a rest. The police followed the sound, drifting up and past the hiding place where Cary and Marlowe remained huddled.

The detective called out, "I'll keep calling. Fan out."

Marlowe wheeled around, looking on all sides of them. Two cops drifted down toward the creek. Two CSIs nosed past them, staring off toward the sound of the phone. The only clear spot on any side of them was where they had all come from.

Marlowe took hold of Cary's face and pulled her close. "You're about to think this is crazy. Just trust me." He grabbed her by the wrist and pulled her through the bushes toward the car. They stooped and ran around the front of the car next to the creek and came up on the far side. Sliding down with their backs against the far side of the car, they froze and listened.

They could hear voices calling out and responding through the woods. The chirp still cut through everything. Marlowe mumbled, "Sweet shit, that's a loud ass ringtone."

Cary leaned against the car and looked back over her shoulder at the open trunk. She convulsed in breathy sniffles. A trail of blood led away from the car and into a little puddle. Marlowe slapped a hand over her mouth and made eye contact. He put a finger to his lips and pointed toward the bridge. He made a hand motion to go under.

A police officer sang out, "Got it!"

A cacophony of footsteps cracked and echoed through the trees, and Marlowe whispered, "Now," jerking Cary up by the elbow and leading them both into ankle-deep water under the bridge. He pulled her up into the dark nook on the near side of the bridge, pressing their bodies into the moss and mud until they couldn't be seen. The movement sounded nearer. They were making their way back toward the car.

Marlowe leaned out on the far side of the bridge to stare up the road which curved farther into the woods. A farm truck slowly rumbled its way toward them. Marlowe poked Cary in the side and pointed. "Here's our ride. Be ready."

He led them up the far side embankment. It was away from the crime scene and slightly obscured, but if they missed the truck they would still be exposed. He put a hand at Cary's back and pushed as the truck eased onto the bridge. "Don't miss this," he barked into her ear.

Junk littered the flattened bed of the truck. Cary got a good start and made one hop up, rolling over a metal rod and into an empty space. Marlowe followed by sliding in next to her and lying low as the truck bounced around the bend and toward the railroad tracks.

When they reached the tracks, the truck eased to a stop before crossing. Marlowe sprung to action. He leapt over Cary and rolled onto the ground on the driver's side. The driver spun around, shocked, and started to move forward. But Marlowe ripped open the driver's door and pointed a gun at him. "Stop the truck, man! Stop!"

The jerking stop flung Cary forward. She sat up and looked at Marlowe. Her mouth hung open, her brow wrinkled in confusion.

Marlowe motioned with the gun. "Out of the truck. Don't do anything. I'm sorry. We need your truck. Now get out. Come on, man."

The driver was an older man. Dressed like a farmer. He climbed out with a grunt of effort. "You don't have to do this, son."

Marlowe waved him on, rushing him. "Yeah. I do. And I ain't your son. You got a cell phone?"

The man moved back from the truck and frowned. "What?"

"A cell phone, motherfucker. Do you have one?"

The man nodded.

"Cary!" Marlowe waved Cary down. "Give her your phone, man."

The man pulled a cell phone out of his pocket and handed it to Cary. She nodded and mumbled, "I'm sorry."

Marlowe jumped in behind the wheel, and Cary rushed around to the passenger's seat. The old man leaned up toward Marlowe through the open window and muttered, "That *son* comment weren't no race thing. I'm just old. And you're young. And—"

The wheels spun and vaulted the truck up and over the tracks. Marlowe wound his way back to the freeway and sped up. Cary had sat, church-still the whole way. She looked over at the gun sitting between them on the seat. "Why the hell do you have a gun?"

Marlowe looked down at the gun. "I should have told you."

"Yeah. You should have."

"Look, I'm not dangerous or anything. I've been looking for my brother. He runs with some rough crowds. It's protection. Nothing more."

Cary made brief eye contact and looked down into her lap. "Why were you at Dollar General?"

Marlowe shook his head. "What?"

"You said yourself. It's the whitest part of the city."

Marlowe sniffed. "Maybe I came from a white girl's house."

"I'm being serious."

Marlowe nodded. "Yeah. Well, I told you. I was looking for my brother. I got a little turned around. Lucky coincidence for you."

Cary laughed. "Not so lucky for you, huh?"

He joined her in laughing. A little humor worked wonders at repairing the mood. "Nah. Not lucky at all."

"So what now?"

Marlowe had worked his way back to the city and pulled into a gas station parking lot. He reached over and picked the gun up, shoving it back into a deep pocket of his jacket. "Well, we in it now, girl. Got no choice."

Cary shook her head. "What choice?"

Marlowe shrugged. "You said it yourself. We either find the other Cary Trubody, or we go all the way to the top. Figure they'll be looking for a white girl with a black dude now, so we might as well split up. Give me that phone."

Cary handed him the phone, and he dialed his own number, then handed it back. He pointed at the farmer's phone. "I'm gonna look for the other Cary. You gonna go find the chief of police. Whichever one hits first, we call." He opened the truck door and got out.

"Wait, what? How will you—"

He waved a hand at her. "Don't worry about me. I got people. I'll find a ride. You take the truck. But remember, it could be reported stolen any minute. You need to ditch it pretty soon. You got cash. Take cabs if you need to."

Cary nodded, her eyes glassy and dazed, red rimmed from thoughts of Johnna. She mindlessly pulled out money and counted out ten one-hundred-dollar bills, pushing them toward Marlowe.

He shook his head. "Keep it. You may need it more than I do."

Cary frowned at the money and swallowed a lump of some lingering doubt. "And what the hell am I supposed to say to the chief of police if I find him?"

Marlowe smiled. "Try telling him that story about your crazy-ass brother and the bears and shit. Worked on me."

Chapter 13

Detective Bright Hudson stood in the middle of some hickville woods holding a phone out in her palm. She struggled to balance on heels, but goddammit, she still wore them. And a dress. Every day. She never wanted any of the men who worked under her to forget for one second she was all woman.

"We got the phone, Bright." Carlos Moya walked toward her holding a disposable mobile phone with a loose blue plastic glove. Carlos was the only member of her team she let call her Bright. She always hated the name. Her mother had been some spaced-out moony feminist who named her Bright New Day. Some accused her of marrying her ex-husband merely to get the name change. She dropped the New at the same time. But Carlos was mild-mannered, polite, artsy. He would doodle in meetings and leave them on Bright's desk at the end of the day with some smartass comment. She liked that. And him.

She hit End on the call and held a gloved hand out for the phone. Carlos gave it to her gently, like it was alive. Bright pulled up the call log and examined the list. "The first call." She looked up at everyone gathering around her. "The first call got declined." They stared at her like slack-jawed simpletons. "They're still here! Comb every inch of these woods. Somebody call and get a car up there by the tracks. Nobody in or out. You know the drill. Go, go, go."

Everyone scattered. The CSIs scanned the terrain for any signs of anything. The detectives went out guns drawn. Bright watched them go and tapped an index finger on her lips, thinking. She made her way back down to the crime scene. The twenty foot perimeter around the body in the trunk rested quiet and empty. Hers. She coveted this moment while everyone else searched for someone who slipped away long ago.

She walked to the car and stood at the trunk, staring down at the girl's body. Someone mangled the poor thing. Bright guessed at what happened. He made a mess of the girl's throat, strangling her at least a couple times—clutching and adjusting and twisting. He used something heavy to crush her face and windpipe, too. And a small stab wound pooled blood all over her torso. A deep red dot and bright red fan bleeding out down her dress like a melted crayon. Somewhere along the way she lost one of her shoes.

Bright looked around the base of the car. She didn't find the shoe, but she found blood. A pool of it right outside the trunk, and, as she looked more closely, blood straggled off everywhere. Drops and splatters and trails. One led off toward the bridge, so she followed it. She moved carefully, making sure not to screw up her own crime scene. Footprints jumbled all over. She couldn't make sense of anything on the ground except this blood. Blood always made sense.

She made her way almost to the bridge when the blood stopped in another pool. A much larger pool. A *this is where she died* pool. A voice up ahead startled her. "Boss?" A CSI hunkered under the bridge like a little troll. "I think I found something."

Bright made her way over to him, trying and failing to keep her shoes out of the water. His flashlight beam illuminated a strappy high heel with something poking out of the toe. She squinted. "What is that?"

The CSI looked up at her. "A shoe."

Bright rolled her eyes. "I know it's a shoe, jackass. What's in it?"

The CSI leaned over the high heel until his face almost scraped against the loose strap. He looked back over his shoulder at Bright. "Screwdriver. Bloody."

Bright felt like saying a line out of a cheesy cop show. Some bullshit about Cinderella or something. But she didn't have it in her. "Take pictures. And bag it." She dictated softly and sadly. Like a funeral director ordering a sandwich.

She made her way back over to the car. Carlos examined a wad of duct tape hanging off the tailpipe. Bright stood over a hose tossed a few feet from the car. She noticed Carlos staring at it, too. Carlos shook his head. "You think this was all a suicide attempt?"

Bright chuckled. "Not unless she stabbed herself with a screwdriver and climbed into the trunk."

Carlos pointed toward the front of the car. "I was more thinking murder-suicide. Registration says Cary Trubody."

Bright nodded. She walked to the open driver's side door and looked around inside the car. She called back to Carlos, "You got gloves on?"

Carlos stood from his crouching position and eased past her. He followed her site line and reached down to the floorboard with a gloved hand.

Bright leaned over his shoulder. "What is that?"

Carlos held up a broken zip tie. "Zip tie. Cheap kind." He pointed to a shoe in the backseat. "I saw the match in the trunk. Laces undone." He waggled the zip tie. "Somebody friction-sawed this."

Bright nodded in appreciation. "Clever."

Carlos nodded toward the body. "Not clever enough, I guess."

Bright frowned and shook her head. "She had on heels. Something went all kinds of fucked up." She pointed toward the loose shoe. "And I think Cinderella there fucked it up."

Carlos grinned. "You want me to hum a theme song?"

Chapter 14

Sameer must have driven every block of every street in Midtown. Harper's Village was nothing more than a loosely-named neighborhood. Even a born-and-raised local might not be able to tell where it began or ended. So he spent his entire afternoon and into the evening popping into every coffee shop in Midtown to ask after a group of budding filmmakers.

Although he turned up a couple of "maybes," no one seemed to remember seeing a group exactly like he described until one of his final stops. He agreed with himself to try four more shops before calling it a day. The second of those four gave him a barista who eagerly nodded at the mention of the group. She told Sameer to come back the next morning around ten. He would be sure to find at least a few of them circled up out on the patio.

The news picked up his spirits a touch. He began to understand what Seamus loved about journalism. The lead definitely provided a rush. And the constant motion—up and moving, moving, moving. Sameer had spent the last five years of his life at a computer, writing code.

Before landing his programming gig, he'd done a three-year stint as a flight attendant. Although he enjoyed the opportunity to travel, the job itself mainly consisted of slowly walking the same aisle over and over for hours on end.

Chasing leads proved more manic and devoid of the sense of pattern ruling his normal life. Even in the pit of fear and panic and heartbreak, Sameer caught himself erupting in adrenaline smiles every now and then.

But home—home brought back the sorrow. Everything half empty. The garage. The little shelf inside where they took off their shoes. The hooks where they hung keys. The kitchen table. The couch. The bed. Everywhere he looked was filled with empty space. The movement helped, he decided. He knew it was illusion. Like taking a long, winding, roundabout path to avoid sitting still a few extra seconds at a red light. But stopping and enduring the cold beside him where a person should be? The notion chilled him and made him choose the illusion.

So he threw on some exercise clothes and went for a run. He showered. He took his dinner onto the back porch and ate standing. After hours of nervous motion, he fell asleep for a couple of hours in a lawn chair. In the morning, he threw on clothes, spending as little time inside as possible, and left for the coffee shop two hours before the barista suggested.

Whole Bean Coffee Shoppe offered a wide array of coffees from around the world in addition to its highly-touted "locally sourced" pastries and breakfast dishes. Sameer opted for a familiar Pakistani coffee with cinnamon and cardamom. He hadn't taken his coffee this way since childhood and his grandmother would pour him a cup, always adding a little extra cream and some sugar. By the third cup, he grew a touch jittery.

Sometime around 10:30 the first of the group wandered onto the patio. Sameer didn't realize at first, but he flagged the guy as a possibility. The lanky black guy wore full hipster regalia: skinny jeans and thick glasses and an unnecessary scarf. Eventually, two others joined who fit the bill. Another black guy with a little more hip-hop in his hipster. And a white guy with a pretentious beard and coiffed hair who looked overly proud of himself for having two black friends.

Sameer sat back and listened at first as they talked about politics and laughed about some inside joke he didn't understand. When the conversation shifted to a discussion of a movie they had seen recently, he leaned forward. Something about the way they talked gave Sameer enough evidence to believe this was, in fact, the group.

He walked up to their table a little more rapidly than he intended. He held out a hand as if he were formally introducing himself in some Renaissance era royal festival and immediately cursed himself inwardly for doing so. "Good morning, gentlemen. My name is Sameer Zardari. I am looking for a group of young men who make movies. Or, well, films, I'm sure. My hope is that they may be able to assist me in locating a missing person. I noticed you discussing film in a way not entirely dissimilar to the way I would expect such a group of young men to discuss film. So I theorized you might be this group, which I hope is accurate."

They all blinked at him. Hip-Hop Hipster laughed. "You been hitting the coffee pretty hard this morning, huh?"

Sameer closed his eyes and shook his head. "I'm sorry. I'm sorry. Yes. That was awful. I'd like to go back."

White Guilt grinned. "Go back? Like, take two?"

Sameer nodded. "Please."

They blinked at him some more before shrugging and all three pointing at him.

Sameer nodded a thanks and took a deep breath. "Good morning. My name is Sameer Zardari and I hate to bother you. I was wondering if I could ask you a couple of questions about a missing person you may have seen."

They all three clapped in soft applause, and the Lanky Hipster pulled a chair over to offer him. Sameer sat and thanked them. He reached into his pocket for his photo of Seamus, but before he could present it Lanky Hipster blurted out, "So you're looking for Do Right?"

Sameer paused with the photo held to his chest. "I'm sorry? Do Right?"

Lanky Hipster nodded. "Yeah. You said missing person. And you're looking for us. I figure you must mean Do Right."

Sameer shook his head and frowned.

White Guilt leaned forward. "We have a friend—Do Right is what he goes by. He hasn't been seen in a few days. His brother has been asking about him. Are you a private investigator or something?"

Sameer couldn't help but beam with pride a little at being confused for a private investigator. He laughed. "No, I'm not. At all." He slid the picture across the table. "And I'm afraid I don't know your friend. I'm sorry. I'm actually looking for my husband, who has also been missing for a few days. I was told someone in your group knew him." He tapped Seamus' face on the photograph.

All three of the men leaned over the picture and sat up, nodding. Hip-Hop Hipster pointed back at Seamus. "Yeah, yeah. The reporter. Irish name."

Sameer grew wide-eyed and nodded. "Seamus Fitzgerald, yes."

They all nodded. Hip Hop Hipster continued, "Yep. Seamus. He worked with Do Right. He ran into me and Do Right shooting some footage over in Dollar Hill. We got to talking about politicians and corruption and conspiracy theories and shit. He asked if either of us would be interested in working with him on a documentary. I was working on a thing at the time, but Do Right jumped on it. They been working on it for about a month since then."

Sameer scribbled notes in a leather journal he had remembered to bring with him this time. "Do you know what it was about?"

They all shook their heads. Lanky Hipster chimed in, "He never said. I guess we figured it had something to do with crooked politicians, based on our first conversation. And they spent a lot of time over in Dollar Hill. They went down there looking for Booker one time." The other two nodded and agreed.

Sameer's head shot up. "Yes. Booker. I've heard his name before. Do you know why? Or where I can find him?"

Lanky Hipster cocked his head. "We've been knowing Booker for a long time. Used him in shots from time to time. He's a guy with a lot of stories. He told one about saving a girl from being choked out by a judge or a senator or some kind of crazy shit. Your husband came and had coffee with us one day. Booker came up, and he got super interested in his story. He asked Do Right to help him find Booker."

White Guilt nodded in remembrance. "Last time I saw him, Booker had moved into a homeless camp in Old Town. The old Parker Building down there. It's run down and boarded up. Homeless kind of took it over as a squatter camp. Booker is supposed to be there."

Chapter 15

Cary fought with the stick shift, grinding her way out of the parking lot as Marlowe laughed at her in the rearview. Remembering how to drive a standard kept her distracted from the suspicion eating her insides like a cancer. She hadn't wondered why Marlowe showed up at the Dollar General at four in the morning. Running for her life left little room for ponderance. But driving gave her time. And she spent the luxury of time wondering if she could trust anyone left alive.

Of course, passing two cops pushed all of her ponderings out of her head. Even if the farmer didn't report the truck stolen yet, the decrepit clunker likely boasted expired tags and a broken taillight. She would be pulled over within the hour.

The roads were getting more familiar. Cary drove with muscle memory, taking the path she took a hundred times—before dates and after Sunday brunches and at the end of long workdays—toward Johnna's house. She got within a block before waking up from road hypnosis and comprehending what a bad idea it was. Johnna lived with her grandmother, who knew Cary, but who knows how the old lady would react to all this. Cary wheeled the truck into a car wash and parked in one of the stables, concealed from view.

Whether he could be trusted or not, Marlowe wasn't wrong. They ran out of options somewhere between the diner and the woods. If he really went to look for the "other" Cary Trubody, then she needed to do her part.

She pulled out the old man's iPhone and scrolled through his handful of apps looking for Google. "Of course," she muttered to herself. "Why do all old people use Safari?" She opened it up and searched for the chief of police.

The first result showed a fifty-ish, salt-and-pepper-headed white guy named Ken Webster. He sported a mustache and looked a little like a Tom Selleck body double. Cary stared at his picture for several minutes, trying to get a read. Maybe the episode of *Blue Bloods* her mom made her sit through influenced her thinking, but her gut told her he wasn't a bad guy. His eyes looked trustworthy.

She next searched Ken Webster AND address. Unsurprisingly, the chief of police kept his home address hard to find. Fair enough. Ken Webster AND appearances.

Yahtzee. Ken Webster would be attending some gala that night.

The gala would be hosted by a local high school—a celebration of some partnership between the school and the police force. Cary looked down at her filthy, tattered jeans and T-shirt. Her "I'm a lesbian" army-green field jacket. She talked into her lap, "Betting this is not what they mean by semi-formal." But "open to the public" buoyed her spirits. One step at a time. She could spend the next few hours figuring out the next one. For now, she needed sleep. A quick nap under the cover of the car wash cubicle. Cary laid her head back and drifted off in seconds.

When she woke up, the disorienting feeling of regaining consciousness in unfamiliar surroundings made her jump alert. The cab of the truck turned into a disco. Red and blue lights oscillated on both sides of her. Confusion beat out reason, and the lights were an annoyance—a mystery. The stickiness of sleep peeled off of her and Cary saw in a convex mirror above the car wash stalls what caused the lights. Two cop cars had pulled over a motorcycle. They were questioning the guy. One of the cop cars was pulled up next to the front of her truck.

Cary instinctively grabbed at the keys but stopped. The cop's front bumper jutted out in front of her enough to keep her pinned in. So she opened her door and stalled again, looking behind her. The cubicle opened to an alley leading to a main road. Cary held her door open and listened. She could hear the cops asking the man if he had been drinking, telling him to have a seat. Radio static crackled as one of them called in to check something about the motorcycle driver. A raspy female voice interrupted the cop by calling out in a bored tone, "Be on the lookout for a 70s model Chevrolet flatbed truck, green with white stripe. Driver is a black male, possibly accompanied by a white female. Driver is armed."

Cary sighed, "Well, balls." She eased out of the door and crept backwards toward the alley. She put on Marlowe's Dodgers cap and popped her jacket collar. When she hit the alley, she broke into what felt like a stroll—hands in pockets, head down, casual. Other than the car wash, this was a residential area for the most part. She stifled all tact and restraint on her walk toward Johnna's grandmother's house.

Johnna and her grandmother lived in a baby blue two-story in the curve of a quiet street. Ms. Langley always hung an elaborate wreath—one for any season— on the navy blue door. Nanna Langley was sweet lady. She baked and wore house coats she sewed herself and did all the things grandmothers are supposed to do. At any given moment, she would be in her recliner watching some screaming preacher on television. However, she was also about the biggest liberal anyone ever met. She supported Johnna's relationship with Cary when no one else knew about it.

Graffiti Creek

Cary pulled off her cap, shoving it in a pocket, and tapped on the door loud enough to be heard over a TV. It took three times, but Ms. Langley finally came to the door. She flipped a deadbolt and opened it right up—a trusting habit for which Johnna always scolded her. Ms. Langley squinted through her little, round grandmother glasses. Cary waved. "Hey, Ms. Langley. It's me. Cary."

Ms. Langley flapped her hands out. "Oh, Cary, honey. Come in here." She pulled Cary through the door in a half-hug. "I haven't been able to reach Johnna, sweetie. Is she with you?"

Cary swallowed. "Can we go sit down, Ms. Langley?"

The old woman offered her a cup of coffee, which Cary accepted. Even with an hour nap, Cary was frazzled and bucking up her eyelids with a finger every few minutes.

As Ms. Langley left for the coffee, Cary thought about what she planned to do. How could any of this be explained? When the coffee came, they sat and sipped at it for a moment, Ms. Langley blathering about her morning. Cary interrupted her. "Ms. Langley, I need to talk to you about Johnna."

Ms. Langley wrinkled her face into a worry like Cary had never seen. "Do you think she's okay, honey?"

Cary opened her mouth and stopped. She looked down at her coffee. "Yeah. Yes, ma'am. I'm," she rubbed at an eye, "I'm sure she is."

Ms. Langley let herself smile. "Have you talked to her?"

Cary nodded. "Yes. I have. It's why I'm here. She, um, she needed me to pick up a dress for her. Do you mind if I," she motioned upstairs.

"Of course. Of course, dear. Go right ahead."

Cary thanked her and started up, trying not to think about Ms. Langley's parting plea of "Please have her call me."

Johnna's room was small. A child's room. Johnna grew up in the room and changed few things over the span of two decades. Before they started dating, Johnna spent a couple of years in a relationship with a guy. The sexy, hip aspiring filmmaker, in the end, panned out to be more interested in his YouTube following than in Johnna.

They had been friends, all three of them. Cary liked the guy fine. They would text back and forth about movies every now and then. But when Cary and Johnna admitted to him they were in love, everything sort of fell apart.

He took it harder than expected. Kicked Johnna out, which left her no choice but to move back to her grandmother's. Nanna Langley kept her room as a shrine to her sweet Johnna. When she moved back, Johnna left most of the band posters up for nostalgia.

Cary walked over to the bed and picked up a framed photo of the two of them. The ex-boyfriend took it at a film festival. Cary smiled thinking about how they ditched him at some art house screening to go catch a James Bond movie. He got so pissed. Called them *tasteless*. Johnna leaned into Cary's ear and whispered, "I think you taste wonderful." Cary turned bright red from a mixture of embarrassment and fear at being discovered. Everything felt so dangerous and exciting during that time. *Dangerous* had such a different meaning to her then.

She went to Johnna's closet and flipped through dresses. She recalled one being too big for Johnna. She kept meaning to get her grandmother to take it in, but Cary bet on her not following through. She found it shoved to the back. Simple. Black. She held it up against her and found her theory to be correct. It might be a touch tight, but it would work.

As she turned, she noticed, for the first time, the drawers. Johnna's drawers were all open, with clothing spilling out. She walked gently around the room and took it in. Things were moved around—strewn about. The laptop lay open and left on. Johnna might be free-spirited, but no one would ever accuse her of being sloppy. In fact, she obsessed about it at times. She could be a neat freak. She assigned everything a place, and things belonged in their place. Someone searched this room.

Cary draped the dress over her arm and hurried down the stairs. She started, "Ms. Langley, has anyone—"

She came upon Ms. Langley standing by an old-fashioned phone table, watching out a window. Their eyes met, and they both looked down at the phone. A little white card sat next to it. They locked eyes again as Cary walked over and picked up the card—a business card for a police detective named Mark Thompson. Cary held it up in front of Ms. Langley. "Did you call him? Does he know I'm here?"

Ms. Langley looked flustered. She stuttered out, "I—I—I...honey they...he wants to find her like we do."

Cary dropped the card and swore. She ran for the door, but a car already pulled up and parked at the curb. Cary spun and looked pleadingly at Ms. Langley. The old woman looked from Cary to the car and back. Tears welled up in her eyes. She shook her head subtly in a form of silent apology and shot a glance to the back door. Cary followed the look and sprinted.

She burst through the door in a dead run. She scanned wildly for an escape route. A gate in the corner of the yard led to a neighbor's yard. Cary followed the path into the next yard, continuing to search. A door opened to an attached garage. She clambered through it and slid down next to a car. Cary panted and clutched the dress against her. She breathed it in, hoping for a scent of Johnna to calm her.

Cary reached up for a door handle. The backseat driver's side door was unlocked. Cary climbed in, lying in the floorboard and pulling at the door until the stifled click told her the latch had caught. On the far side of the car, giggling voices bounced out a door from the house. Two teenage girls talked in *likes* and *reallys* about something nonsensical. They flitted into the car on either side of the front seat. As the passenger reached to buckle her seatbelt, she caught sight of Cary and jumped. Both girls swiveled and stared at her with shocked fear.

Cary pulled out several hundred dollar bills. "Please. I'm not a bad person. I'm not going to hurt you. Please." She held the money up to confused glares. "There's a man. He wants to hurt me. Please." She waved the money again. "Please."

The two girls shared a look commemorating a hundred moments. Moments of men who wanted to hurt them. The passenger snatched the money and nodded to the driver, who started the car.

A beat later, Detective Mark Thompson in his cheap suit stood at the driver's side window tapping on it with a large ringed finger. The girl jumped again and rolled down her window. The detective sulked at her. "Has a woman come through here?"

The driver froze, but the passenger, once again, leaned across her. "Yes, sir. She scared the shit out of us." She pointed. "She ran through here and headed out onto the road."

Chapter 16

Jonathan Epstein loved few things in this world. He loved zippered pullovers. They felt like wearing a hug, and they were not too unflattering to his rather large belly. He loved steak sandwiches from a diner around the block from his office, and street tacos out of a truck across from the diner. Thus the big belly. And he loved to golf. More than anything, he loved to golf.

Bright Hudson claimed few friends. And Jonathan Epstein most certainly did not make the cut. They barely liked each other. But in her divorce, Bright demanded her ex-husband give her the membership to the most exclusive country club in the city. Among other amenities, the club boasted a world-class golf course, for which Bright found absolutely zero use. So her membership went straight to Jonathan, and he relished it, playing at least twice a week. In exchange, anytime she wanted, Bright got to demand a meeting for a cup of coffee. They would always meet in the same spot: the Starbucks across from the coroner's office, where Jonathan worked.

Bright sat at a table in the back in a quiet spot close to the bathroom. When Jonathan came in, two coffees sat waiting. She took a sip from hers as he sat down. "Who's doing the autopsy?"

Jonathan sighed into the chair across from her. "Not me. I listened in, but it's early. I'm not sure how much I can tell you."

Bright shrugged. "Anything will help."

Jonathan took a pull from his coffee. "Well, cause of death is a weird one. Looks like she got choked by hand. The killer might have thought it did the trick. But some time later, she got roughed up a bit—punched in the face, at least. Then stabbed in the chest with, most likely, the screwdriver you found in her shoe. And for a final death blow, she got her throat crushed. Maybe by foot...brick? Something heavy."

"In that order?"

Jonathan scrunched his face up. "Probably."

Bright nodded. "Anything else?"

"She's missing a fingernail. Defensive. The whole nail—ripped completely off."

Bright shook her head. "Nobody found a fingernail. Was she moved?"

Jonathan cocked his head. "Could be. The trunk seemed too clean. Struck me as odd. She did not bleed in it, scratch it up, kick out a light. Nothing. But she wasn't bound. And she left enough blood at the scene to suggest the stabbing happened there."

"Guy or girl?"

"Hands that strangled her are male. They're big. Strong."

Bright chewed at her coffee cup, in thought.

Jonathan leaned across the table to get her attention. "That's all I got."

Bright waved him off, dismissing him. Jonathan stood and gladly started away, leaving Bright to sit and contemplate. He stopped at the counter to drop a dollar in the tip jar and looked back at Bright. "Oh yeah. The screwdriver."

Bright looked up and raised her eyebrows.

Jonathan took a step back toward the table. "Yeah. Very weird."

"How so?"

"Well, it comes from a set, but a tool kit makes no sense in that trunk. There were no other tools, no clutter, no road kit or anything. The screwdriver doesn't fit."

Bright nodded. "Yeah. But it could've come from anywhere, right?"

Jonathan shrugged. "It could. Yes. The thing is…I know it came from a set. The kind you keep in the trunk with road flares and shit. I own one just like it."

Bright frowned. "You own a screwdriver exactly like the one we found in the creek?"

Jonathan laughed. "Yeah. You do, too. We all do. They gave them to us from the department."

Chapter 17

The girl driving shook, almost crying. "Who was that guy? Your husband?

Cary stayed in the floorboard. "No. Not my husband."

The passenger pulled out the money and checked it, then put it back in her pocket. "That guy reeked of cop. What'd you do?"

Cary cocked her head. "You're quick, aren't you? I didn't do anything. Big misunderstanding. What are your names?"

The driver's voice still quivered. "Haley."

The passenger looked almost bored. "What's yours?"

"Cary." She paused. "Probably best to keep it at first names."

The passenger smiled wryly. "Fair enough. Grayson."

Cary sat up a little. "Well, Grayson. I need a favor. One that pays. How much did I give you?"

Grayson smacked at a piece of gum. "Four hundred."

Cary nodded. "I've got four hundred more. I need a ride. You girls know Roosevelt High School?"

Haley chirped. "Yes. I used to date a guy who went there."

"Good. I need you to drop me off there and pick me up later."

Grayson raised an eyebrow. "Right now?"

Cary struggled her way into the backseat. "Before seven. Give me maybe until eight."

Haley looked back. "That's in four hours."

Grayson leaned onto the console. "Why do you need to go to a high school at night?"

"There's a gala. Some policeman's thing. I'm not sure what it's called."

Grayson smiled. "I know it's not the Policeman's Ball."

Cary squinted at her, and then bit. "How do you know?"

"Because policemen don't have balls." She slapped Cary on the knee and laughed. "So that's the dress, huh?"

Cary laughed along and nodded. "Yeah, I need a place to change, I guess."

Haley made a sour face over her shoulder. "You need more than a place to change."

Cary shot her an affronted look. "What?"

Haley raised her eyebrows and smiled. "We need to go to the mall or something." She motioned toward Cary's face. "You need…lots of things."

Grayson clapped her hands in feigned chipperness. "Makeover! Makeover!"

Cary rolled her eyes. "I'm going to go ahead and hard pass on the mall. Without getting into it, people might be looking for me."

Grayson smirked. "Yeah. So you go to a dinner party with a bunch of cops. Makes perfect sense."

"I'm not scared of cops. Well, not all cops. Only a few." Cary frowned. "Balls. Hopefully, they won't be there."

Haley flashed another patronizing smile. "I'm just saying."

Cary started something, but Grayson interrupted her. "Haley's not wrong, you know? Whatever you did—" Cary flashed a look and Grayson held her hands up and corrected, "Or didn't do. And whoever it is looking for you. They're looking for," she motioned up and down Cary with a finger, "you. Now, my friend here may seem a bit spacey and shallow, but you give her a couple of hours in the mall." She winked and made a clicking sound with her mouth. "You won't even recognize yourself."

Cary bit her lip and thought.

Grayson added, "Of course, that'll be another hundred."

Cary sighed. "Oh, of course."

It had been years since Cary felt like "one of the girls." She never got into the shopping-nails-hair-makeup frenzy too much anyway. But after spending the better part of a day trying to avoid getting murdered, a little pampering provided, despite all of her instincts, a nice release. She traded the oversized pockets of her jacket for a clutch which complimented her dress. All three girls got makeovers and manicures and shoes and pretzel bites, Cary's treat. They whipped up a regular goddamn sleepover in the middle of the day.

At the end of it all, Cary found a full-length mirror in a Macy's and stood staring into it. "Fuck me."

Grayson leaned onto her shoulder. "Oh, he'll want to."

Cary cut her eyes at her. "I'm gay."

Grayson shrugged. "He'll still want to."

By the time they drove toward the school, the little digital clock in the dash read a quarter past seven. Cary kept checking the time on her stolen phone until Haley scolded her. "Stop! You can't be on time. You look desperate when you're on time to an event. And you sure as shit couldn't be as early as you wanted to be. You would have looked like a murderer."

Grayson spoke out of the side of her mouth. "Which she might be."

Haley rolled her eyes. "Please. She's not a murderer. She wears Crocs."

The girls laughed in agreement, and Cary piped in. "They aren't Crocs. The Crocs company manufactures them, but they aren't, like, *Crocs* Crocs."

The girls nodded exaggeratedly and kept laughing.

Cary added, "I'm not a murderer."

Haley cruised through a neighborhood across from the school. She stopped in front of an empty house—a for sale sign sat out front in an unmanicured lawn. Haley looked back at Cary. "I'll drop you off and pull back around here. We can sit and wait."

Cary shook her head. "You don't have to wait."

Haley closed one eye. "I think we do. You were running for your life earlier. I'm not sure you can assume this goes well for you."

Cary looked over at the high school. "Fair point."

The girls dropped Cary off at the door. The high school expanded across a few blocks in a multi-building behemoth of structure. Lights looped and hung along a walkway leading to what looked like the primary building—two or three stories and brick, but newer than the buildings around it. High school students stood at the doors as greeters. People traipsed in and out, holding drinks, carrying on jovial conversations about mundane topics.

Cary's nerves felt like a wet sack of joy buzzers. She jerked at every passing hello. Inside the doors, she took a moment to close her eyes and collect herself. This could never work if she came across like a lunatic. Luckily, none of the faces looked familiar. She hoped this would be the last place any of her pursuers would expect her to be. And even if they showed up, the diner proved to her they couldn't make a move around other cops, of which this place had an abundance.

Never before had Cary put any stock into the old "looks like a cop" label. Grayson had pegged Mr. Cheap Suit for one in the garage. And now, she had to admit, these guys all looked like cops. The crowd consisted of white men and their wives. Although a few outliers mingled around, along with a few female officers of rank, the plus ones stood out from the invited like parents at a park. Cary accepted a flute of white wine from a tray. Holding something made her feel more at ease.

She scanned the room for Ken Webster. She pulled up a photo of him on her phone, and she kept stealing glances of it in her clutch. It didn't take long. Ken Webster and his wife were toward the front of the large lobby where the event centered. A massive, curved, glowing blue tile wall ran the entire height of the building along the far side. And the Websters stood in the glow of it, chatting with a steady stream of people.

As she made her way toward the police chief, two spots of tan caught her eye. The two tan suits flanking the room stood out from all the black and navy. They both scanned the crowd. Searching. Looking for Cary.

She turned her back to them and swore to herself. *They can't hurt you in a crowd*, she thought. The mantra didn't grant her quite the solace she had hoped for. Cary downed the rest of her wine and started back for the doors. Her only hope was Marlowe would come through with plan B.

About ten yards from the door, before Cary emerged from the crowd, a woman burst through the doors. Her jeans and sweatshirt stood out like sardines in a fruit tray. Not to mention she was female, and black. But Cary didn't need any of those for the woman to grab her attention, because she recognized her. The cop from last night. Doyle.

Cary spun back around and marked the two fat detectives. Doyle held at her back, surveying the crowd. They triangulated her. One of Cary's bosses used that word far too often, and it came back to her in the moment like acid reflux. She looked for doors. Doyle was posted by the main set. The two dicks stationed themselves up in front of what appeared to be the only other exits to the outside. Over to one side of the triangle of death a hallway stretched off into a darkened school. And then there stood the Websters. Her first option became her only option.

Taking a second wine, Cary wove back through the crowd toward Ken Webster. Two older men held him engrossed in conversation. His wife hung at his elbow, sipping her drink with a blasé expression. Cary stood behind the two old men like she was waiting in line. When they moved on, she stepped forward with, "Excuse me. Chief Webster?" But before it registered, he turned to a louder voice guffawing something at him.

Mrs. Webster laughed. "Oh, sweetheart. You have to be more forceful. He can be an oblivious jackass. Like a thirteen-year-old boy in math class." She motioned toward the loud man talking to her husband. "He's always going to get distracted by the class clown."

Cary smiled politely. "He has a lot of demands on his attention. I understand."

Mrs. Webster looked her up and down. "That's a darling dress."

Cary glanced down. "Thank you. It's—it was my friend's."

"Well, she has great taste." Mrs. Webster extended a hand. "Karen."

Cary switched her wine to her left and shook Karen Webster's hand. "Cary. Trubody. Lovely to meet you."

Karen cocked her head. "'Lovely to meet you?'" She let out a breathy laugh. "No one says that anymore."

Cary shook her head. "I don't say it either. I have no idea why I did."

They both laughed and let it bleed into a conversation about cocktail parties and wine and shoes. All the while, Cary tried repeatedly to get the police chief's attention only to fail each time. Karen set her empty wine glass on a passing tray and put a hand on Cary's arm. "You let me find a little girl's room, hon. Then I'm coming back here to force the insufferable ass to talk to you."

When Karen turned to head for the restroom, a figure stood menacing in the woman's wake. Detective Dick had spotted her. He spoke into a cell phone and moved toward her. To her left, Ken Webster continued talking to a revolving door of old men. She turned right and hurried after Karen Webster. "I think I'll join you, if you don't mind."

"Of course, dear." Karen linked arms with Cary and they walked down the hallway which darkened into the rest of the school.

The noises of the party died away, swallowed by the acoustics of the cavernous lobby. Cary and Karen walked swiftly. Behind them, Cary heard the footsteps of boots. The hallway grew darker. Karen babbled on about something, but all Cary could hear were boot steps. They turned a corner and everything got even darker. Light burst out of two doorways ahead of them on the left. Cary could see the male/female restroom icons above the doors. The echoing of the steps grew faster, closer. Cary could sense someone behind them as they swerved into the open restroom.

Once inside, Cary swirled around and took Karen by both arms. She looked around Karen to the door and found nothing. She whispered. "I have to tell you something."

Karen's face blanched in surprise but instantly grew concerned. "What's the matter, sweetheart?"

Cary breathed in rapid pants. "This is going to sound insane, but I have nowhere else to turn. I'm being targeted by police. Only a handful of them. They think I'm someone I'm not. Or maybe I have something I don't have. And all this can be cleared up, but I need protection. I need help. I need—"

"Cary, honey. I—" Karen stopped. Her eyes quivered. She looked as if she may vomit mid-sentence.

Cary shook her head. "What's wrong?"

Karen's mouth hung open, as if searching for a word she couldn't remember. Blood pooled around her teeth and on her bottom lip. She coughed involuntarily, spraying blood all over Cary's face. The bathroom echoed with a wet sucking sound. And Karen collapsed into Cary, almost knocking them both down.

Detective Dick hovered over her. Holding a bloody knife and staring at Cary. He didn't smile. Or threaten. His stare said, *Look what you made me do*. He reached a bloody hand across Karen's body and stroked Cary's cheek. He turned and rushed out of the bathroom, turning away from where they had come, his footsteps disappearing down the hallway.

Cary let the weight of Karen take her to the ground. Dick had stabbed her behind the ear. And Karen Webster's ear bled like a leaky sink. Cary desperately tried to put pressure on the wound and talk to her and flip her over. Anything. Everything.

"Mrs. Webster? Mrs. Webster? Please. Please. You're okay. I'll get help. You'll be okay."

She looked around in a frenzied search for a way out of this. Dick had left the knife lying in front of them. And on either side of the knife dawned a shadow. Cary looked up to find to party guests standing in the doorway. She shook her head at them. One of the women let out a scream like a hurt animal. The other looked sick and held a hand up in fear. She cowered away from Cary, saying, "What did you do?"

Cary started to say something, but they had turned in a run back toward the party. To alert a room full of police.

Chapter 18

Marlowe sat in a booth of the convenient store where Cary left him. The steamy food counter of the gas station served fried chicken and potato boats and taquitos. Marlowe spent his only cash on a cardboard tray of fried okra.

He and his brother loved gas station fried okra when they were kids. Gas stations were about the only place you could find real fried okra. They fell in love with it spending summers with their grandmother in Alabama. Fried okra tasted like Southern summers spent getting chased out of the kitchen with a wooden spoon. Marlowe's brother was a next-level wizard at crashing through the kitchen and coming out with a blistering handful of okra. They would sit out under a big oak tree and lay the greasy pieces out between them right in the grass. His brother would smile bigger than Huck Finn with his bare feet and blue jeans cuffed up to his knees. He always loved it down South. The lazy rhythm appealed to him.

He rolled the last piece of okra between his fingers and fought back tears. His phone vibrated in his pocket. Shelley rattled at him before he could answer. "'lowe, where you at? I've been worried."

Marlowe repeated her name to calm her down. "Shelley. Shelley, I'm okay. I'm at a gas station over on Yarberry. The one with the okra me and Do Right like." He hung his head. "Liked."

"You don't know he's dead, 'lowe."

"I do, Shelley. I don't know how, but I do. And I was thinking, if we can find his body, I want to bury him next to Grandma."

"Stop! I'm not ready for that yet!"

"Shelley, they killed him. And they're going to kill you, too, if you let them. *That's* what *I'm* not ready for. I lost my little brother. I'm not about to lose my baby sister, too."

Shelley sniffed into the phone. "You won't. I'm doing everything I'm supposed to. But Marlowe, I can't let them hurt somebody because of me."

"I ain't worried about somebody else, Shelley."

Shelley's breathing faltered. "Marlowe. Please tell me she's still with you."

Marlowe held the phone down and brought it back up. "We had a truck. A truck I took from some old guy. She left me here and took it."

"What do you mean you 'took from some old guy?' You stole a truck?"

"Yeah. I stole a truck. It was life or death, Shelley. They got me in this now. And I'm about to get us both out."

"Where is she, Marlowe?"

"She talked it out and reasoned that she only has two ways out of this shit. One was to go all the way to the top. She figures the chief of police can't be crooked, so maybe he'd listen to her. She went to find him."

"Shit." Shelley's end of the line buzzed with silence. "She—she won't be able to go up and—" Shelley sighed. "There's some gala at Roosevelt High tonight. All the bigwigs will be there."

Marlowe swallowed. "Yeah. I looked it up."

"Marlowe. They can't find out where she's going."

He sighed into the phone. "They already did, Shelley."

"Shit. Shit!" Shelley hung up.

Marlowe sat and stared at his phone until Shelley called back. "I'm sorry, Shelley. But all I'm worried about right now is—"

"What are you supposed to do?"

"What?"

"You. You said she thought of two things and left you at the gas station. To do what?"

Marlowe laughed a little. "She figures there must be another Cary Trubody out there. They must have gotten mixed up. I'm supposed to find the other one."

Shelley let out a breathy laugh. "Jesus."

Shelley hung up and threw her phone across the room. Marlowe talked to her like they were still kids. He always took on a tone like some kind of church deacon. She laughed to herself and thought, *That boy ain't sat through church a day in his damn life.* Marlowe always felt responsible for everything. Like part of his job was to hold up the sky. Their momma even kidded him about his sense of burden. Called him Atlas. It wasn't until studying mythology in high school when any of them got the joke.

Those early days wore hard on Marlowe. Their momma worked two jobs back then, and Marlowe ran baths and fixed lunches. He kept the weight of the sky off Shelley and their brother so they could play through life.

At least Shelley straightened up. While she still lived at home, their momma married a rich man whose house she cleaned. Everything got so much easier for their momma once she took on a rich man's name. He was a nice man. Shelley let him adopt her. Figured she'd score herself some of the rich name. Didn't take long to learn the name didn't do much by itself. So Shelley put herself in a position to earn the respect she wanted. She ran for class offices. She got into college on a scholarship. She did pre-law and joined the Academy. And, by God, she shined her badge every night before her shift.

Their brother, though, he never straightened his path. Couldn't pull his head out of the clouds, as they say. Or maybe he couldn't pull the cloud out of his head. When they were little, their momma bought him a shitty video camera from a pawn shop for Christmas. He ran all over the neighborhood filming every move they and their friends made. They recreated more movies than Shelley could count. And he kept at it all the way through high school and into a couple of failed attempts at college.

Kids in the neighborhood took to calling him *Spike Lee*, and then *Do the Right Thing*, and, finally, *Do Right*. Dante loved it. He never went anywhere without a camera in his hands. Shelley used to call it his albatross. Film was supposed to lift Do Right out of his own shit and to a better life. But he ended up obsessed with filming the shit he was living in. And now she started to fear the same conclusion Marlowe had reached: Do Right's obsession might have gotten him killed.

Chapter 19

Officer Doyle had worked three nights in a row. She planned on sleeping through the afternoon. But instead she was fishing through her laundry room for a shirt and a pair of jeans. Living alone meant laundry at her own pace, and her pace was *smell it before you wear it.* She managed to dig up a dingy blue T-shirt and a gray hoodie. She could throw on a cap and look as inconspicuous as she could as a young black woman. The gala didn't start until 7:00, so she had hours to track down Cary before then.

But those hours whittled down to nothing. She tried any and everywhere Cary might go, but to no avail. Tired and starving, she sat outside Roosevelt High School and watched the police elite file in looking uncomfortable in black suits. She was on the verge of dozing off when a car pulled close to the main doors and dropped off a lone woman. Although the woman cleaned up and dressed for the occasion, Doyle knew immediately she had found Cary.

Doyle parked in a visitor lot between two SUVs, staying out of sight. Checking to make sure she had her gun tucked into the back of her pants, she jumped out of the car and took several quick breaths to steady herself. The entrance was a good thirty feet to her left, so she darted up to the side of the building, far from the madding crowd. As she searched for a way in, a voice barked from over her shoulder sending her flipping around with a hand under the back of her hoodie.

Mark Thompson walked up, laughing at her. "Holster it, Doyle. What the hell are you doing here?"

Doyle tried to avoid eye contact. "I caught sight of Cary Trubody. I've been following her ever since."

Detective Jolly walked around the side of the building. "She's in there?"

Doyle looked around, startled. "Yeah. Yes, sir. She is."

Jolly nodded, looking around her at the crowd.

Thompson ducked his head and cut his eyes at Shelley. "You realize we need to talk to this young lady. Right, Doyle?"

She nodded. "Yes, sir. I made an attempt to confirm her whereabouts and then I planned on calling you."

Thompson curled a lip and sucked at his teeth. "Good, Doyle. Makes me happy to hear that."

Jolly stepped between them and past Shelley to get a better look at the crowd. "What's she doing in there?"

She looked back and forth between them. "I'm—I'm not sure, sir."

Thompson shrugged. "Don't matter. We need to stop her."

Doyle cocked her head. "With all due respect, sir, how can we do anything with this many officers around?"

Thompson sighed, "I don't know. But we gotta."

Jolly spoke away from them, "What we need is for all of them," he pointed toward the crowd, "to want this bitch as bad as we do."

She shuddered. "And how do we do that?"

Jolly looked over his shoulder at her.

She closed her eyes and swallowed. "Sir."

Jolly grinned. "Leave it to us, sweetie. You just help us find her."

Thompson said, "Jolly and I will head around to the side entrances up front. Doyle, you guard the main doors. Make sure she doesn't slip back out the way she went in."

Doyle pointed up and down at her clothes. "I'm not exactly dressed for an event like this, sir."

Thompson laughed. "Looks a hell of a lot better than the dress you'll wear to your brother's funeral, Doyle. Now, help us find this bitch, unless you want to go ahead and start picking it out."

Chapter 20

The beauty of being a computer programmer was not getting any harsh looks for holing up in an office and doing weird shit. Sameer proved to himself he couldn't go back to an empty home. Instead he took the notes from Seamus' desk Margaret copied for him and went up to his office.

The building always hummed with the buzz of computer monitors and the clickety-clack of keyboard taps at any hour. Coders worked when they worked, and management let the work happen in whatever fashion those coders chose as long as everything got done.

Sameer wheeled a large corkboard on casters into his office and retrieved colored note cards and push pins from the storage closet. He cleared his work table and laid out the Xeroxed notes so every page was visible.

He started by seeking out names. Seamus had horrible handwriting, but after twelve years together Sameer knew the scribblings as well as his own. He fished through his stack of notecards for all the red ones and put one name on each card with a black Sharpie. When he found it, he would add a title or position next to a name—usually judge or senator or district attorney and the like. After he fished out every name, he pinned them to the board, spread out from the center.

He used green note cards for places, like the Hill Street Cafe and something called Graffiti Creek, among others. One note stumped him: a Post-it with "Thompson and Jolly" scribbled on it. They might be names or the name of a place, maybe a bar or a law office. He set "Thompson and Jolly" aside along with a confusing note reading "Bright New Day = Bright Hudson," with a phone number. Sameer uncovered several phone numbers. He put them on yellow cards and pinned them near the names, when a name linked up with a number.

After pinning up all the cards he could make sense of, Sameer fished a spool of yarn out of his desk. He had found the yarn when he took the job and always found it too odd to throw away. Sure enough, here he was with a legitimate use for it. He began winding fuzzy thread from push pin to push pin, associating names he had connected together.

Hooking the string around the Booker card, he pulled it tight around the Do Right card. He added a phone number, which he did call, but it went straight to voicemail. Using a blue card, he wrote "Story about saving sex worker from judge or politician." He collected all the red cards with names he discovered to belong to judges or politicians. With a handful of pins, they fanned out in a cluster under his new blue card along the thread between Booker and Do Right. Sameer had only begun and his head already spun. He continued connecting whatever he could (not much) until he ran out of information. Then he went to his computer.

Sameer Googled one name after another, adding information as he found it—this guy is a state senator, this one is a federal court judge, and so on. Bright Hudson ended up being an attractive blonde police detective, but he couldn't find the meaning of Bright New Day.

There was an old, shut-down bar called Thompson and Jolts, as well as a law office called Thomas, Jolly, and Jones. Sameer made a red and green card for the names. He added some information about the bar and a phone number for the law office, along with basic details about long-time partners Bradley Thomas and Angelica Jolly.

On the third page of search results, he found one last possibility—an old article about a robbery investigation which quoted two police detectives named Mark Thompson and Richard Jolly. He went ahead and added a red note card for each of the men, placing them in the corner of the board with other disconnected cards.

The Bright Hudson card stymied Sameer. Seamus had scribbled a phone number along with the name. Most of the phone numbers appeared to belong to contacts. And Margaret said Seamus claimed to have a police contact. However, he was also investigating police corruption. So Bright Hudson may either be the first call Sameer should make, or the last.

For the time being, he put the card in the inside pocket of his jacket. He also pocketed a yellow card he made for a phone number from a disposable phone. Margaret copied the number alongside a receipt for one, so Sameer assumed they connected. He didn't want to call this number yet either. If it rang in Seamus' pocket at the wrong time, a simple phone call would prove disastrous. Besides, it might be months old or may rest in the hands of someone other than Seamus.

Another mysterious note not placed on a card was a hyperlink to a YouTube video. Sameer settled in at his computer and typed in the link. The channel belonged to one of the filmmakers from the coffee shop—Sameer recognized his picture. The video was a thirteen minute, overly artistic film set to some sort of industrial punk music. Snippets of interviews popped up every few minutes with locals sermonizing about the steady decline of culture in the city. Sameer couldn't connect the propaganda film to anything.

Until the end.

In the final seconds, as the closing credits flashed up intermittently on screen, there was one long shot of a homeless man on the steps of a museum. Sameer hit pause on a closeup of the man's face. The small black man with glasses had to be Booker. Sameer printed the screenshot and pinned it under Booker's card. Finally, he made a green card for the Parker Building, connecting the location to Booker and adding the address he found online.

Chapter 21

Cary clutched at Mrs. Webster, shaking and pressing against the spouting wound behind her ear. She pleaded, *Hang on* and *Help is on the way* and *Please*. But it was no use. Karen Webster had been reduced to a gurgling plash of blood. Her eyes lost focus and her breaths turned into whistling coughs—final and all expelling her initial gasp.

Cary let her lie back onto the tile floor. She stood and looked around at the blood. So much of it. More than should have been in one person. Cary surveyed herself in the mirror. Took in her blood streaked arms, the smears across her face, the sticky dark mass across the front of her dress. She was showered in blood. In the moment, it hadn't felt like it.

Her mind was steadily blocking out pieces of what happened. The corners of her eyes filled with flashes of white. Loud shouts and footsteps started their stampede down the echo chamber of a hallway. The knife. Mrs. Webster—now still—a body. The blood still flowing, running in rivulets down a drain in the floor. Noises grew louder. Tears sprung to Cary's eyes, clearing paths in the blood on her face.

She ran. Her feet slipped on the bloody tile, and she crawled for the door. Scrambling to her feet, Cary started for the hallway leading into the darkened school. Her heels made sharp clacks on the linoleum floor, so she hopped forward, pulling them off one at a time. Wielding them by their straps, she sprinted down the hallway.

Voices shouted, screamed, wailed. Someone bellowed out Karen's name in a horrible wail. More footsteps. Cary slammed into doors and slapped at door handles. Everything was locked. She came to an open stairwell and took a sharp left into it.

The stairs led up into blackness. Her bare feet smacked out a reverberating pattern of a woman on the run. A cadence of pure terror. She bounded out of the stairwell onto the second floor. Classrooms stretched out down a dimly lit hallway. The edges of the ceiling had soft fluorescent lights glowing every few feet.

Cary hit more doors until one gave. It opened with a whoosh, rattling a door on the far side of the room. It was a science room, with lab tables spaced out instead of desks. The lab tables jutted out from the walls on both sides like kitchen islands. Stools clustered around each one.

Cary ran to one and cleared out the stools. She crouched into the cave beneath an overhanging workspace and pulled the stools back around her. They made a honking sound as they raked across the floor, and Cary cringed. She tensed and leaned into shadow.

Footsteps pounded outside in the hallway. Cary held her breath. She had been practicing it since she was five. Her dad played hide-and-seek with her all the time. He would creep around her and growl. When she was still a novice, she would pick the laundry hamper every time. Her dad would lurk around it for a requisite amount of time and then rip it open to her delighted squeals. As she got older, she learned. And she would always double-back on him, waiting for him to check one spot before running to hide there.

Police voices, confidant and authoritative, rang out up and down the hallway. Shouts of *Clear!* came from empty rooms. Cary trembled, wet with blood, holding her shoes and her purse like stuffed animals. Her ears locked on the door to the classroom, but sound erupted right in front of her.

The door on the far side of the room rocked open and a flashlight beam shot across the room. Cary bit a finger to keep from screaming. The light scanned the room. Cary glimpsed the outline of a man from where she hid. He held the flashlight along the sights of a handgun and swept the room with soldier precision. The light scoured one side of the room, above table tops, then the other. The man took three shuffling steps forward and kicked a stool out from in front of the lab table at the back of the room. He shot light under the table and continued, noisily scattering stools and checking under tables.

One by one by one. The gun jabbing under them with each stop of movement. He was fluid, efficient. And he was across from Cary, on her row. The empty table next to her had an extra stool, and it spun in the center of the floor. He crab walked over to Cary. Stood in front of her. Took a stance of action. And he kicked, sending a stool touching the tip of her foot careening off into an adjacent table. The light leaned down.

Another noise brought his focus up and away, swinging his flashlight beam toward the door to the hallway, which popped open with a shout of, "Hey! Martin! You got a flashlight? We need to clear under the stairs!"

Martin snapped to react, running toward the voice with a, "Yes, sir!"

In front of Cary was open space leading toward the far door where Martin had entered. It opened to a room. A room which had been cleared. She pushed up onto her knees and crawled to the open door. It led to a common space connected to several science labs. Cabinets of equipment and chemicals lined the walls.

Cary eased the door closed behind her and scooted on her ass back into a storage space. She edged her way along a table, wedging herself in a dark crevice between the work table and a storage cabinet. A tall box sat on the table, and Cary positioned herself behind it. She could peek around the far side of it, but, other than her legs under the table, she couldn't be seen.

She held still until her muscles ached. In the distant reaches of the hallway, more calls of *Clear!* rang out. A cop game of Marco Polo. How long would it take? At what point should she move? And where would she go?

The thoughts were lonely. And the only company they found were soft, creaking footsteps. Someone was near. They prodded around the science storage room, moving boxes and opening cabinets.

Cary snuck a peek. Detective Dick. She made out his profile by the soft light from the chemical cabinet. He came closer, making his way, table by table, across the back of the room.

Cary had no emergency exits. No back doors. She found herself cornered, pinned into a dark crevice and hoping for the best. She made no plan for the worst case scenario, but it arrived regardless.

Dick stood at Cary's table. He drummed his fingers on the side of the box. The big, meaty hand planted itself right in front of her. Dick used it to brace himself as he grunted and leaned down to check beneath the table.

Cary had one chance. She took a high heel and came down hard onto the back of Dick's hand. It went deep. Found bone, or maybe even the table below. Dick let out a heaving grunt and his knees buckled. Cary swept the box aside with one arm and rolled over the top of the table. She landed on Dick's back and kept rolling until she was on her feet and past him. He made a swipe for her with his good hand, but he was still reeling. It was feeble and fruitless.

Cary landed in a full run, but made it only three steps. The looming shadow of Mark Thompson was blocking her straight ahead. He chuckled, the round outline of his stomach bouncing. There were doors on either side of her. To her left, the classroom where she first hid. To her right, another class which should lead to the other hallway. But both doors stood ten feet off. Mark could close on her before she reached either escape.

She whipped her head around. Dick was working his way to his feet behind her, cursing and whimpering. Mark took a lumbering step forward. Cary found to her right a row of chemicals in corked bottles arranged in a neat little line, each with a yellow sticker warning of some hazard or another. She gripped her shoes and purse in the same hand like a baseball bat. And she swung. Connecting with the first bottle, she followed through as hard as she could, sending chemicals and shattered glass raining onto Mark Thompson's face. He squawked and recoiled into the darkness before her.

And Cary wasted no time. She bolted to her right and through the door into another science classroom. Hiding was over. It was time to run. She burst out of the classroom into the hallway. Cops roamed around, scattered in both directions.

In less than a second, one called out, "Spotted!" Other voices followed. Shadows danced on both ends of the hallway.

Cary whipped around and scanned the walls around her. To her right was a fire extinguisher encased in glass which read, *In case of emergency, break glass.* Cary mumbled, "Well, it's worked so far." And she hit at it three times with her shoes until it gave.

What followed was an absolute eruption of sensory overload. An alarm howled in chirping barks. Overhead sprinklers blasted a shower of freezing water. And emergency strobe lights throbbed and blinded everyone in the hallway. Cary stumbled forward, pawing at the wall for an exit. She found another stairwell, leading back downstairs. Her hair matted to her face and her teeth chattered. She slipped and toppled down the stairs, landing in a roll on the midway landing. The next flight she took in almost one leap.

When she hit the bottom, she threw a shoulder into the door. It flung open and laid an older policeman flat. He groaned up at her as she leapt over him and continued running. Police were everywhere, shielding their faces from cold water and flashing lights. Cary kept trying doors until one gave. She fell into a classroom and raked water from her eyes. Through the sounds of the alarm, shouts resonated and scuttling dress shoes slapped wet linoleum. No backdoors this time. The room was empty, save a few mismatched stools discarded into the empty classroom. This was the end of her escape attempt. Her legs ached. Adrenaline was beginning to wane, leaving her sapped and nauseated.

Cary stood in the middle of the room and cried. Behind her, the door clicked open softly. She turned and held up her hands in surrender. Officer Doyle closed the door behind her. Her ballcap was dripping wet. Cary waved both hands, one holding her shoes, the other her purse. "I'm done. I give up. It's over."

Officer Doyle reached to her back and came out with a handgun. Cary wrinkled her face in confusion. Doyle raised the gun, leveling it at Cary. Cary wrapped her arms in front of her face and cried out, "What are you doing?"

Officer Doyle half-whispered, "Duck."

Cary didn't hesitate. She fell to her knees and covered her head. She heard three shots ring out above her. Officer Doyle planted all three in the corner of the giant window behind Cary. Doyle shoved the gun back in her waistband and swiped up a stool with one hand. She paused to look down at Cary. "Be ready to run."

Doyle threw the stool into the window, widening the shattering break started by the bullet holes. She scooped up another stool and kept at the window until almost all the glass fell to the ground. Cary stared back at her in wonder. Doyle waved a hand at her. "Come on! They heard the shots. We've got to go!"

Cary reached out and took Doyle's hand, letting the officer lift her to her feet and help her through the broken window. Doyle followed her out and they stood in the grass trying to feel out their surroundings. Doyle looked back at the building. "We're on the north side of the building. I'm parked south. There's no way we'll make it to my car."

Cary looked west and spotted Haley and Grayson parked about a block up the road she was facing. "I have a ride. Come on." She led Officer Doyle in a dead run toward the waiting teenagers, parked and blaring some rap song to which they were singing along and dancing.

Doyle gawked at where they were headed. "Please say you're shitting me."

Cary looked back over her shoulder. "Don't be so quick to judge. They'll give you a makeover, if you want."

Chapter 22

Detective Bright Hudson stood outside the high school staff restroom and chewed the lip of her coffee cup. She had been inside—saw the carnage. School officials turned on all the hallway lights per her request. Carlos Moya gathered the two rattled witnesses into a small office for questioning. The scene was a bit chaotic. It took four men to pull Ken Webster away from the scene. And the place bubbled with veteran cops. Every swinging dick in the building felt like they could stroll right in and solve the case at will.

Not that they had much case to solve. Multiple people had seen Karen Webster walking to the restroom with a younger female in a black dress. The two witnesses had walked in on a younger female in a black dress alone with Karen Webster in the restroom. Karen Webster lay stabbed, the knife rested next to her, the younger female fled the scene covered in blood.

Bright was waiting on two things. She had assigned several uniformed officers to clear her crime scene—an unenviable task, having to ask a party full of high-ranking officers to clear out. And she had sent a young patrol officer named Lindsey back to the station to print a picture for her. She needed the DMV photo of the owner of the car by Graffiti Creek—Cary Trubody.

About ten seconds before Bright lost all patience, the hallways cleared. Quiet settled in around her. She set her coffee cup on a water fountain and moved into the bathroom.

The body sprawled out in the center of the room, surrounded by blood. Bright kept to the outside edge, taking careful steps on clean tiles. Karen Webster lay slumped onto her side with her face pressed to the floor. A single gaping wound shone visible behind her right ear. The medical examiner might uncover other wounds, but this one would do it. From the looks of the blood pattern, one slash caught the carotid artery.

Blood had sprayed forward. Bright moved around to the front of the scene. A shadow broke the pattern. A clean silhouette. Like a snow angel. Someone stood in front of Karen Webster while someone else stabbed her from behind. Carlos Moya appeared at the door of the restroom. Bright glanced up at him. "Three people," she said casually.

Carlos glanced around. "Three people?"

Bright nodded. "There were three people. Look at the blood splatter."

Carlos nodded. "I noticed. But the witnesses only saw the girl."

"Is my picture here?"

Carlos pulled a printout from behind his back. "I haven't shown them yet."

Bright stepped toward him and flapped her fingers, calling for it. She took it as she brushed by him on her way toward the office where the witnesses were detained. It was a small office around the corner—a counselor's office or some sort of parent center. The two ladies sat huddled on a couch. They had both been crying. One looked over fifty, the other could be either side of forty. They both gave off a Junior League vibe—blonde and fake, reeling from spending years relying on looks only to find it fleeting. Now they scrambled for something else to define themselves with, but only came up with wine and shoes and charity raffles. Bright resented these women. She wished different, but her resentment didn't care.

They both startled when Bright barged in, Carlos at her heels. "Tell me what you witnessed. Every detail."

The older of the two looked around Bright at Carlos, the crowd-pleaser—so easy going and gentle. "We already told—"

Bright leaned into her gaze. "Don't look at him. Look at me. I want to hear it again."

They both looked at each other and stammered. Bright rolled her eyes and pulled a chair up to sit in front of them, hold a hand if need be. "I apologize, ladies. It's very stressful, I know. Let's start with your names. Introductions. I'm Bright. Detective Bright Hudson."

The fortyish-year-old sat up. "I'm Billie Mitchell. My husband is over vice."

Bright nodded. "John. I know him well. Good man."

The other cleared her throat. "Dorothy Peavy. My—my husband and I are donors to the program here at the high school."

Bright patted her knee. "Which is wonderful. We all thank you." They all shared polite nods before Bright broke the facade. "Now, if you could walk me through the murder you witnessed, that would be great."

Dorothy tittered, flustered, but Billie closed her eyes and nodded. "We walked together to the restroom, because the hallway was so dark. I don't know how much we can tell you. We turned the corner and…" She trailed off into a half cry.

Bright turned her head away and rolled her eyes. "And what, Mrs. Mitchell?"

Billie swallowed. "There was so much blood. The woman, with the knife."

"She was holding the knife?" Bright squinted.

Billie nodded, but Dorothy spoke up. "No. She had dropped it on the ground, I think."

Bright leaned toward Dorothy. "You think?"

Billie shook her head. "I thought she was holding it."

Bright looked back and forth between them. "Can the two of you do me a favor? Show me with your hands. How big was the knife?"

The two women held their hands out. Billie showed the length of a machete, while Dorothy held her hands about six inches apart. Bright nodded, shooting a look back to Carlos. "Thank you, ladies." She pulled out the picture, holding it more to Dorothy than to Billie. "Did you see this woman?"

Billie muttered something about it *happening so fast* and there being *so much blood*, but Dorothy nodded vigorously. "Yes. Yes, I believe so. More made up, but I think it might be her."

Bright nodded out a *Thank you* and placed the photo on a table. "Did the woman say anything to either of you? Threaten you at all? Anything?"

Both women shook their heads.

Bright frowned. "What *did* she do?"

Billie started a couple of different sentences, but Dorothy interrupted. "Nothing. She looked scared."

Bright cocked her head. "Scared?"

Dorothy nodded sadly. "Yes. She was sitting there holding poor Mrs. Webster. Karen and I go way back."

Bright held a hand up. "Wait. Holding her?"

Dorothy nodded, thinking back. "Yes. The young woman sat on the floor with Karen sort of crumpled into her lap. The woman held Karen's head, like she was talking to her."

Bright nodded again, staring off into a spot on the floor. "Thank you, ladies. If you don't mind, we may ask you to repeat some of this one more time. I'm going to send someone in to record it all."

They both protested, but Bright snatched up her printout and started away, pulling Carlos with her. They went back to the restroom. Bright handed Carlos the printout of Cary Trubody's driver's license and stepped carefully into the ladies' room. She looked around, up, down, everywhere. Her eyes stopped on a smear of blood on the door frame. It was high up, maybe six feet. She stood facing the body. Turning, almost in a run, Bright placed a hand within inches of the door frame, bracing herself to bolt out the door. Her hand hovered level with the smear of blood. She motioned for Carlos to enter the room as she, herself, backed away.

Carlos walked in, unsure of what he was acting out. He held his hands out and shook his head.

Bright pointed at a spot looming over the body, with his back to the door. She placed herself at the far end of the restroom, watching. "There. Right there. Looking down at her. How tall does the DMV say Cary Trubody is?"

Carlos studied the printout. "It says she's five-three."

Bright nodded. "How tall are you, Carlos?"

Carlos hung his head and licked his lips. "Are you giving me shit, Bright?"

Bright shook her head without cracking a smile. "No. Promise."

Carlos grimaced. "I'm about five-five."

Bright cocked her head at him.

"I said about."

Bright grinned. "Fair enough. I want you to turn, like you're running out of here. And put your hand up like you're about to grab the door frame to brace yourself as you run out."

Carlos did as instructed. When he held his hand out, Bright yelled for him to freeze. His hand froze a good six inches lower than the blood smear. Bright nodded. "In these heels, I'm six foot." She pointed at the smear. "My hand was perfectly even with the bloody handprint."

Carlos looked up. "Third person?"

Bright nodded. "Third person."

Carlos looked back at the printout. "But tell me this. Why, if you're Cary Trubody, do you come to the one place with more cops than anywhere in town? I mean, you just killed your friend or girlfriend or whatever, right?"

Bright raised her eyebrows. "Or maybe you witnessed it. Maybe you need help."

Carlos nodded. "I get that. I do. I'm not convicting her. But if you're going to take the time to get all dolled up and come to this thing? Why not call 911?"

Bright shook her head. "Did any other witnesses notice Cary Trubody at the party?"

Carlos took out a spiral notepad. "I talked to one guy. One of the ones who watched her walk off with Mrs. Webster to the bathroom. He said Cary waited to talk to Chief Webster. But started talking to Mrs. Webster because the Chief was preoccupied with other guests."

Bright squinted. "So 911 wouldn't give you the chief, huh? You need to go all the way to the top. Why?"

Carlos laughed. "She's nuts."

Bright shrugged. "Maybe. Why would you?"

Carlos scrunched his face up and shot her an incredulous look. "Why would I what?"

"Need to talk to the Chief."

Carlos shook his head. "I wouldn't. No way." He shrugged. "I mean, unless I needed to rat on your ass."

Chapter 23

Cary and Officer Doyle fell into the backseat on either side of the car. Haley spun around in a squeal. "What's going on? Who is she? You're all bloody!"

Cary held both hands up, shaking her head, "It's not my blood."

Haley scrunched her face up. "That doesn't make it better!"

Doyle stole a look out of the back window and shouted, "Just drive!"

Grayson cocked her head. "We don't even know you."

Doyle whirled around, gun drawn. "Drive."

Haley screamed and punched the gas hard enough to send everyone lurching back.

Cary placed a hand on Doyle's arm. "I don't think you need—" She motioned to the gun with her head until they both looked at it.

Doyle put it away and mumbled an apology.

Cary worked to catch her breath, but managed, "Why did you help me? Officer Doyle, isn't it?"

Grayson wheeled around. "Hold the fuck on. She's a cop?"

Doyle looked back and forth between Grayson and Cary. "Yes, I'm a cop. But not like them. They were going to kill you. That's why I helped you."

Cary shook her head. "I didn't kill Karen Webster."

Doyle hung her head and nodded into her chest. "I know."

Grayson leaned forward, almost grinning. "Who's Karen Webster?"

Cary cut her eyes at her. "The police chief's wife."

Grayson nodded. "Wow. Your meeting didn't go like you drew it up, huh?"

Doyle sighed. "They'll all be looking for you now. The whole city."

Grayson laid her head down on the back of her seat. "You know how when people psych themselves up to do something. And in their head they're all like, *What's the worst that could happen?* Yeah. Whatever you thought in your head. This is so much worse."

Haley looked back, near tears. "Where am I going? I don't mean to pressure. But I don't do well driving aimlessly around town."

Grayson chuckled. "Very true. She'll drive us to the police station."

Cary frowned. "But you were there. Last night. You identified me. How do you know who I am?"

Doyle looked out every window of the car in rapid succession. "That's not important. We need to go someplace safe."

Haley whimpered, "I think she was joking, but all I can think right now is police station. For real. Like when someone says don't think about a pink elephant and all you can do is—"

Doyle leaned up to the front seat. "Does one of you have a credit card?"

Both of the girls laughed. Grayson said, "Yes, sweetie. We have a credit card."

Doyle slumped back. "Drive us to a hotel. Any hotel. Rent us a room in one of your names and we can clean Cary up." She looked over to Cary. "Can anyone connect you to the two of them?"

Cary shook her head. "I don't even know their last names." She shrugged. "Of course, I'm not sure how you know me, so maybe I'm connected to more people than I thought."

In less than a minute, Haley had found a hotel and pulled in. She dropped Grayson at the front and circled around. Grayson came flouncing out with a key card and jumped back in the car. "I asked for a first-floor room around back. She probably thinks I'm a hooker."

Haley pulled around to the back and parked as close to the door as possible. She looked back at Cary with a grimace. "We can go buy you some clothes."

Cary patted her old jeans, T-shirt, and green canvas jacket. "This'll be fine. Thanks for everything, girls."

Doyle looked to Cary. "How long have you been with them?"

Cary shrugged. "Four hours maybe."

Doyle turned to the girls. "If anyone asks, you drove her to a bus station. Nothing more. You thought she was leaving town."

They both nodded, as Cary and Doyle eased out and ran for the door before anyone could see them. The room was the first one inside the door. They managed to slip inside before being spotted by anyone. Doyle put the "Do Not Disturb" sign up and flipped on the bathroom light. "Clean yourself up."

Cary threw her things down on a bed and stood resolute. "No. I want some answers first. What the hell is going on?"

Doyle rolled her head around. "There will be time for answers later. We need to clean the blood off you and keep moving."

Cary shook her head. "No. We will make time now. We will make time right the fuck now!" Cary grew increasingly hysterical, pointing at some invisible line in the carpet. "Now! Right now! I need you to tell me why this is happening!"

Doyle stepped up and took Cary by both arms, at the elbows. "Okay. Okay, Cary. You're right. Let's sit down and talk."

Cary was shaking, crying. She let Doyle take her by the hands and guide her to the bed. They sat in silence for a moment, letting Cary breathe and calm down. When she had caught her breath, she laughed. "I remember when I was about seven or eight, my parents took me to Disneyland. It was the first time I can remember staying in a hotel. The second morning, after spending a whole day there, I got up way before they did. I was so excited to go back. I sat on the end of their bed and ate two bags of cotton candy for breakfast. When we started for the car, I puked all over myself in the parking lot. We had to come back to the room and clean me up. I was crying hysterically. Sobbing and hyperventilating. I was so scared we weren't going because I was sick."

Doyle smiled. "Did you get to go?"

Cary nodded. "Yeah. An hour later than planned, but we went. My favorite vacation. We took many after that. When I was old enough to appreciate things more. But I always loved the Disneyland trip the most."

Doyle put a hand to Cary's back. "Does your family live here?"

Cary shook her head. "No. The only family I had here was Johnna."

"Your friend? The one with you last night?"

Cary shot her a look. "Yes. The one your partners killed."

Doyle's eyes teared and she turned away. "I'm sorry, Cary. I didn't know. I would've stopped them if I could."

Cary shot up and backed away. "Why? What is this to you?"

"I made a mistake, Cary. I was scared. They asked me if I recognized you as the person they were looking for and I said I did. It was wrong, okay. I understand now. And I regret it. It's why I've been looking for you. I'm trying to make it right."

Cary screamed, "You can't make it right!"

Doyle ducked her head and cried. "Yeah. I know that. And I'm sorry. I had no idea what they would do."

"What's this all about?"

"I'm not entirely sure, Cary." She squinted at Cary. "What about you?"

Cary threw her hands up incredulously. "Me? How the hell would I—if you're 'not entirely sure,' then I promise you, I am entirely not sure."

Doyle nodded. "Okay, okay. I'm not accusing you of anything. I'm only saying, they think you have something. Is there any way you could and not realize it?"

Cary's eyes teared pleadingly. "What? Have what?"

"Did you receive any unusual text messages yesterday?"

Cary shook her head. "What? No. I don't remember getting anything—" She paused in thought. "Wait. Yeah. I guess. Maybe. But it was nothing."

Doyle stood up. "Maybe not. What was it?"

Cary shrugged. "No. I mean exactly that. Nothing. An errant text from an old friend. Someone who would never text me. But it was an empty text. I didn't even reply."

Doyle frowned. "Empty? You're sure?"

Cary nodded. "Yeah. Like I said, a mistake. Wrong Cary Trubody."

Doyle stepped forward and patted her on the arm. "All right. I'm sorry, Cary. I want to help pull you out of this."

Cary let herself collapse on the officer's shoulder and they fell to the bed. Doyle held Cary in an embrace as Cary sobbed. And she sobbed for almost half an hour. No words. Pure shock. Doyle soothed her with shushes and smoothed her hair. "Cary, people are trying to kill you. I'm assuming you saw Mrs. Webster die. You're in shock. This is normal. And we're getting you out of this mess. But to do that, I need you to pull yourself together. Can you get it together?"

Cary patted at her eyes and drowsily said, "Yeah. I can. This is just a lot."

Doyle laughed. "No shit. You're one tough bitch."

Cary mumbled, "I guess."

"No guess. Most anybody would've folded by now. They'd be dead after the first trip to the woods. I was trying to follow. At a distance. I had a hunch where they were headed. Those guys been taking people out to Graffiti Creek for years. Or at least rumors say so. I was so scared. I thought I had… I thought…" She trailed to the hum of Cary's soft snores from her shoulder.

Eventually, they both dozed. For hours. Daylight was starting to seep in through the curtains when the ding of a phone woke them both with a start. They fumbled at pockets and purses and pulled out identical phones. Doyle held hers up and raised her eyebrows.

Cary rolled her eyes. "Yeah. Mine's stolen."

Doyle gave her a look.

"It's a long story." A message from Marlowe had popped up on her lock screen: *Found the other Cary Trubody. She'll meet you. One hour.*

"Holy shit. He did it! My friend. He found the other Cary Trubody. He set up a meeting for me. In an hour."

Doyle took a breath. "That's—that's great, Cary. Tell him to send us the address." She held up her phone and said, "Send the place to my phone. I'll put it in my GPS." She called out a number as Cary texted Marlowe.

Doyle's phone made a noise and she read her screen silently. She nodded. "Okay. We got it. You clean yourself up and we'll head out."

Cary nodded and dropped her phone on the bed. "God. This feels like hope. The first hope since all this started." She pointed at her purse and a stack of towels on the other side of Doyle. "Hey, can you give me my purse and a towel?"

Doyle set her phone down next to Cary's and reached around to grab the towel and purse. She turned to hand them to Cary, who took her purse with one hand and snagged the towel while scooping up Doyle's phone with the other.

Cary went into the bathroom and started the shower. She let the steam build up around her as she listened at the bathroom door. Within two minutes the door to the hotel room clicked closed. She stepped out to find Doyle gone, with her clothes. Cary stared down at her tattered dress. "Balls." She opened up Doyle's phone to find the text from Marlowe. His name was in the phone. She hadn't said his name. The text read, "Old Town. Parker Building."

Chapter 24

Carlos Moya had worked his way down to about four cigarettes a day. One of those remained as his early morning smoke with a cup of coffee. His favorite and the hardest to give up. Something about coffee and cigarettes felt very milk-and-cookies for Carlos. And mornings needed a zen moment like smoking—a time when nothing else could happen, nothing matters for these five minutes except this Pall Mall.

But after about three minutes, Bright Hudson pulled up at his curb and peered at him over a pair of oversized sunglasses. Carlos held out his cigarette and sighed at it. He dropped the half-smoked butt into his coffee with a depressing *pfft* and started for the car.

Although Bright's eyes hid behind the sunglasses, they looked about as puffy as Carlos'. They had been at Karen Webster's crime scene until the wee hours of the morning. Carlos knew Bright had said they would go notify the girl's next-of-kin first thing. He had merely hoped first thing didn't mean *first thing*. But Bright rarely said anything if she didn't want it taken literally. Carlos rubbed at his mussed hair and sucked at the teeth he'd forgotten to brush. "So do we need an ID?"

Bright studied street signs. "No. We know it's her. This is a notification call. And we can run through the usual shit, given the chance. 'Anybody who might want to hurt her' and all."

Carlos nodded. "Mom?"

Bright shook her head. "Mom died young of a brain aneurysm. She lived with her grandmother." She glanced at a scrap of paper in her cup holder. "Brenda Langley. Girl's name was Johnna Kitteridge. Grandmother is the only living family. Father unknown. Had a sister, but she died in a car accident a few years back. One aunt who died around the same time from what looks like a suicide."

"Jesus. The luck of this family." Carlos noticed a pack of gum next to the scrap of paper and helped himself to a piece. "So what's her connection to our Cary Trubody?"

"They were in a relationship, according to Kitteridge's Facebook page."

Carlos chuckled. "Of course they were. Shit. This'll be fun. We get to tell an old lady not only was your granddaughter gay, but her gay lover might have stabbed her to death."

Bright eyed him. "Yeah. Let's hold off on that bit for now."

Brenda Langley's kitchen glowed as they pulled up in front. The old woman's frame passed back and forth several times, enough for Bright to cock her head at Carlos and kill her engine. They had to ring the doorbell twice and knock once before Mrs. Langley sheepishly opened the door. Bright had her badge out and apologized before introducing herself. "Mrs. Langley? I am so sorry to disturb you so early, ma'am."

Mrs. Langley frowned at them in silence until Carlos pulled out his badge as well. She frowned even more. "Yes? What's wrong?"

Bright put her badge away and smoothed her skirt. "I'm Detective Bright Hudson. This is my partner, Carlos Moya. Can we come in for a moment?"

Mrs. Langley started to step aside but held onto the door frame. "Is it Johnna? Oh, Jesus. Is it Johnna?" She repeated the phrase over and over until Bright stepped in and caught her by the arms.

Bright helped her to the living room and sat her on the couch. "Breathe, Mrs. Langley. Breathe." Carlos hurried to the kitchen for a glass of water. "Do you need to lie down?"

Mrs. Langley shook her head frantically. "I need to know what happened."

"When is the last time you spoke with your granddaughter, Mrs. Langley?"

The old woman closed her eyes and shook her head. "A couple of days ago. Has there been an accident?"

Bright nodded. "Yes, ma'am. Johnna was killed sometime early yesterday morning."

Mrs. Langley started into a sob, but held off with an incredulous look. "Killed? How?"

Bright grimaced. "We can talk about that. But I want to make sure you're okay first." Carlos arrived with a glass of water and a damp rag. Mrs. Langley waved off the water but took the rag and held it across her forehead. Bright placed a hand on her shoulder. "We're going to take as much time as you need, Mrs. Langley."

There passed a rather tumultuous few minutes of tears and wailing and fears of fainting. Carlos hovered in the most uncomfortable of fashions, while Bright struggled to keep mustering up a little more compassion. After the old woman settled into a rhythm of sniffling and wiping at her eyes with the rag, she righted her breathing and she said, softly, "Tell me."

Bright nodded. "We don't know as much as we would like. We're hoping you might be able to fill in a few gaps for us."

Mrs. Langley rolled her head around and waved the rag. "I can try."

Bright nodded to Carlos, who sat with a pad and pen out and ready. Bright turned to the old woman. "Did your granddaughter know a woman named Cary Trubody?"

Mrs. Langley nodded. "Yes. They were in a relationship."

Bright raised her eyebrows. "Lovers?"

Mrs. Langley chuckled. "If you want to call it that, yes. Cary was Johnna's girlfriend. They hadn't told everyone yet, but they've been together for several months."

Bright nodded. "Well, we found your granddaughter in Cary's car. It was abandoned in the woods. Johnna's body was in the trunk."

Mrs. Langley started to sob again but held herself together. "Cary—Cary came by here. Yesterday."

Bright and Carlos shared a look. "Cary Trubody came here?"

Mrs. Langley nodded. "She came looking for something in Johnna's room. An address or phone number or something. I called the other detective like he told me to. But Cary ran. And I let her. Maybe I shouldn't. Did Cary—"

Bright held a hand up. "Wait, Mrs. Langley. Slow down. What other detective?"

The old woman rose and walked over to a phone table. She returned with Mark Thompson's card, which she handed to Bright. Bright studied the simple white business card and passed it over to Carlos. Mrs. Langley pointed at the name. "He showed up sometime yesterday morning. He said he was trying to find Cary and hoped Johnna could tell him where she might be. He told me no one was in trouble, but they might be in danger. Made me promise to call him if Cary showed up."

Bright shook her head. "And that's it? He left?"

Mrs. Langley nodded. "Yes. It concerned me, of course. And when Cary showed up later in the day, I called him. Like he asked."

"What did Cary want?"

"She said she was trying to catch up with Johnna and she needed an address or maybe a phone number—something. She went up to Johnna's room. When she came down a few minutes later, she had a shirt or a dress with her. I," she ducked her head, "well, I suppose I sort of tipped her off about the detective. I directed her to run out the back as he pulled up out front. I tried to stall him, but he chased her out into the yard. But she got away. He came back through a couple of minutes later and left."

Bright shook her head. "Why help her get away?"

Mrs. Langley frowned. "I didn't trust him."

109

"Why not?"

Mrs. Langley swallowed and stifled tears. "He told me to call if *Cary* showed up. Not Johnna."

Bright hung her head and nodded at the ground.

Mrs. Langley leaned over toward Bright. "Detective Hudson? Who hurt my Johnna?"

Bright shook her head. "I'm not sure yet, Mrs. Langley. We are trying to find out. Do you mind if we look around a little bit?"

Mrs. Langley nodded. "Of course. Johnna's room is the first on the left upstairs."

Bright nodded for Carlos to head up. She turned back to Mrs. Langley. "Can you show me where Cary went?"

Mrs. Langley rose and walked toward the back door. She opened it, revealing a rather large backyard beyond a porch full of wind chimes. "She took off this way. I didn't see beyond that. I'm sorry."

Bright patted her arm. "Don't apologize. This has been very helpful."

Bright stepped past her into the backyard. She took her time, walking and looking. Several times she glanced back at the house, imagining the moment. Cary was scared. Frantic. Panicked and desperate. Bright scanned the fence until she found a gate leading into a neighbor's yard. She walked toward it and pushed. The rusted chain link squeaked open.

Bright followed the path into the next yard. Only one pathway led to anything other than dense bushes or more fence or brick structures. She snaked her way down this logical trail. The neighbor's carport was bricked in with an opening about midway. When Bright turned the corner, she found an empty space where a car had been, a car had painted over an old oil stain with circle after circle of newer stains.

After a moment, Bright turned to head back to the house, but the sound of a car pulled her back. When she got back to the garage, two young girls hopped out of a car. Bright flashed her badge, startling them. "Sorry, girls. I'm checking out the neighborhood."

One of them looked purely frightened. The other seemed harder. More cynical. The harder one grinned. "Okay. Carry on, officer."

Bright turned, but paused. The girls hadn't disappeared through the door yet, and Bright called them down. "I'm sorry, girls. I hate to bother you. I'm—"

The cynical one spun. "Checking the neighborhood. Got it. Thanks."

Bright smiled. "Yeah. We've had this guy impersonating a cop. Harassing young women. Real creep. Have either of you seen anyone who might fit that description?"

They shared a look. The scared one turned her doe eyes to Bright and started in with, "Actually—"

The other one grabbed her arm. "Some guy drove all slow down the road earlier. Looked creepy. Could be your guy. But we didn't get a good look."

Bright grinned and nodded. "Okay. Thanks, girls. You've been very helpful."

When Bright got back inside, Carlos was asking Mrs. Langley, "Ma'am, was your granddaughter messy? Did she keep a messy room, I mean?"

Mrs. Langley laughed. "Lord no. She was a touch OCD."

Carlos nodded and jotted in his notepad. "Have you been into her room lately?"

Mrs. Langley shook her head. "No. I respect her privacy. I seldom go in there."

Bright and Carlos thanked Mrs. Langley for her time and made sure she had someone she could call to be with her. Practically as soon as she answered, the doorbell rang. As friends arrived, the detectives saw themselves out. They only asked Mrs. Langley to keep everyone out of Johnna's room. On the way to the car Bright shot Carlos a look. "The girl's room is messed up?"

Carlos nodded. "A little, yeah. Like somebody was looking for something."

"Cary?"

Carlos shrugged. "Could be. But it doesn't sound like she stayed up there long enough to do this."

"We'll need to gather it all. Computer?"

Carlos nodded. "I did a quick check. Nothing jumped out. But somebody can comb through it back at the station. You find anything?"

Bright quirked her mouth. "Maybe. I think Cary hitched a ride out of here with a couple of neighbor girls. I got the plate. I want somebody to run it down. Then I might take a run at them. One would break pretty easy."

Carlos climbed into the car. "Have you worked with this Thompson?"

Bright nodded. "A time or two, yeah. He's been around for a while."

"Do we talk to him?"

Tapped her fingers on the steering column for a second before starting the car. "Not yet. But I want you to see where he goes."

Chapter 25

Carlos made detective before he turned thirty. It had been a private goal of his. He was the first in his family to go to college. His dad gave him an endless string of shit about using an expensive degree to become a cop. He and Bright shared the latter in common.

They both earned law degrees and had family members who thought they underused them. Carlos, however, possessed nowhere near Bright's ambition. But his dad wasn't about to pay for him to stop at an art degree. Practicing law had always been out of the question. Carlos needed something to do with his hands. He needed to solve puzzles and move around.

Honestly, he couldn't be sure Bright even knew he held a law degree. She would be about as disappointed in him as his dad if she knew. Because Bright would be moving on into politics someday. Carlos? He kept himself content poking around at mysteries all day and going home to his canvases and palettes of color.

But he hated this shit. Waiting. Sitting and waiting and waiting and waiting. Mark Thompson was supposed to check in at the station by 9:00. Carlos had been camped out in an unmarked Taurus since he and Bright left the old lady around 8:00. Mark Thompson was late.

Carlos finished his coffee during the first half hour, and now he doodled on his cup, trying to fight off the thought of finding a restroom. He was starting to consider using the cup for something other than doodling when a car pulled up into a handicapped spot near the door.

Carlos kept watch from an inconspicuous parking spot down a row of unmarked cars. Mark Thompson and his partner, Richard Jolly, stepped out and lumbered inside to check in and pick up their assignments for the day. They looked similar. Jolly stood a bit taller, but both of their bellies protruded as they waddled around like scotch-soaked stereotypes. Watching them made Carlos wad up the last of a breakfast pastry in a napkin and shove it into a trash sack.

Thompson and Jolly disappeared into the station. They would be at least thirty minutes to an hour. Could be much longer. He might be sitting and waiting half the day. He decided to take what might be his one window of opportunity and run for the restroom.

Carlos passed the detectives' car and ran in to use the restroom in the station lobby. Rushing back out to resume his position, he passed back by the car and paused. No cop locked his car when he parked right outside the station. Carlos decided to test the hunch. The driver's door popped open.

Cigarettes and stale coffee wafted up into his face. Carlos settled into the seat to avoid drawing attention. He pulled down the sun visor. Flipped through the glove box. Poked around in the middle console. Nothing. Bright mentioned what she picked up from Jonathan Epstein. The screwdriver might have been police issue. He popped the trunk and got out to check it.

Sure enough, there sat the emergency kit the department issued to everyone. He leaned in and pried it open. The Phillips head screwdriver lay pressed into the slot where it belonged. Most of the kit seemed untouched. The jumper cables looked like they had been pulled out and thrown back a time or two. But the flares were still there. The tools looked clean. The flashlight untouched. Wire clamps in place. The only other thing disturbed was the bag of zip ties.

Carlos picked up the bag. It had been opened, and a few were missing. Cheap zip ties. Not police issue. He pulled one out and held it. It appeared identical to the one he found in the floorboard of Cary Trubody's car.

He pulled his phone out and snapped a quick picture of the trunk. Easing it shut, he thought to snag a picture of the plate, too—in case he lost them. As he prepared to take the picture, he happened to look up and find Thompson and Jolly strolling out of the station.

Carlos spun on his heels and started back for his car. He made it about eight steps before he heard, "Hey!"

He stopped, frozen. Carlos turned to face Thompson, who stood next to the car cocking his head at Carlos. "Were you taking a picture of my car?"

Carlos looked at him and swallowed. "I—I was only going to—"

Thompson shook his head. "Going to what? Huh? Asshole?"

Carlos laughed. "My sister. She's in a wheelchair." He nodded at the handicapped sign. "That kind of shit pisses me off, you know?"

Thompson and Jolly looked at each other and laughed. "You gonna write me a ticket?"

Carlos scratched at his head. "I was thinking about reporting you."

Jolly held a hand up, bracing it with his other hand. "Well, you see, dip shit, I got this handicap. I can't…I can't," he worked at his hand until his middle finger shot up. "I swear, I can't keep this finger down." He and Thompson howled with laughter and climbed in the car.

Carlos hurried to his car and waited a minute before pulling out. He may have avoided disaster, but they would sure as hell notice him now if he followed too close. Luckily, they turned out of the parking lot and headed back toward him. He could ease unseen through the lot and exit from a different spot. As long as he didn't pop out right behind them.

Carlos crept to the other exit until he saw Thompson's car flash by. He let a couple of cars fill the space between them and pulled out. It was not his first time following a car. He kept Thompson and Jolly in sight without getting too close. But they were cops; he needed to keep a pretty good distance.

Thompson made no unexpected moves—keeping to main roads most of the time. Carlos lost him twice, but only briefly. They wound around to a part of the city known as Old Town, which made sense.

Old Town consisted of a knot of run-down buildings, with homeless squatters everywhere. Homeless murder cases happened routinely. They were awful—full of nowhere leads and suspects without any actual names or records. But two homicide detectives—or vice or anything, for that matter—pulling into Old Town was a common sight.

Thompson and Jolly took a slow cruise around the Parker Building, an old hollowed-out office building with homeless crowded in like campers at a national park. They were definitely watching for someone, but it might be anyone. They pulled around to an attached parking garage and parked behind it. Their car sat obscured from view of basically everything, tucked in behind the parking garage. Carlos had no hope of following them into the little alley lot they parked in. But he still kept them in sight as he made passes between neighboring buildings.

The two detectives got out of their car and started around the parking garage. Carlos surveilled them until they slipped into a back entrance of either the Parker Building or the garage itself. He found a row of spaces on a side street running along the side of the parking garage. He could just lay eyes on the back of Thompson's car from where he parked.

He killed his car and got out, easing the door shut. Carlos stayed at the side of the parking garage, creeping up to the corner. Peering around the edge of the building, he surveyed both Thompson's car and the door they must have used to enter the Parker building.

Carlos looked around at the ruins of a former city hub. About twenty yards back from Thompson's car perched a rotten stack of wooden pallets next to an old dumpster. He checked up at blackened and broken windows of the Parker building, and over at the darkened caves of space in the parking garage. Seeing nothing, he crouched and ran over to the pallets.

Carlos slid in behind the dumpster and worked his way over until he found a perch behind all the rotten wood where he could peer through to the buildings. After about fifteen minutes, the detectives came out and hopped in their car. Carlos cursed to himself and glanced over the corner of the garage obscuring the view of his car. But Thompson drove straight for an entrance into the parking garage and disappeared into the cavernous relic of ramps and shadows.

Chapter 26

Cary stared at her second stolen phone in two days. Old Town was familiar enough. What used to be a bustling swath of downtown was now basically abandoned. A bit of a ghost town. The Parker Building didn't ring any bells, but she figured a cab driver would know it. And she might not have clean clothes, but she did still have a couple thousand dollars in her tiny clutch of a purse.

Officer Doyle would figure out the phone switch any second. Cary was dying to get some answers as to why Marlowe's name showed up as a contact in Doyle's phone. But she was more anxious to talk to the other Cary Trubody and clear all this up.

Cary wasted little time. She grabbed her purse and shoes, running barefoot out the door. Instead of slipping out the back, she chanced her appearance in the lobby. It was mid-morning, according to the time on Doyle's phone, so maybe it wouldn't be too busy.

She eased carefully around each corner, making sure she didn't run into Doyle on her way back for her phone. Although she caught an odd look or two, no one stopped her. Outside the front doors, she found a cab parked a few car lengths down the curb. The cabbie was leaned against the car reading a newspaper.

Cary fished a hundred dollar bill out of her purse and approached the cabbie. He eyed her up and down before looking at the bill. When he did, it was pure skepticism. Cary pushed the hundred closer to him. "Half this should get me to Old Town. The rest is tip. Work for you?"

The cabbie folded his paper and rubbed his chin. He looked back at the doors to the hotel. "You run from someone?"

He had the same accent as a couple of Nigerians Cary had worked with once. But he was older. Wore little reading glasses he took off to better examine the offer. Cary shook her head. "No. No, I'm just in a hurry. Can you help me?"

The cabbie sucked at his teeth and accepted the bill like it was alive. He nodded. "Okay. Okay, I drive you."

Cary jumped in the back of the cab and let it start rolling before adding, "Do you know the Parker Building?"

The cabbie eyed her in the rearview mirror and nodded. "Yes. But you don't want Parker Building. All homeless. All run down. Bunch of homeless living in tents."

Cary could sense things getting more and more difficult. "I know. But near there. My friend is going to meet me. If you could drop me off, that would be great."

The cabbie kept looking back at her. "Your friend is homeless?"

Cary laughed. "No. No, he's not."

The cabbie nodded. "I think he is. All homeless. All homeless. Your friend? He's homeless."

Cary collapsed back into the seat and tried to enjoy a moment of quiet as they drove. She considered messaging Marlowe, but if Officer Doyle somehow knew him, it meant he knew her as well. This could all be a trap. If she had any options, she would be considering them.

The streets were abundantly clear when they drove into Old Town. The surroundings blanched out like a shitty arthouse movie. There was still traffic, but it was more sparse and suspect. Everyone looked like they were cruising for drugs or sex. Lots of ducked heads and popped collars. The cabbie stopped near a corner at a broken meter. He pointed at an old building on the next block. "Parker Building. Big one with the broken windows." He sighed. "Why not let me drive you somewhere else? Call your friend."

Cary mumbled, "No, this is good. Thanks." She shot out of the car and walked off from the cab as he looked after her with worried eyes.

The Parker building appeared to be more than deserted. It was sad. Like some hulking person who had lost something. Some carcass, with the homeless like ants scuttling in and out of it. Cary leaned against an old storefront and examined it. The front of the Parker Building was all windows, most of which had been boarded up. One piece of plywood was pried loose at a corner. She noted an old man as he worked his way inside. Moments later a woman slithered out. Cary rubbed at one of her bare feet.

She glanced down at herself—her ruined dress, all torn and bloodstained. Her hair and makeup were a shit show. She was barefoot, holding heels like some deranged and jilted lover. There was little reason to lurk in the shadows. She fit in perfectly. Even Marlowe might not recognize her right off. But Officer Doyle would because of the dress. Either way, outside she was exposed. Whatever the inside of the building looked like, no question, it offered her more of a chance to move around undetected.

Cary started across the street toward the Parker Building. She muttered nonsense to herself and waved a hand around. Before slipping through the loose plywood, she slipped back into her heels. Cary hated heels. But stepping on cold pavement was one thing manageable, stepping on a discarded needle was not.

One good thing about the homeless: they don't stare much. As a group of people who have been routinely stared at, they keep their eyes to the ground in front of their feet. Girl in a bloody cocktail dress and heels talking to herself? Not my business. Cary was able to move about the first few ambling people without so much as a glance.

The first floor of the building was a hollowed-out lobby. It had once served as either an office building or a hotel. Skeletons of reception desks flanked the belly of space stretching out in front of Cary. There was a smattering of tents set up across the open area. They were all make-shift and ready to be packed up on the run.

At the back of the lobby, an ornate staircase led to a landing and curved around to the second floor. From the outside, the building looked to have about fifteen stories.

There was a structure next to the Parker Building, which connected at multiple points up and down the side of the building. This structure was most likely a parking garage. Cary hadn't seen any cars parked around the building as they were driving in, but anyone could've parked in that garage.

Making her way toward the stairs, Cary shot a cursory glance toward a trio of homeless men huddled around a barrel. There was no fire in their barrel at the moment, but it was obvious there had been from the charred black edges. Two of them smoked cigarettes, but no one spoke. Most of the lobby's windows were boarded, blacking out its edges. The only light billowed down the wide staircase from the second-floor landing, where windows lined one side. Light spilled out onto the tile floor and spotlighted a trail of bottles and food wrappers and lost articles of clothing. Cary crept up the stairs with one hand on the railing. She darted looks over her shoulders the whole way up.

The landing gave her a view of the second floor. Two hallways stretched in either direction. They were dark, like the lobby, but with shots of light every ten feet or so. Open doors gave off boxes of sunshine like searchlights. Cary hung onto the railing before starting up for a moment. She scanned back and forth, up and down the stairs, looking for anyone different—someone less tattered or acting as uncomfortable as she felt.

After a full minute of zero movement in either direction, she made her way up to the second floor. The hallway looked to make a circle around the building. There was nothing to do but make the round and start looking for the way up to floor three. The ornate staircase only went to the second floor. The rest of the way would be some stairwell.

She had a sense of where the parking garage was from where she stood, and she figured on it being on that side of the building. So to start, she went to her right. Abandoned offices lay open on either side of the hall. The first three were empty. The next five each had one inhabitant.

They would always look up once, startled, and then return to studying their shoes or busying themselves with whatever they had been huddled doing before she passed. Cary jumped at every person she came across, but they were all quite obviously homeless. Most were men. But as she turned the corner, along the back stretch of the building, she came across a woman sitting alone in a small office.

She was younger than most—maybe late twenties. She had a bedroll and a spray of magazines she was flipping around in to kill the tedium of the morning. Cary paused and thought, *What if the other Cary Trubody is homeless. Maybe that's why Marlowe set the meeting here.*

The woman gave her several quick glances. Cary stood in the doorway—almost too long. The woman exhaled loudly and slapped her magazine shut, looking up with a curled lip. Cary squinted at her. "Is your name Cary by any chance?"

The woman grinned. And laughed a little to herself. She shook her head, not in an answer, but more in disbelief. She looked back up. "No. It's not." She reached over into an open bag beside her and pulled out a metal spoon. She leaned back near a radiator behind her and tapped the spoon against one of the pipes running off into the walls. The taps rang out and echoed off into the building. She continued, clanking steadily in a rhythmic *ping-ping* pattern, grinning at Cary all the while.

Cary nodded and backed away from the door. "I'm sorry. I didn't mean to bother you. Sorry." She kept nodding and mumbling apologies out into the hallway and hurried to keep on her path around the second floor.

Cary passed a few more empty rooms, shaking her head and frowning at the steady pinging behind her. Rounding the back corner, she discovered several men on this side standing at their doorways. The first she passed stared at her—more than anyone had yet. He studied her face. The next did the same. And the next. Cary stumbled and looked back. The men were sliding out of their doorways and falling in pace behind her.

With her head turned, she didn't see the mountain of a man who had stepped out into her path. She collided with him and bounced back, apologizing. Four men now approached behind her. She made a step to excuse herself around the huge bearded man in front of her. He looked like he should have owned a bar at one point in his life. Big, round head, with scruffy hair jutting out in every direction. Meaty hands. He wore an old army field jacket similar to the one Cary often wore, but he had it over a white tank top. Even had a towel tucked into the front of his tan canvas pants like a bartender would.

He held something up next to her face—a piece of paper. Or maybe a photograph? A big smile revealed a rotten row of bottom teeth and betrayed a face full of wrinkles and scars. He looked past her, at the men gathering speed at her back. "Yep," he said. "It's her alright."

He shoved the photo into a jacket pocket and placed a hand around the side of Cary's head. The hand swallowed her from the fingers curled around the knotty base of her skull to the grimy palm pressed into her cheekbone. The man squeezed and threw Cary, headfirst, into the room to her left.

She tumbled into a sideways roll sending her all the way to the far wall, landing in a sitting position beneath a window. Cary shook her head hard, trying to lose the electric gnats at the corners of her eyes. The giant took a step inside and kept smiling. Cary tried to scuttle backward, pushing with bare feet. He had picked her right out of her shoes. She gaped as the four men following her kicked them out of the way coming to the doorway.

Her back pressed harder and harder against the wall. Her eyes cleared and she rummaged for anything around her. The giant kept smiling. He was talking. Something like "hold still," but Cary was close to going into shock. Everything was moving slower. Shapes around her were huge—the walls, the window, the trash, the broken boards littered about the place. She reached for one jagged piece of wood and gripped its smooth end. She placed her other hand at its base and looked up at the looming figure above her. He was a blur of green and white and beard and smile. She focused in on the greasy towel hanging at his belly. And she lunged.

She put the pointy end of the board toward the towel, braced it with her hand at its base, and shot upward. It was a leap, all leg muscle. The board met something soft and Cary pushed against the resistance. There was a massive grunt over her head and she followed through until the board slipped from her hand and she rolled around the giant, toward the door. She came up in the middle of the four men, who stared past her, stunned. Cary looked back once to see the giant doubled over, moaning in pain. She didn't hesitate. Taking advantage of the moment of surprise, she shoved past the men at the door and fell into the hallway.

Cary stumbled into a wall and tried to move forward. Her head was fuzzy. Everything was still crooked and caricatured. The hallway stretched to a pinhole. Shouts of "Hey!" rang out to her right. Her knees started pumping, pushing her in a slide down the hallway wall. She hit a doorframe and tried to swing around it. A woman sprang out of the door with her hands up like claws. She went for Cary's eyes, but Cary ducked. She put her shoulder into the woman's midsection and pushed her into the other side of the doorframe. The woman huffed and went limp. Cary dropped her and tried running upright.

Another two men appeared in front of her, blocking the hallway. Cary looked back to see the first four running toward her. When she turned back, one of the men in her way crumpled into a heap on the floor. The other shot around to find a small black man with glasses holding a huge pipe. The little man connected with the second guy's face, sending him into a similar pile next to his friend. The little man waved Cary forward. "Come on, girl. Run. Goddammit, run!"

Cary jumped over the two men on the floor and accepted the little man's hand. She tried to say "Thanks," but nothing came out. Her mouth felt like she'd been chewing on insulation. The little man pulled Cary along the hallway, waving the pipe threateningly at a few others, keeping them in their rooms. They passed an old, rotted-out elevator and a doorway with a picture of stairs on it. The little man got Cary back to the big stairway to the bottom floor, but the trio around the barrel had started making their way up.

They eyed Cary, and one pulled out some sort of blade. Cary swiveled to the little man. He looked defeated. He was shorter than Cary, with a wiry frame and wiry glasses and the wiry beginnings of a beard. He looked like a bookseller. Or a watch repairman. He pulled a picture of Cary—her DMV photo—from his pocket and handed it to her. "Girl, you got a couple of cops been passing this thing out. Offering up a grand to anybody who lays you down."

She looked past him at the door to the stairs. The four men had caught up with her, blocking the door. Cary and the little man edged back toward the big staircase. He gripped his pipe. They stood back to back and braced for a fight. From the lobby, shots rang out—three quick barks. Everyone spun around and looked down at Officer Doyle standing with her gun pointed at the ceiling. The men on the staircase scattered up and disappeared down the opposite hallway. Cary spun around to find the four men all running and ducking into rooms. Her savior stood by her for a moment, but as Doyle started up the steps, he dropped his pipe, apologized weakly, and fled down the hall. Cary turned back to Doyle. "You left me!"

Doyle still had her gun drawn, pointed loosely at Cary. "I'm trying to help you, Cary."

Cary looked from her to the stairwell door. Doyle marked the look and put her gun away, starting into cries for Cary to wait. But Cary took the chance to break for the door before Doyle could reach the landing between floors. She grabbed the little man's pipe on her way. The doors to the stairwell were double doors, so she shoved the pipe through the handles on the other side. The makeshift barrier might not last, but it would slow her down.

The stairwell was pitch black, and she had lost her clutch in the attack. She had to paw around for a way up. The only chance she had was to find one of those connections to the parking garage and work her way back down to the street from there. At the third floor, she found another set of doors. She kicked them open to let in a bath of light. Two floors up she could make out a door facing away from the building. This had to be it. She scrambled up the next two flights until she could feel around for the door. Once open, she could see the picture of the car and the word *Parking* on the inside of the door.

The garage was vast and open. The walls went up to about waist level and then opened up for about five feet before the next level started. Cary ran toward a ramp angling down. In the center of the garage, a silo shot upward. On each level was a door with a picture of stairs leading to a closet-like space. A second stairwell ran through the middle of the structure. Before she reached the door, Cary heard the squealing of tires coming up the ramp. She ducked into the stairwell and started down.

She was frozen by heavy footsteps beneath her. As soon as she stopped, so did the footsteps. They both sat in silence, squealing tires still resounding off concrete walls outside. A soft voice called out, "Cary? Is that you?"

Cary trembled. And started easing silently up the stairs. She could hear the engine of a car outside the door, so she continued up as quietly as possible. The voice called out, louder, "Cary? We only want to chat. We can work all this out, okay?"

A footstep. And another. The voice called her name again softly, sweetly. Cary continued taking slow and silent steps upward. Another footstep. Faster. Another. Running. Cary turned and bolted, taking steps two at a time, her dress stretching against her thighs.

The voice called out something into the clicking static of a radio and tires squealed again outside. Cary ran, passing door after door. Her side ached, threatening to split wide open. Her head still buzzed from being thrown. The stairwell ended with one final door. She burst out onto the roof of the structure.

The roof was one sprawling parking lot stretched out to the horizon in every direction—streets and lots and buildings beyond like an infinity pool of pavement. Cary wandered around in the open space with her head in her hands. Behind her, Thompson came crashing out of the door. A car squealed into view from a ramp at the center of the lot. Cary edged toward the building's edge. Jolly jumped out of the car, leaving it running. He and Thompson both eased toward Cary with their hands out, shaking their heads, smiling, soothing.

Thompson nodded at her. "Let's talk, Cary. Come on. Get in the car."

Cary peered over the edge. A lone car sat parked down in a string of spaces on a side street. "You think I'm crazy?"

Jolly shook his head. "No. I think you're scared. So let's work this all out, what do you say?"

Cary turned on both of them. "I have it. I have it, okay. I do."

They froze. Dropped their hands. Stared at her. Thompson said, "Have what?"

Cary swallowed. "What you're looking for." She searched her brain for anything anyone might have said. "He sent it to me."

Jolly laughed. "Bullshit."

Cary shook her head. "I had another phone. You didn't know about it. I got it from Johnna's house."

Jolly looked at Thompson, who shrugged.

Cary pointed toward the Parker Building. "My purse. I dropped it when one of the assholes you sicced on me attacked me. On the second floor. Toward the back of the building."

Thompson rolled his head around. "Well fuck." He looked at Jolly. "Keep her here. Let me go check it out." He started for the stairwell.

Jolly called out, "Don't have a heart attack on the stairs, fat ass."

Thompson flipped him off and disappeared through the door.

Jolly looked at Cary and jerked a thumb toward the car. "Want to wait in the car?"

Cary shook her head.

"Suit yourself." He started to walk toward his car.

Cary called out, "So Doyle? She's with you?"

Jolly stopped and called over his shoulder, "Who?"

"Doyle. The cop. Young black woman?"

Jolly turned around. "Yeah. What about her?"

Cary shook her head. "Is she with you or against you in all this?"

Jolly looked confused. "She's nothing. What the hell are you talking about? She helped us identify you, yeah. But that's it."

Cary shook her head. "No. That's not it. She's still all in this."

Jolly hung his head. "Jesus. When?"

Cary peered over the ledge again. She pointed. "Right now. She's here. I see her car right down there."

Jolly cursed and started marching toward Cary. She eased out of the way until he got close. As he got even with her, Cary jumped into his legs, crouching and putting her whole weight into his knees. She grabbed at his coat and pulled him forward, letting his momentum propel him.

Jolly hit the ledge and teetered over. Cary rolled onto her back and kicked upward with everything she had, connecting with his face and chest. Jolly gasped and continued falling, flipping over the side and vanishing into silence.

A moment later, the silence was replaced with a thudding crash and the resonating whirl of a car alarm.

Cary panted and shivered. Thompson had to have heard the struggle. She whirled around and looked at the running car. Scrambling to her knees, she ran for the car. She jumped in and grabbed at the gear shift. The unmarked police car started rolling as she reached for the gas pedal with bare feet. She looked into her rearview and caught a glimpse of a befuddled Thompson crashing out of the stairwell door as she sped down the ramp.

Chapter 27

Officer Doyle ran after Cary, throwing herself into the barricaded door. After a few tries, she gave up and sprinted down the main staircase. She found a door to the stairwell on the first floor. The door was jammed shut with old boxes on the other side. She had to give the thick metal door several shoulders before it gave enough for her to fit through. Above her, she spotted Cary dashing out a door headed away from the building.

Directly in front of her was a door with a car and the word *Parking*. Doyle leapt over the boxes and hit the door in a run. The parking garage was dim, but enough light spilled down the ramp from the upper levels for Doyle to make her way across the empty spaces. In the middle was a small stairwell running up the center of the multi-level parking facility. Doyle reached the door and paused. She took out her gun and sucked in several sharp breaths.

The door opened quietly enough. On higher levels, footsteps and voices bounced off the walls. They wouldn't be able to pick out her clomping over those echoes. Thompson was calling after Cary. She recognized his voice.

Doyle kept to the edges of the stairs and worked her way up behind Thompson. He was a couple of flights below Cary from the sound of things. And Doyle was a couple of flights below him. She didn't stand a chance of doing anything in these enclosed, dark confines. Even if she worked up the nerve to take a shot, she had no way of keeping it from missing and ricocheting up toward Cary. So she kept a steady pace at a short distance behind them.

When Cary reached the end of the line, she burst out onto the top level and light exploded down the well like a blown dam. Doyle flattened herself against a wall, but it didn't matter. Thompson was focused on catching up to Cary—Doyle got an eyeful of him huffing his way up to the open door.

Tires squealed above and Doyle heard Thompson trying to talk to Cary. She snuck up to the top level and watched out the open door. Jolly had driven up, and they were both easing toward Cary, who stood at the edge of the roof. Doyle crouched and held her gun close to her cheek, ready. She stepped out, unseen, and worked her way around to the far side of the stairwell. Pressed flat against the far wall, she listened.

Cary was conning them. Separating them. Doyle wasn't sure if Cary knew what she was doing, but this might give them a fighting chance. Thompson's footsteps diminished headed back down the stairwell, and Cary kept on, undeterred. She was reeling Jolly in. Moving him away from his car and toward her. If he got distracted enough in the conversation, Doyle might get the drop on him. Maybe convince Cary to get into Doyle's car with her and burn out of there.

Doyle started easing around the edge of the protruding stairwell structure, gun still at the ready. As she eased around the edge to put Jolly in her sight line, Cary moved. Jolly went over fast—flipped almost. Doyle dropped her gun and stood shocked in the silence. Then, *wham.* Jolly hit something hard. A car. The alarm rang out everywhere. Cary started scrambling for the car, and Doyle took a step toward her. But Thompson was noisily pounding back up the stairs.

Doyle ducked back down around the structure and held her breath as Cary sped off in Jolly's car. Thompson stammered and cursed, screamed after her in futile yips. He looked over the edge and mumbled something in unintelligible sobs. Doyle eased up to her haunches and held her gun back out, ready again for anything. But Thompson went bounding back down the stairs without ever seeing her.

She put her gun into the back waistband of her jeans and inched over to the ledge of the roof. Sneaking a look down she could just make out the outline of Jolly's body smeared across the hood of a parked car. It looked like a cop car. But if Thompson and Jolly had their car in the garage, then…

A figure was running from behind a dumpster and pile of pallets toward the car. Doyle didn't recognize him, but he was definitely a cop. And he was steadily talking to someone on a phone or a radio.

"Shit," she whispered to herself. She pulled Cary's stolen phone out of her back pocket and searched the recent numbers. The most recent she recognized as Marlowe's.

He answered on the first ring. "Cary?"

She rolled her eyes. "No. But she is alive. No thanks to you."

"Shelley?"

"Yeah. You got a car?"

He breathed into the phone. "Yeah. I borrowed one. What's going on?"

"No time for explanations. I need you to pick me up at the Parker Building. Now."

"Dammit, Shelley. Why'd you have to go there?"

"You better be glad I did. Might have saved that girl's life."

He sighed. "Shelley, I'm worried about *your* life right now."

"Then come pick me up, asshole. Out front. In, like, thirty seconds."

He mumbled a curse and fumbled the phone. "On my way."

Shelley Doyle ended the call, erased any signs of Marlowe's number, and tossed the phone on the ground. She took off back down the stairwell, using the first door available to switch over to the Parker Building stairs. She made it to the first floor, heaving and almost ready to vomit. Climbing over the boxes, she slipped into the lobby.

Jolly had fallen off the back of the garage, farthest from the front doors of the Parker. It wouldn't take them too long before they started poking around in this direction. Not to mention, Thompson was still lurking somewhere, and she had successfully pissed off about eight or nine homeless men. She slunk through the lobby, gun drawn. Several homeless men gave her a wide berth. No sign of Thompson. Sirens. In the distance, but behind her, toward the garage. She made it to the loose plywood and took a peek out. No sign of anyone.

Putting her gun away, she slipped out and made a full sprint across the street. She slid into a crouch in a hollowed out nook of a neighboring building. A couple of police cruisers zipped by, but didn't slow before taking the corner toward the garage. Within a minute or two, a little black Chevy Equinox rolled up, pausing and looking at the front of the building. Shelley ran for it, hoping. She hit the passenger door and jerked it open. Marlowe jumped and yelped.

Shelley hunched down in the seat. "Go, go, go, go."

Marlowe sped off and took his first opportunity to turn away from the scene. He looked over at Shelley as he drove. "Are you okay?"

Shelley eased up into her seat and fastened her seatbelt. "Yeah. I am now."

"What the hell happened, Shells?"

Shelley shook her head. "Everything went south. I tried to take your bullshit and make something out of it. I told her to have you send the address to my phone. My other phone. Not the number you have."

Marlowe laughed. "I figured she had switched to a new phone. I wouldn't have sent it."

She nodded. "I know. But it didn't matter. She switched phones on me. Got the address and came anyway."

Marlowe shrugged. "She's crafty."

"No shit. But they were gonna kill her, 'lowe."

He looked at her and hung his head. "That ain't what they said."

"Well it's what they did! They killed the girl's friend!"

Marlowe bit his lip. "Yeah. I saw the body."

Shelley slapped at his arm. "Then you know we got to end this, Marlowe! Nobody else is getting killed because of me. We got to find Do Right and end this shit."

Marlowe looked at her and shook his head. "Shelley. Do Right's dead."

She looked away and back, pointing a finger. "Don't say that."

"What you think, Shelley? They gonna kill all these people to cover up some shit he did, but not kill him?"

She shook her head. "What's this all about then, huh? If they killed him then why not let it be done?"

"Thompson says they think he made a copy. They think he sent it to Cary."

Shelley frowned. "You and I both know he wouldn't."

Marlowe shrugged. "No. He wouldn't. But it don't mean he didn't make a copy."

Shelley flopped her hands in her lap. "So what are you saying?"

"I'm saying we offer to find the copy. We hunt it down. We hand it over. And they leave you alone, me alone…"

"Cary alone."

Marlowe nodded. "Yeah. Everybody."

Shelley closed her eyes and nodded. "All right. Call him. Tell him we'll do it."

Marlowe cocked his head. "I can't. They burned the phone they used. Told me if I needed them again it would have to be face-to-face."

"How we supposed to do that?"

"There's a chat room on some site they gave me. I go on there, post a location and a time, and meet them. They said to give an hour lead time. So we'll meet them. Somewhere public. And we'll end this shit."

Chapter 28

Mark Thompson left his partner with Cary Trubody on the roof of the parking garage. He secretly hoped Dick would put her down while he was gone. The girl had become a pain in his ass. He had enough of those already. Huffing on those stairs on the way up reminded him of a few of them.

Pausing at a landing between floors, Mark pulled a pack of American Spirits from the inside pocket of his sports coat. Four cigarettes and a disposable lighter rattled around in the pack. He lit one and scoffed at the Indian on the packaging. Fucking hipster cigarettes.

His girlfriend bought them for him—said they had less tar, not quite as horrible as his normal brand, which cost half of the American Spirits. He shook his head. To Mark, her logic sounded about like cutting back on drinking by switching to light beer. But she did it out of love. No doubt about it.

For reasons Mark would never understand, the girl loved him. They met when her kid witnessed a mugging. The victim got stabbed in the neck and ended up dying the next day. The kid was five. Mark managed to pull in a transient to pretend to have seen what the kid actually observed. It kept him from having to testify and made his mom incredibly grateful.

Mark may not have helped the girl and her kid for gratitude, but he sure didn't reject it. She was fifteen years his junior and drop dead gorgeous. And she imagined something in him which two ex-wives and a slew of passing acquaintances never did. Most of what she envisioned had to do with the kid. The little shit was nine now and Mark would be goddamned if he hadn't fallen in love with the kid every bit as much as the mom. He never gave kids much thought. A fact which ended one marriage and didn't help the other. The job always seemed like a cruel thing to put on a kid.

The job ruined everything it touched. Like a cancer. Dry rot. Being a cop ate away at your whole family from the inside out. Give it enough time, and a detective's beat would leave nothing but hollowed out bones and crumbling wood. Cigarettes and booze and fast food were bush league threats. The job could seize a heart before they got the chance. In every conceivable way.

Mark smoked and thought about his make-shift family at home. He had a year—one goddamn year—and then he would draw a little pension and go cut lumber at a Home Depot or some shit. Teach history to middle schoolers. Deliver packages in dopey brown shorts. Anything. Anything would be better. He'd get married and settle and raise and do all those things a man's supposed to do. Cut out the smoking and cut back the drinking and eat a salad every now and again. He'd do it better than his dad or any of his uncles or his grandfather.

He dropped his half-smoked cigarette and ground it out with a toe of his loafer. None of that would happen if they didn't clean up this mess. Sweat beaded up across his forehead at the thought of huffing it back down those stairs. But before he traveled another flight, he heard screams from above him. He paused and listened. They didn't sound female. And then, *crash*! A car alarm swirled to life.

Mark grunted back up the stairs and stumbled out the door, pulling his gun from its holster. Jolly was gone. Mark ran for the edge of the rooftop parking lot where Cary stood. He skidded to a stop and leaned out over the edge, looking down. His partner was painted across the hood of a parked car—a cop's car from the look of it. He swirled around and found Cary fighting his car into gear. Tears swelled into the corners of his eyes. When he called out, his voice cracked. He raised his gun, but stopped. He thought of the cop whose car had just been smashed. Who was down there?

Lowering his gun, Mark sank down with his hands on his knees. He pushed vomit back down his throat. No time for this shit. He needed a car—an exit plan. He holstered his gun and ran for the stairs. Weak heart be damned, Mark threw his forty extra pounds down three and four steps at a time.

Jolly fell to the west. The entry to the Parker Building was north. The parking garage had an old maintenance entrance near a loading dock to the south. He had to make it out through there and find a car somewhere on the streets of Old Town. Two blocks south was a shelter. They usually had seven or eight employees parked in a lot out back. If he remembered right, a couple of them drove old, shitty cars he could jump-start by popping off the steering column.

By the time he came falling out of the stairwell, Mark was wheezing. His chest ached and his gut burned. Stumbling past the loading dock, he almost laughed. *Perfect. Have a heart attack and shit yourself, why don't you? You fat bastard.* An old gate lay bent over enough to walk through. Before he did, Mark stopped and listened for sirens. They were coming, but they were all north. He gambled right.

He crossed the street and hit an alley running between forgotten buildings. Past one more street and there was the shelter. Mark hung back at the corner of the nearest building. He could see the whole employees' lot from where he lurked. At least two cars looked old enough to hotwire—an ugly ass tan Celica and a little Ford pickup. He pulled his gun and worked to catch his breath. He'd have to break a window. Picking a damn lock took too much time.

Before he broke for the lot, a teenage girl came trotting out with a couple of jugs of tea. She went straight for the Celica and started it before moving around to the back to put the tea in the trunk. The girl went trotting back in for another load, leaving her car running.

Mark looked up. "Are you fucking kidding me with this? Don't make it easy. I'm an asshole." He laughed to himself and ran for the car. He grabbed the tea and set it on the ground, shut the trunk as softly as possible, and hopped in the driver's seat. He watched for the girl, but he rounded his first corner before anyone appeared.

Once on the road, he let himself cry. Jolly was a horrible person but a great partner. The guy was a war vet. It did something to him. He didn't value life the way normal people did. What he valued was loyalty. And he was the most loyal motherfucker on earth. Jolly was the guy you called to help bury the body. With him, it was never a question of why. He didn't care. If you were his people, he took care of you. All the way down the line.

The problem with Jolly was he took it too far. He didn't have to kill Karen Webster. It was a batshit crazy move—psychotic. But Mark couldn't help letting one thought take over his mind: Jolly killed Karen Webster, and Jolly shot Dante. Even if he couldn't catch up with Cary and shut her down, Mark might skate on everything. There would be suspicions, sure, but not enough to convict him or pull his pension.

Mark slammed his hand into the steering wheel and cursed at himself. What was he thinking? Jolly laid everything on the line to pull them out of the hole they dug together. It was the difference between the two of them. Mark could talk it. He broke a few fingers every now and then to make a guy say what they needed to hear. But Jolly was nuts. A man with no dimmer switch. And everything he had done for the past two days he did to help them out of a bind. Mark cursed himself again for being so quick to use his partner's dead body to step out of his own grave. He couldn't do it. He still needed Cary.

By now the whole force would be looking for her. She would be implicated in the deaths of her friend out by Graffiti Creek, Karen Webster, and now Jolly. Mark knew they'd be looking for him, too. If they caught up with him now, it would look fishy. But if he tracked down Cary, put her down in self-defense? Well, he would look like a cop trying to do right by his partner. Everybody would respect that. He might get looked at pretty hard, but it would drag out for months, maybe a year. If the world would hold together for ten and a half months, he'd offer to retire and they'd jump at the bait. Mark Thompson may not receive a hero's send-off, but he didn't mind. Heroes die bloody. Cops with a little dirt on their hands make it home in time to wash up for dinner.

If he was going to find Cary, he would need a few things. With his car gone, he needed a police scanner. He couldn't keep one step ahead if he didn't know where they were headed. He would also need some help. Reynard was still as much on the hook as he was, so he could count on him. Doyle was a wild card, but Marlowe was still useful. Cary possibly still trusted him, and all Marlowe cared about was getting his sister out of the crosshairs. Mark needed to convince him she was still in them. He also required a little walking around money. If they were going to start looking for him, he needed to stay off the grid until he could put Cary's neck in his hands.

Among the many perks of being partnered with Dick Jolly was the petty cash account he kept at a local bank. Jolly busted this bank president with a hooker when he worked vice. He recognized him from one newspaper photo of the grand opening of Spring Valley Bank and Trust. Mark glossed right over shit like newspaper clippings and lobby photos of board members. But not Jolly. The guy always worked an angle. And letting SVB&T's president off with a little ribbing and a slap on the ass got Jolly and his partner a petty cash account at the downtown branch. They couldn't go crazy, but there was always a few hundred available for an emergency. Mark had used it to pay a bum to testify in place of his girlfriend's kid. Now he needed a couple hundred bucks to keep his credit card from showing up anywhere.

He called Reynard on his way and told him to meet him in the parking lot. While waiting, he strolled in and went to the designated teller. They were always changing, but this month it was a cute blonde college student with a titty tat peeking out of her blouse. She was sleepy-eyed and snarky. Jolly claimed to be in love with her. Mark sauntered up to the counter and tapped on the desk with a grin. The teller looked down at his two outstretched fingers. She jerked two hundred dollar bills from underneath the counter, jotted something down on a notepad, and Mark was on his way back to the Celica.

Reynard was waiting for him when he got out. He leaned against the Celica and smirked. "Nice piece of shit, Thompson."

Mark scowled at him. "It's Detective, Reynard. Shut the fuck up and get in."

The two men got on either side of the front seat. Reynard glanced around casually. "Where's Jolly?" Mark shot him a look and he hung his head. "*Detective* Jolly."

Mark shook his head. "Don't worry about Jolly. Did you get my scanner?"

Reynard handed over a radio he unclipped from his belt. "I checked the message board. Your boy wants to meet."

Mark's eyes widened. "Who?"

Reynard searched for the name. "Marlin, Martin, Marty…"

"Marlowe?"

Reynard pointed. "Marlowe. Yeah. The brother."

Mark nodded. "Good. Message him back." He pointed toward the bank with his head. "Tell him to meet me here. ASAP. In the lobby."

Reynard pulled a cellphone out and started typing. "Want me to stick around?"

Mark shook his head. "No. I got this. I need you on the house. Good old fashioned stakeout, Reynard. Consider it a promotion."

Reynard rolled his eyes and climbed out of the car. He called back, "Promotion my ass. Watch your six, *Detective* Thompson. And when you see Jolly tell him to suck my nuts." He grinned and headed back to his car.

Mark smiled back. And then hung his head and let himself cry while he waited.

Chapter 29

Cary tried to focus on driving. The top of her head tingled with sweat and her brain filled with white noise and electric fuzz. Her tires screeched around the curves of the parking garage, but the road noise was overshadowed by a steady buzzing. A hum mixed with the shushing of a thousand locust wings eating at her thoughts. Her hands slipped on the wheel, jerking the car. When she erupted out of the garage into the street, she slid into a curb before spinning forward again.

Detective Jolly was dead. He had to be. Although she couldn't look, the sound was horrific. It was the last noise she remembered over the rattling static in her head. No thought substantiated what she did. It was pure survival. Jolly, and the homeless giant, and Johnna… Johnna. Cary felt responsible for all of them. They were all dead. They had to be dead. No one could take a jagged board to the gut. No one could fall like that. He hit a car, she thought. The car alarm—she remembered the wailing now. And Thompson, screaming. He sobbed.

Cary shook her head. *No. Don't feel bad for the asshole. He wants to kill you.* As she drove, she started feeling around in the console, the glove box, anywhere for something useful. She didn't even know what she was looking for. And whatever it was, she didn't find it. The two detectives were slobs, but they didn't leave a trail of anything useful.

Doyle and Marlowe. She needed to find them. They may not be trustworthy, but Doyle saved her ass back at the Parker Building and Marlowe had helped her out of several tight spots. They were all she had. If there was another Cary Trubody, which she began to doubt, then all of this began with her. She needed to know why. And Doyle and Marlowe held more information than they let on. One of them tipped off Thompson and Jolly. And they definitely knew each other.

Cary took a sharp turn and heard a thudding rattle from the dashboard. She had been hearing the noise all along, but her brain just began to catch up. She pulled off into the parking lot of a fast food joint and parked. She fished around on the dashboard until she came back with a cell phone. It had to be Jolly's. He must have left it in the car.

She pulled up his contacts, but they were a sea of initials and numbers and code names. There was no way to decipher Jolly's system in time to do anything with it. She tapped the phone in her hand trying to think what would be available. Jolly was obviously a paranoid guy. Not the type to have an informative text or email. Sure enough, both were empty. So what do people forget to clear? She spent thirty valuable minutes lost in a Facebook app which yielded nothing. Jolly wasn't the sharing type. Cary opened up Safari and flipped through the most recent pages: a lunch menu, a PDF of a police briefing, and an Internet chat room. Jolly didn't strike her as the chat room type either.

Opening the chat room link up didn't help much. It was on a Reddit thread. The message board heading read, "Ask a plumber…" Cary scrolled the messages and found nonsense. They weren't even questions. Pure gibberish: a number or a location. Maybe arranging meets? The last one posted minutes ago. It read, "Spring Valley Bank, downtown, lobby, now." It came from someone called "Gr8t8" in response to a post of a simple string of three question marks. From "Leander."

Cary sat back and thought. Leander. Where was the name from? She recognized it. There was a Leander in mythology. Hero and Leander. She sat up. *Hero and Leander* was also a poem. By Christopher *Marlowe*.

She sped off in the direction of the bank. She had been there before. They offered to put fifty bucks in your account if you opened a checking with them. Anyone who'd been a poor twenty-something like Cary was familiar with Spring Valley Bank and Trust. Marlowe had to be meeting Thompson. Things had taken a shit turn, and they needed to regroup. She would much rather be going to find Doyle, but she would take whatever she got. And she had Thompson's car. Maybe it would give her some leverage.

The bank's parking lot was full enough for Cary to slip into a spot and hang back, unseen by anyone in or close to the building. The lobby of Spring Valley was huge, with several seating areas—comfortable chairs positioned around coffee tables littered with glossy magazines. Offices lined the lobby on all sides in an open plan. People huddled over desks to discuss loans and financial problems in private, but Cary had been in there before.

The thirty-foot ceilings swallowed all conversations. Spring Valley Bank and Trust had all the sound qualities of a large library. Along one wall sat a row of kiosks, but Spring Valley had an old-fashioned vibe. They still had about seven tellers lined up and waiting to pull the next number. She positioned herself where she could see most of the lobby and the front doors. And within minutes they slid open for someone familiar.

He got out of a car somewhere up the rows; Cary couldn't tell which one. Luckily, he never turned back to see her, either. Mark Thompson surely would have recognized his own car. He shuffled inside with the beginnings of a limp—not like he had hurt himself, but more the way Cary's uncle used to walk when his sciatica acted up. Cary followed Thompson as he hobbled over to a chair by a front window and plopped down with a foot on a stack of magazines like he owned the place. He sat and rubbed at his temples, waiting on someone else to show.

And they did. Marlowe drove up in a little black SUV. He parked and hopped out, headed for the front doors. Right behind him was Doyle. They were together. Whichever one of them she hoped she could trust walked arm-in-arm with whichever one of them she knew she couldn't.

The meeting between the three was terse. Cary felt the tension from across the parking lot. As she monitored them, she chewed at a thumbnail. This was it. She was out of people. There was no other Cary Trubody. No one on the police force, not even the chief—especially not the chief—was going to help her. The cavalry would not be showing up. Marlowe double-crossed her, Doyle abandoned her, Johnna died, and *that* fat jackass was still trying to kill her.

Cary caught sight of herself in the rearview mirror. She sighed. "Screw this." She reached over, popped the trunk, and got out. Moving around to the back of the car, she started fishing around. What she hoped to find was shoved off to the side under an old police department sweatshirt. A shotgun. The only thing Cary ever learned about guns she assembled from a single duck hunting trip she went on with her grandfather when she was twelve. This shotgun was a pistol grip—it looked like something the dirty cops kept off of some street thug. But the principles had to be the same. Besides, she didn't need shells; merely the threat—a way out once she got in.

With the gun tucked up under her ripped dress, Cary started the long walk to the front doors of the bank. This was insane. But what was left for her to do? She had been running for two days now. It was time to stop running. If Thompson wanted her dead, she was going to make him kill her somewhere it would be captured on film. These cops did anything they wanted, but once she caught them on film they'd go from gods to monsters in one viral video. It was the least she could do. For Johnna.

By the time she got within twenty feet of the doors, Marlowe, Doyle, and Thompson all turned to stare at her with wide eyes. She read Thompson's lips as he shook his head and said, "What the fuck?"

Cary kept the shotgun concealed in her dress as she worked her way inside and over to the last empty chair around the table by the window. Her back was to the window, with Marlowe across from her. Doyle was to her left and Thompson to her right. Doyle and Marlowe sat up with their hands or elbows on their knees, but Thompson kicked back with his legs crossed. Cary tried to mimic his posture without revealing the gun up her dress. She looked at each of them. "You guys didn't tell me you started a book club. I want in. What are we doing? Romance?" She raised her hand. "Who likes erotica?"

Doyle cocked her head at Cary. "Cary, what the hell are you doing here?"

Cary shot a look at Doyle. "I'm getting answers." She looked at Marlowe. "Starting with how you know this asshole."

Marlowe looked affronted. "Hey!"

Cary leaned forward. "Don't *hey* me! You set me up! There is no 'other Cary Trubody,' is there?"

Marlowe hung his head. Thompson grinned like a damn Bond villain. "What do you girls say we keep our voices down so we don't get kicked out? I doubt anyone but me wants to continue this conversation somewhere more private."

Cary turned to Thompson. "Shut up. You tried to kill me." She thought. "Three times, I think. You don't get to talk."

He shrugged. "Four." He waved a hand between Cary and Marlowe. "But continue."

Cary looked back at Doyle and pointed at Marlowe. "Who is he to you?"

Doyle nodded. "My brother." She frowned at Marlowe. "And all *this asshole* has been doing is trying to protect me." She looked back at Cary and sucked in at her lips. "I'm sorry, Cary. Nobody ever wanted you to get hurt."

Thompson raised his hand. "Um, I did."

Doyle and Cary both said in unison, "Shut up."

Cary shook her head at Marlowe. "Why me?"

Marlowe grimaced and looked to Thompson. "They think you have something."

Cary squinted at Thompson. "What?"

Doyle said, "The text you got—the one you thought was meaningless. It was from mine and Marlowe's brother."

Cary shook her head. "Dante?"

Marlowe nodded. "Yeah. Do Right—Dante—he had something they wanted. They think he made a copy, but we don't know where it is. They think he may have sent it to you."

Cary laughed. "It was a blank text. Dante was Johnna's ex-boyfriend. I doubt he would trust me with much of anything after his girlfriend left him for me. It was a mistake. This is all one big mistake."

Thompson raised his eyebrows. "*She* left *him* for *you*? Oh, this just got a fuck ton more interesting."

Doyle leaned across the coffee table toward Thompson. "Shut up, fat man. You hear her? She doesn't have it. Now, you tell me where my brother is and let this shit go."

Thompson smiled. "Oh, I'll tell you where he is. All the different places he is. Give me the copy he made first."

Doyle reached around for a gun and froze.

Thompson jerked to life and made a similar motion. "Go ahead, Doyle. Let's hash it out right here, right now. In front of all these people. That'll fix this right up, won't it?"

Marlowe put a hand on Doyle's leg. "Shelley. It's okay." He looked to Thompson. "So let's say we find it? This copy. Me and my sister—" Shelley and Cary shot him looks. "And Cary. We all go on with our lives?"

Thompson cocked his head. "You two? Yeah. You're good. Cary here? She's got shit to atone for, don't you, Cary?"

Cary swallowed and looked at her lap. "He was going to kill me. You were both going to kill me."

Thompson leaned forward until Cary was able to catch a whiff of the cigarettes on his breath. "Listen, bitch. You're going to burn for this. I'm going to walk you in myself." He smiled. "Or drag you in." He looked around. "Hell. You gotta walk out of here sometime."

Doyle kept her hand on her gun. "No. She walks out now. We'll look for this copy you think exists. But Cary goes. Now. let her walk."

Thompson scrunched his face up like he'd sucked on a lemon. "Fuck you, Doyle. You aren't writing the script on this one. I'm telling you how it goes. Don't worry about her. You worry about you and what's left of your family."

Cary blurred out into a swirl of voices. Thompson and Doyle argued and postured and threatened. Marlowe tried to make peace, but even he ruffled at the mention of Dante and what Thompson might have done to him. They started to catch a few stares from the patrons of Spring Valley Bank and Trust. And Thompson was right. What had she been thinking? She'd be lucky to make it out of this bank alive. The only way he wouldn't put her down in the parking lot was if she walked out…in handcuffs.

Cary looked up at all three of them. "No. Fuck all of you. Let me tell you 'how this goes' for once." She stood up and pulled the shotgun out of her dress. The distinctive and frightening *chick-chuck* of cocking it echoed throughout the lobby. Cary stood on the coffee table and screamed out. "All right, everybody be cool, this is a robbery! Any of you fucking pricks move, and I'll execute every motherfucking last one of you!"

Chapter 30

Cops had mobbed the Parker Building by the time Bright arrived. She parked a little ways up the road and walked the last bit with both hands in the pockets of her obey-me-red quarter-length trench coat. She weaved in and out of swarming CSIs and uniforms. Bright kept her eyes trained up, studying the upper floors of the building and the higher levels of the garage.

She had made it all the way to the back of the parking garage when a sharp cry of "Detective Hudson!" broke her concentration. Glancing right, she spotted Carlos Moya with his hands cupped around his mouth. He hung at the far corner of the parking structure and waved her around before disappearing out of sight.

She followed Carlos until she rounded the corner and got the full sight of the actual crime scene. Blood had sprayed out in a fan around the front of the car. Dick Jolly's body was sprawled out with limbs jutting out of a dent in the hood and windshield. His head was buried inside the car, but his hands were both visible, flopped up backwards at odd angles and hanging there frozen in some sort of mangled gesture.

Something about the hands was more jarring to Bright than seeing dead eyes. The hands always seemed to be mid-grasp, like they were still trying to reach for someone. With his oddly angled legs and dangling shoes slipped half-off and shattered glass sprinkled into the blood splatter like glitter. The whole scene looked like some sort of avant garde art piece.

Carlos stood between Bright and Jolly's body, rubbing his head with a shaking hand. "Yeah," he nodded at Bright's wide eyes, "it's a regular Gallagher show. I'm sorry, Bright. I was watching. But I couldn't do anything."

Bright stepped over and put a hand on Carlos' shoulder. "It's okay, Detective Moya. Walk me through what happened."

Carlos nodded again and sighed. "Yeah. Well, I followed them—"

Bright held a hand up. "Them?"

Carlos closed his eyes and cocked his head in apology. "Sorry. Shit. I followed Detectives Jolly and Thompson from the station, but while at the station I had checked their trunk for a missing Phillip's head." He looked at Bright and shrugged. "It was there, by the way. So, they made me. Or, well, almost made me. I shrugged it off as me being as asshole."

Bright laughed, "Easy enough to do."

Carlos shook of some of his visible nerves with a chuckle. "Yeah, well, they bought it at least. But I had to keep a distance after that." He pointed back to the dumpster and pallets. "I hid out back there to watch the building when they entered."

Bright stopped him again. "Entered which building?"

Carlos shook his head at his own carelessness. "They walked into the Parker, but then drove into the garage. I waited, watched. Nothing. No Cary Trubody, no sign of the two detectives, nothing." He pointed to the roof of the parking garage, which stood about two thirds as tall as the Parker Building itself. "Finally, I heard a car—like, tires squealing. I caught sight of figures on the roof of the garage. It looked like—could've been a woman. Hard to tell. Next thing I knew," he held his hands out toward Jolly's body.

Bright shook her head. "Was he pushed? Did he jump?"

Carlos shrugged. "No clue. There was a shout, but it was him. Sort of as he fell. It was awful, Bright."

Bright looked back at the buildings. "Did we sweep the buildings?"

Carlos nodded. "Yeah. No sign of Thompson or his car. No sign of Cary Trubody, if it was even her." He pointed. "They found a homeless guy stabbed with a board. Caught him in the stomach. He was bleeding out in a second-floor office. We bused him to Harper General."

Bright raised her eyebrows. "Conscious?"

Carlos shook his head. "He will be, but you know these guys, Bright. He won't give us shit."

Bright hung her head. "Yeah. May not be connected."

Carlos cut his eyes toward her and reached in his pocket. "Oh, he's connected." He pulled out a sheet of paper and handed it to Bright. "EMTs found this on him."

Bright frowned from the photo in her hands to Carlos. "This is Cary Trubody's DMV photo."

Carlos nodded. "Yeah. We found them on seven or eight homeless in the Parker."

Bright looked back at the Parker Building. "So Thompson and Jolly come looking for her here? What made them think she'd be here? The whole department is looking for this girl. I haven't heard any tips put her here."

Carlos cocked his head. "I didn't think so, either. And I watched these guys go in. It wasn't like they were looking for anybody. It was more like," he trailed off into a shrugging shake of his head.

Bright nodded at the photo. "Like they were lying in wait for somebody."

Carlos grimaced. "Yeah. Exactly like that."

A uniformed officer approached them and pointed over his shoulder with a thumb. "Detectives? We found one who'll talk."

Bright handed Carlos the photo and pointed past the cop with her head. "Lead the way."

The entire Parker Building had been cordoned off with yellow police tape. All the way to the road, which included an old bus stop at the far corner of the front of the Parker. The bench was enclosed with plexiglass on all sides and over the top to shield waiting bus riders from the elements. Old advertisements for a local news station were fading and peeling from the sides.

The uniformed officer led Bright and Carlos around to the front of the bus stop. There they found a small bespectacled man clutching a cup of coffee with both hands. The cop leaned toward Bright and Carlos and spoke into his own shoulder. "We had to put a little bourbon in his coffee, but he's willing to talk."

Bright scrunched her face up. "Where'd you get the bourbon, officer?"

The cop smiled. "Let's all agree you'd be better off not knowing."

Carlos scoffed and moved around them to approach the man on the bench. Bright hung back, dismissing the officer with a condescending wave of her hand. Carlos smiled and nodded in greeting to the man. "Sir. I'm Detective Moya." He turned and motioned to Bright. "This is Detective Hudson. You mind if we ask you a few questions?"

The man studied them both in a practiced way. It was the look of someone who didn't forget faces. He pulled the lapels of his jacket—a worn, brown tweed sport coat—closer together with one hand, while taking a sip of Irish coffee with the other. "I'll help if I'm able. Don't want you blaming the girl for this."

Carlos frowned. "What girl, sir?"

The man motioned back to the building. "White girl. Running from those cops."

Bright moved past Carlos and sat next to the man. "What's your name?"

The man grinned. "Now, Detective Hudson. You and I both know I ain't giving you my real name. And you got nothing to get it with. I'm a ghost." He glanced back at the Parker Building. "We all are."

145

Bright smiled and nodded. "Fair enough. What do I call you?"

He sucked at his teeth and took a sip. "People have taken to calling me Booker. It'll do."

Carlos wrote the nickname down in a notepad, fruitlessly. Bright said, "Okay, Booker. Tell me about this girl. What did she look like?"

Booker squinted. "She was about five-three. A little hippy, if I can say so without offending anyone. Dark headed. She was a bit of a mess, but pretty enough. She had nice eyes. Like some kind of sad wolf. Looked the color of swimming pools."

Bright smiled. "You said she looked a mess. How?"

Booker shrugged. "Just a mess. Hair was roughed up. Makeup smeared. Looked to have a little blood on her in places. She had on a ripped up dress. Black cocktail dress of some kind. She even had on heels before somebody came along and knocked her out of 'em."

Bright shook her head. "Who knocked her out of her shoes?"

Booker took a sip of coffee and shook off the mention of the man. "Ah. Don't worry about him. This big fella they call Tex. But your girl's no daisy. She put him down. I think he's dead."

Bright grinned. "He's close." She held a hand out to Carlos and he handed her Cary's picture. "Is this her?"

Booker nodded. "Yep. Those two cops were handing her picture all over the place. Promising cash to anyone who could put her down."

Bright frowned. "Put her down?"

Booker nodded and pulled a finger across his throat. "Wanted dead or alive. They holed up in the garage and told us the first bum to bring her to them could walk away with a cool grand. Said it like that. Called us bums. Screaming it out and tossing those photos into tents."

Bright put the photo in her pocket. "What did these cops look like?"

Booker shrugged. "Fat white guys. Cops."

Carlos snickered under his breath and Bright shot him a look. She turned back to Booker. "And someone did? Take her to them?"

Booker shook his head. "I don't think so. I helped her all I could. Until the lady showed up with the gun."

Bright shook her head. "What lady?"

Booker shrugged again. "Not sure. She looked a little like a cop, too. Young black girl. Real pretty, but a hard ass. You know what I mean. Looked like the type of girl who'd be a whole lot of fun until you looked over in bed one night and realized you hadn't been fucking her. She's been fucking you." He looked Bright up and down. "You kinda look like one of them women yourself, Detective."

Carlos snickered again and Bright cleared her throat. "And what did this woman do?"

Booker shook his head. "Chased us all off, that's for sure. I was keeping the crazies at bay, but they were closing in around us. This girl showed up and fired a few shots off. We all scattered. The two ladies had a little yelling match. The black girl with the gun called your girl Cary. They recognized each other. But Cary, she took off up the stairs. Other girl tried to follow, but she got blocked out. Took off looking for another way up. Last I saw of either one."

Bright patted Booker's shoulder. "Thank you, Booker. This has all been very helpful. I'll send the officer over to refill your," she smirked at his cup, "coffee."

Booker grinned. "Thank you, Detective."

As they walked away from the bus stop, Carlos flipped through his notepad. He found a page and tapped at a note with his pen. He held the page up toward Bright. "I knew that rang a bell. I asked everyone at Roosevelt High if they noticed anyone else at the event who seemed out of place. And Joey Young gave me this. You know him, right? He's over the evidence locker. Been around forever."

Bright rolled her eyes. "What did he say, Moya? Either spit it out or stop moving your notepad so I can read."

Carlos pointed to a line on the page. "He said he witnessed a young black female enter the event. He took notice because she was dressed all wrong—had on jeans and a sweatshirt and ballcap. But the ballcap? It was a PD cap. He said she looked like a cop. I sent him home to study his department directory and see if he recognized her."

Bright frowned at him. "Call him up. Find out if he did."

Carlos nodded and pulled out his phone. Bright walked on ahead of him back toward the scene. This was growing. Thompson and Jolly didn't have the best reputation, but if Booker was right, they had definitely crossed a line. And if they crossed, when? With Johnna Kitteridge? Karen Webster? Had Cary Trubody actually done anything? Bright was beginning to wonder if maybe Cary was an innocent wrapped up in the wrong shit. But even so, she had to find her.

Bright's phone startled her with a steady chirp. She pulled it from a jacket pocket and answered with a curt "Hudson." There was a faint, audible breath at the other end. Bright repeated, "This is Detective Hudson. Who is this?"

No answer.

She listened to the silence and started to turn and look around her, but she was distracted by a uniformed captain on the scene waving her down. She hung up her phone and waited for him to come near before greeting him. He cut off her small talk abruptly with, "The name of this girl you've been looking for? Cary Trubody, right?"

Bright paused and nodded. "Yes. Why?"

The captain laughed and held out his radio. "Because she tried to rob a bank a few minutes ago."

Chapter 31

Sameer was beginning to feel some pressure at the seams of sleep deprivation. For the second night in a row, he slept in a chair. This time it had been his office chair. He dozed off after spending hours Googling one name or location after another. Several times he found himself getting lost on a Topix discussion board before concluding it was filled with Internet trolls and crackpots. But anything was better than trying to sleep in his own bed. The first night Seamus didn't come home he had been worried, but not panicked. The nature of a journalist's job, he knew, meant sometimes chasing a lead into the night. And, to be fair, he had spent a late night or two trying to finish one last line of code. He and Seamus both enjoyed the freedoms of not having kids or pets and the comfort of trusting one another absolutely. So on the second night, he was still able to fall asleep. The next morning was when concern inevitably turned to fright. Seamus would have called, or at least answered a text.

Most of the places on Sameer's board led nowhere. He located them—random bars or storefronts or intersections. Graffiti Creek turned up as a local name given to some vandalized bridge over a stretch of stream out in the sticks. But he had no details to connect those places to any happenings. Sometimes not even a person. And searching people turned up lots of details, but no way of knowing which were sources and which were suspects. The only lead he had to work with was Booker. And an address for the old Parker Building.

After a quick stop home to freshen up and change into an inconspicuous hoodie and joggers, Sameer drove down to Old Town to find the Parker Building. The task turned out to be much easier than he anticipated. The Parker Building was the one surrounded by police cars. Sameer slowed to a crawl as he passed by, but he couldn't tell what had happened. About a block over he parked in an old grocery store's abandoned parking lot and walked back toward the scene with his hood pulled down around his face.

Enough homeless meandered about to allow Sameer to blend in. He found a corner of a building across from the biggest collection of police cars. The sun created shadows for him to lurk within, obscuring anyone's view of him while allowing him a pretty clear shot of what was going on. The comings and goings seemed to center around the back of the building. Sameer couldn't locate the source of the trouble, but his focus was drawn to a homeless man being catered to near a bus stop right across from him.

Sameer reached into the pocket of his hoodie to pull out the information he deemed fit to bring. He unfolded the screen grab of Booker from the YouTube video. There was no doubt in his mind. Booker was right in front of him.

After several different cops spoke to Booker briefly, two detectives came over to speak with him. One was an attractive blonde, possibly Bright Hudson. Sameer studied her intently until the conversation ended and the two detectives started away. He fumbled around for his phone and leafed through his papers for Bright Hudson's card. He punched in the number Seamus had for her. Sure enough, the blonde detective across the street answered her phone. Sameer let a little gasp escape when she did, but he couldn't bring himself to speak. Detective Hudson hung up and continued toward the scene, stopping to speak with another officer.

Booker continued to sit at the bus stop bench and sip on a cup of coffee. Sameer had no idea how to reach him. Before returning his wad of notes to his pocket, he noticed the mysterious phone number. He shrugged and punched in the numbers. Booker jumped. Sameer grew wide eyed as Booker pulled a phone out of a pocket of his jacket and looked around nervously before answering it. They sat in silence for a moment. Booker whispered into the phone, "How you get this number?"

Sameer sucked in air and swallowed. "Seamus Fitzgerald."

He scrutinized Booker as the man hung his head. The hand holding the Styrofoam coffee cup shook. "I can't—I can't talk to you right now."

Sameer nodded like Booker could see him. "Yes. I understand. Are you familiar with the old Holt's Grocery? About a block over from here?"

Booker also nodded. "Yeah."

"I'm parked there. Come find me when you can slip away. Please."

Booker hung up.

Sameer sat in his car long enough to fall asleep. When his passenger side door burst open, he awoke with a start. Once he regained his composure, Booker was sitting next to him staring straight ahead. Before Sameer thanked him, Booker blurted out, "How do you know Seamus?"

Sameer nodded once. "He is my husband."

Booker nodded. "I'm sorry."

Sameer shook his head. "Sorry? For what?"

"I know he's missing. He and Do Right both. Think they got too mixed up in something."

Sameer sniffed and fought back a swell of tears. "Do you think they're okay?"

Booker cocked his head. "I don't know. I wish I could tell you different, but I just don't know."

Sameer collected himself. "I was told you have a story. Something Seamus was very interested in."

Booker nodded. "Some years back, I helped this girl get away from a rough John. Helped her as much as I could."

Sameer frowned. "Why did this story matter to Seamus?"

Booker hesitated. "This girl. She worked for the cops."

"Worked for the cops? Like undercover?"

Booker laughed. "Oh, under covers all right." He shook his head. "No. She answered to a couple of cops. They arranged meetings like the one that night for those kind of guys."

"What kind of guys?"

Booker shrugged. "Important ones. Guys who depend on votes to keep their jobs."

"Do you have any names?"

Booker shook his head. "Nope. I try to keep my head down and my ass intact." He pointed back toward the flashing blue and red lights around the corner. "Thought I could blend in here. But I can't help myself. If I see a young girl in trouble, I can't sit by and watch."

Sameer looked back. "Now? What happened in the Parker Building? Another girl?"

Booker nodded. "Same damn cops. Thought they were after me at first." He shook his head. "But they had their crosshairs set on some new girl."

"And you helped her?"

Booker nodded. "I tried. Best I could. From the looks of it, she managed to get away. One of those cops took a nosedive off the building. Girl tore off after. Didn't see what became of anybody else."

Sameer squinted at Booker, who still stared straight ahead. "Why did you think they were after you?"

"Your husband and Do Right started getting real nervous a week or two ago. Seamus, he came and found me and took me to Do Right's apartment. Said I should keep out of sight for a few days due to this documentary they were working on."

"Do you know anything about the documentary?"

Booker smiled broadly. "Called it 'Chicken Little.' Said it was a working title. I told my story for it. They filmed me talking about it over near Dollar Hill where it happened."

"How long were you at the apartment?"

Booker hung his head. "Few days. Seamus dropped me off there." He looked at Sameer for the first time. "It's the last time I saw him." He looked off again. "Do Right came home and set me up on his couch. Few days later, Do Right came in all crazy. Scared. Upset. He told me it wasn't safe for me there anymore. He grabbed some stuff, like he didn't plan on staying either. Ran down stairs for a bit and then said we got to go."

Sameer nodded. "And he brought you here?"

Booker tilted his head to the side. "Not at first. We made a stop. He was rushing around like crazy, but he pulled his shit together to make one stop. Got himself all proper for a minute. Said he needed to pop in and leave something for his ex-girlfriend. I waited in the car. Then he drove me here and dropped me off. Last I saw of him, too."

Booker shrugged as if to say *that's all I got to say* and started out, but Sameer stopped him by offering a handful of cash. Booker waved it off and smiled, looking Sameer in the eye for the first time. "I hope you find your husband."

Sameer smiled back in thanks. "One more thing. Do Right's apartment? The Girlfriend's house? Can you tell me where they are?"

Booker nodded. "Yep. I got a way with addresses. You got a pen?"

Chapter 32

Cary waved the shotgun around in the air and smiled broadly. She was slightly ashamed to admit it to herself, but robbing a bank was a bit of a rush. Her heart raced and her brain flooded with life and energy. She was hyper alert and electrified with confidence. Shelley and Marlowe both barked out unintelligible questions and objections.

Thompson smiled and reached for his gun. Shelley was on her feet, gun drawn and dangling next to her leg. Thompson laughed and mumbled something about her and Cary both being "crazy bitches."

Cary's senses were jumbled and warped. Screams and voices blurred and the colors of the lobby swirled into a technicolor-explosion-acid-trip.

Thompson stood and pulled at Marlowe's sleeve. He waved at Shelley and grunted, "Come on! Get the fuck out of here!" The three of them scrambled for the door along with several people in the lobby. Others laid down on their stomachs and covered their heads.

From across the lobby, two security guards were drawing their weapons and shouting things at Cary: "Put it down!" "Don't do it!" "Drop your weapon!"

Cary kept her shotgun pointed straight up. As soon as she saw Thompson running for his car, she lowered the gun to the table and clambered down with her hands up. She repeated, "Don't shoot. Don't shoot. I'm surrendering. I'm putting it down."

The next fifteen minutes passed in a frenzied blur. Cary was roughed around and her hands were zip tied—much better this time, police grade zip ties. Multiple uniformed officers bustled in and out of the bank, yelling things out over their radios. By the time Cary was able to focus, she was being half-carried out toward a squad car by two burly police officers. She started trying to talk, twisting her head toward both of them intermittently. "My name is Cary Trubody. Call it in. Tell them you have Cary Trubody." They tugged at her arms and barked at her to shut up.

Once in the car, a woman settled in behind the wheel, with one of the burly cops in the passenger seat. The woman looked back at Cary, who was struggling to sit up after being thrown into the car. The female cop said, "What did she say her name is?"

Cary craned her neck to make eye contact. "Cary Trubody! Call it in!"

The woman looked at her partner and mumbled. "Holy shit. Call it in."

They drove in silence to the police station. When they arrived, as they led Cary to a set of doors, a woman in a red trench coat came bursting out holding up a badge. She stared down the cops in an authoritative stance. "Officers. That's my suspect. I want her in an interrogation room." The woman turned her attention to Cary and softened. "Hi, Cary. We've got a lot to talk about."

Cary didn't have time to respond. She was whisked away by the elbows. It was her first time being whisked and the experience isn't as pleasant as the word makes it sound. She ended up getting tossed into a chair in a stark room. The room consisted of a few chairs and a single table with a box of Kleenex. The female officer released her from her wrist constraints and called out into the hallway, "Ask if they need her restrained." There was a beat and she heard the answer from her partner come back as no. Without another word, the female officer left Cary alone in the room.

In less than a minute, the woman in the red trench coat burst through the door and glided into a chair across the table from Cary. She didn't appear to be much older than Cary—maybe three or four years deeper into her thirties. But she had a gait and the posture of someone in charge. She was sleek and blonde and newscaster attractive. A short Latino man followed her in and took the other chair across the table. He had on a tailored suit with a thin tie, but his eyes betrayed something a little less polished—a kindness not made for police work. Cary preferred to look at him with his half-smile and soothing expression, but the lady in the trench coat snapped her fingers to bring Cary's eyes back to her. "Cary? Cary, you with me?"

Cary nodded.

The woman continued. "Good. I'm Detective Bright Hudson. This is Detective Carlos Moya. We've been working on a couple of cases we think you can help us with."

Moya held up three fingers. "Three cases."

Hudson clucked her tongue and looked at the ceiling. "That's right. *Three* cases." She twisted her mouth. "Four if you count your show at the bank."

Moya nodded. "Oh. And five counting the homeless guy with the stab wound."

Hudson snapped her fingers. "Absolutely. Can't forget him." Hudson pointed at Moya. "Stolen truck."

Moya smiled open-mouthed. "The farmer! Yes. He's pissed."

Hudson nodded. "Very pissed." She turned to Cary. "You've been a busy girl."

Cary closed her eyes and nodded. She smiled. "I can explain well over half of those things."

Both of the detectives laughed. Hudson gestured for her to carry on. "Do tell."

So Cary did. She told them everything, from winning three thousand dollars playing poker at a party all the way to pretending to rob a bank in order to save her ass. She left out the bit about turning Haley and Grayson into teenage getaway drivers, but everything else was there. Moya wrote it all down, flipping page after page of a tiny notepad. Neither detective reacted. They asked a handful of clarifying questions, but nothing probing.

Hudson leaned over and said something to Moya, which caused him to leave and return in a matter of minutes with a yearbook-style directory of police department staff. They showed her pictures of Thompson, Jolly, Reynard, and Doyle.

Hudson leaned back in her chair and glared at Cary. "So this is all one big conspiracy?"

Cary sighed. "I'm not saying the whole police force." She jabbed at the police yearbook with a finger. "I'm saying those four are wrapped up in something."

Hudson nodded. "And you got mixed up in it because of—" she snapped her fingers and fluttered her hand at Moya.

Moya flipped through his notepad. "Um, Do Right."

Hudson nodded. "Do Right."

Cary rolled her eyes. "Dante Holliverse. He's the brother to your Officer Doyle and Marlowe—the guy who I thought was helping me."

Hudson reached over and grabbed Moya's notepad, which didn't seem to bother him. She read over his notes as she said, "So this Dante Holliverse. If he hated you as much as you say"—she cut her eyes up at Cary—"and I imagine you're right, then why would he text you?"

Cary shrugged. "It had to be a mistake. Or maybe he knew Thompson and Jolly would think he had sent a message to somebody, and he picked me because he didn't care if they came after me. I don't know."

Hudson handed Moya back his notepad. He looked at his boss with a question in his eyes. Hudson gave him a slight nod and he turned to Cary. "What did this Holliverse kid have?"

Cary shook her head. "I don't know. They kept saying 'a copy.' I can only assume it might be a video. Dante was always filming. It's why they called him Do Right."

The two detectives shared a look, and Hudson glanced toward Cary to say, "Sit tight." They rose in unison and stepped into the hallway.

Bright leaned against the wall and raised her eyebrows at Carlos. "What do you make of this?"

Carlos shook his head and rubbed the bridge of his nose. "I want to believe her. It scares the shit out of me, but I want to believe her."

Bright nodded and stared off. "Me too."

"Thompson had those zip ties. Everything she says checks out with what we found."

Bright nodded.

"I worked with Doyle. Don't know the other three, but she's a good cop. She may be mixed up in something because of her brother, but I think we can convince her to come clean on what's going on."

Bright looked at him. "If we can find her."

Carlos held up the last page of his notes. "Cary said Doyle said they would look for the copy. If your brother had a copy of something, where would you start looking?"

Bright shrugged. "Wherever he lives, I guess. But don't you figure Thompson and Jolly already searched it?"

Carlos smiled. "You have siblings? Because I do. And I guarantee you could search my brother's room seven times. Turn up nothing. I could walk in and find his weed in thirty seconds."

Bright nodded. "Okay. I'll find the last known on the brother. See if I can catch up with Doyle and this Marlowe."

Carlos frowned. "What do you want me to do? Babysit?"

Bright looked around the station. "Yeah. Only not here. I hate to admit it, but we don't know how deep this goes. Cary might be safer elsewhere until we sort it out. I want you to keep her with you. Get her some clean clothes and keep an eye on her until you hear from me."

Carlos shrugged. "Fair point. How do I take a murder suspect for ice cream?" He closed one eye. "You think it'll tip anybody off if I put on a vest to do it?"

Bright chuckled. "I got her before she was processed. So you just walk out. And, if I'm being honest, the vest always makes you look a little pudgy."

Carlos shook his head. "Pudgy might be better than dead or homeless. Cause this is going to get us fired or killed, I imagine."

Bright curled her lip. "God, I hope the latter. I don't want to change careers at this point in my life."

Chapter 33

Marlowe lost himself in a wall of sound. As soon as Cary's shotgun chewed the air around him with a violent sound of being cocked, he curled up into a tunnel of cotton. Every shout came at him muffled and faraway. Cary was saying something, screaming at everyone in the bank. Thompson reached for his gun. Marlowe looked to Shelley, and his sister had hers out and poised, hanging at her side. His head and neck lolled around like he was drugged. Thompson said something, or maybe Shelley did, or Cary. Someone was pulling him, at his sleeve, dragging him away. Shelley pushed at him to go. He ran for the door and felt his senses start to return. The noises came into focus—people screaming, Cary shouting out for everyone to get down. Thompson was pulling his arm and Shelley was at his back repeating, "Go, go, go, go."

They all stumbled their way into the parking lot. It was eerily quiet. When the doors to the bank slid shut, the world went almost silent. The sirens would come, but not yet. No one else had thought to duck out before Cary faced her inevitable standoff with the security guards. Marlowe glanced back, feeling, for maybe the first time, the weight of his own guilt and responsibility for what was happening to Cary. He started to object, to ask if they could simply leave her.

He turned back to Thompson and his sister to find them facing off, guns drawn.

Thompson snarled, "I should put you both down right here."

Shelley was starting to cry. "What? Like you did Dante?"

Thompson kept his gun trained on Shelley, but laughed under his breath. "Your brother dug his own grave, sweetheart."

Shelley shook and gripped the gun tighter. Marlowe stepped between them with his hands up. "Nobody else needs to get hurt. Put the gun down, Shelley."

Shelley was talking through snot now, spitting and fuming and trying to shout with a cracking voice. "He killed him, Marlowe. They killed Dante."

Marlowe nodded. "I know, Shelley. I been knowing."

Thompson cleared his throat. "I got one chambered for your other brother if you don't put the gun down."

Marlowe swiveled and stared Thompson down. "And then what, detective?" Sirens started to drone in from several blocks away. Marlowe pointed to the air. "You shoot me, Shelley shoots you, cops swarm this bank and start putting pieces together? Is that what you want?"

Thompson shook the gun at him. "I want the copy your brother made of the video. I get the copy, this all stops."

Marlowe nodded. "And we're gonna get it." He looked back at Shelley and clasped his hands together in a plea. "We're gonna get it. Ain't we, Shelley? We're gonna get it and this is gonna all stop."

Shelley closed her eyes and let tears roll. She lowered her gun.

Thompson put his gun away and smiled. "Go find my tape." He turned and ran for a beat-up little Celica and drove off in a squeal as Marlowe helped Shelley to his borrowed SUV.

Marlowe drove away from the sound of sirens as Shelley sobbed in the passenger seat. He zigged and zagged down alleys and back roads until he relaxed into a cruise and turned to Shelley. "Shelley, I'm sorry. I thought I was helping. I didn't know what they were capable of."

Shelley shook her head. "But you were right. About Dante."

Marlowe pursed his lips and nodded. "Yeah. I didn't want to be."

She laughed a little. "I was stupid enough to think they were going to help me find him."

"Is there anybody we can trust? Somebody who can help us?"

Shelley shook her head.

"I'm at a little bit of a loss here, Shells. I don't know how to end this without us getting dead."

She jabbed at her eyes with the cuffs of her sleeves and turned in her seat to face Marlowe. "Do you think Dante made a copy of his film?"

Marlowe shrugged. "You know Do Right. He was always filming everything." He cocked his head and nodded. "But yeah. The things he got on his phone? Stuff he liked? He always copied it to some digital format—something he could edit and do all his shit to."

Shelley nodded to herself. "'s'all we can do, then. We got to find it, 'lowe."

Marlowe frowned. "And just hand that shit over, huh? I been trying to work with these assholes, Shelley—to save you. And look where it got us. Almost got

Cary killed. Got us into some standoff in a parking lot. Getting chased, threatened. What happens when we hand it over?"

Shelley shook her head. "I'm not talking about handing it over. I'm talking about leverage. We find a copy and we might get ourselves out of all this. Cary is somewhere right now trying to make somebody believe a crazy-ass story. We show up, with Dante's film? Her crazy-ass story gets credible real fast."

Marlowe laughed to himself.

Shelley squinted at him. "What? You got a better idea?"

Marlowe shook his head. "Nah. It's not that. I was laughing about you scheming. Like Dante. Remember all Dante's schemes?" They both chuckled and shared a nod before he continued. "I remember one. You wouldn't remember. You were young—doing school stuff. Me and Dante were in prime hooligan age. We got up to all kinds of shit back then. Nothing serious—no drugs or gang banging bullshit. Messing around, you know? Dante always had some scheme on how to get over.

"One time, Do Right, he was out filming what he called "B roll" in this junkyard. And he found this old fish tank. Like, an aquarium, you know? Beat to hell. Dirty. So a few days later, Do Right asked me to drive him and one of our friends to Walmart. I didn't think much about it. I mean, Walmart. What could be wrong with that?

"So I picked up this friend of ours first—Justin was his name. And me and Justin drove over to pick up Do Right." He laughed at the memory, trying to catch his breath to keep talking. "Do Right comes walking out carrying this huge fish tank, all green on the sides and shit. Big nasty thing. And he's telling me to pop the trunk. Of course, I'm asking him why I gotta have this gross-ass fish tank in my car for. And you know Do Right. He kept saying, 'I got this, 'lowe. Trust me, brother.'"

Shelley laughed and nodded. Marlowe continued, "So I kept bugging him and he kept dodging. When I wore him down, he pointed off to some dirt lot and told me to pull in. He got out and called us around to the back of the car and popped the trunk. Do Right points at this fish tank and he's like, 'Boys, we're going to procure me a new fish tank today.' He's all serious. Do Right's like George Clooney in *Ocean's Eleven* or some shit. He gets this stick and starts drawing out a plan in the dirt."

Shelley laughed and said, "A plan? For what?"

Marlowe nodded. "Yeah. Whole plan. So the way he drew it up, I would drop Justin at the front door of Walmart. Justin would walk in, grab a buggy, and go to aisle thirty-seven. Do Right knew the damn aisle numbers. And Justin was supposed to push his buggy around and pick up a ninety-dollar aquarium and put this new fancy-ass fish tank in his buggy. He would walk around so his buggy was facing out on aisle thirty-six. And then leave the buggy sitting there with this new aquarium. Walk away. I was supposed to pick him up at the other entrance, where I would drop Do Right off. Do Right would walk in with his old-ass fish tank in a buggy. Get a sticker from the old man at the door. Tell him he needed to exchange it. And Do Right would proceed to aisle thirty-seven, take the little sticker off of his fish tank, and leave this old stanky aquarium sitting in the middle of Walmart. He'd stroll around to the buggy Justin left, put the sticker on the new tank, and walk right back out. Tell the little old man they wouldn't let him swap it. I pick him up, and we all drive off with a brand-new fish tank for free."

Shelley howled with laughter. She shook her head. "No way that works. Did it work?"

Marlowe gasped, laughing, and nodded. "Hell yeah, it worked!"

They both laughed until they were wiping at their eyes. Shelley said, "Do Right didn't have no fish."

Marlowe shook his head and tried to talk. "No! That's the thing. He never got fish. I went over to his place a couple of weeks later and there sat the fish tank—right in his bedroom—full of socks."

Shelley scrunched her face up. "Socks?"

Marlowe nodded. "Socks. Every pair of socks the boy owned was thrown in there. Filled up damn near the whole tank."

Shelley shook her head. "Why the hell did he keep his socks in a fish tank?"

Marlowe shrugged. "I have no clue. I asked. I looked around at his bedroom furniture. I mean, he had a full dresser and a chest of drawers. I pointed to all them drawers and asked, I said, 'Do Right, you got all these drawers, and you keeping your socks in a damn fish tank?' He said, 'Marlowe, they're drawers meant for more important things than socks.'"

Shelley nodded. "That's Do Right."

Marlowe let his laughter fade into a distant look. "Yeah. That's Do Right."

Shelley stared off and sniffed. After a beat she turned to Marlowe. "Wait a second."

"What?"

"Think about the fish tank story. Those cops—Thompson and Jolly—they would've tossed Dante's place, right?"

Marlowe shrugged. "I figured, yeah."

She nodded. "But Dante had a whole studio and shit, you know? He had equipment and everything. If I tossed his place, I would've looked there. Torn it up, right?"

Marlowe nodded. "Yeah."

Shelley pointed at him. "But would you have searched his sock drawers?"

A huge grin spread across Marlowe's face. "No. No I would not have."

Chapter 34

Officer Jean Reynard sat in his patrol car twirling an electronic cigarette. He hated the thing. It tasted like melting plastic and made his tonsils burn. But he couldn't smoke a real one in the car. There were strict departmental rules against tobacco use.

Jean started smoking at age fourteen. Starting high school in a bigger town—where no one knew your family—came with challenges. All the kids pronounced his name like Gene. They made fun of his throaty Cajun accent. He was a small ninth grader. Short and bony. Jean was the type of kid who showered with his underwear on in gym class. Every day after school a cluster of older kids would group up by a tree down past the practice baseball field and smoke. Jean would wait for his bus marvel at how tough they all looked. So he swiped a few packs of cigarettes from an old neighbor lady and spent a week training himself to smoke without coughing.

The day he tried to join them was a Friday. He missed his bus on purpose and walked down to the tree to light up. A senior with tattoos on his arm stole Jean's cigarettes and pissed on his backpack in front of everyone while they all laughed. Sent Jean home crying with a bloody nose. He had to walk four miles through a couple of sketchy neighborhoods. But he still smoked.

The video had been his fault. He accepted responsibility. Thompson and Jolly picked him out because he had potential as a detective—he was sure of it. After all, he tracked down what the Trubody girl drove. And he zoned in when he spotted it. He also found her house and the little shit, Dante's house. He had done more than his share of the leg work. But when it all started, his job was to clear the area. Make sure none of the local hood rats were scurrying around to size up what was going on. And he did—he hit the neighborhood hard, bracing every kid who even jaywalked. The problem was Dante.

Dante was no neighborhood punk. He was basically passing through. Said later he was shooting what he called "B roll" of some street art. And he was packing it up for the day. His camera was put away, so he snuck about a three minute shot with his phone. Jolly blamed Jean pretty hard, but if it hadn't been for his still-sharp-patrolman eyes, they never would have seen Dante. Jean caught sight of him filming from behind a pillar and gave chase. Dante slipped through a Mexican market and got lost. But Jean put those detective skills to work then, too. He noticed the bag, and he recognized it as film equipment. So he asked around until he found some people who told him about this guy they called Do Right. And he tracked the nickname all the way to Dante's doorstep.

So Jolly could kiss his ass. Maybe he helped mess things up a little, but he sure as hell helped clean up the mess. The girl was the last mistake he planned to make. He had been so sure she was dead. Thompson and Jolly could fuck right off with their condescending bullshit, too. Like they had any room to talk. Maybe if they were capable of cleaning up their own messes he would be a little more willing to take shit off them.

The first time was all about money. Both of those assholes worked vice then. And Jean caught their eye when he went a little too far arresting a mid-level drug dealer. Broke both of his wrists. Jolly let the prick walk to keep him from calling in the ACLU. Jean wasn't even grateful. He was pissed. Broken wrists or not, the shit-heel dealt to teenagers. Seven of them sold for him in local schools. Thompson and Jolly pulled Jean aside and broke down the world for him. Mid-level dealers were interchangeable. Taking out mid-levels was like trying to rid your house of termites with a fly swatter.

They took him under their wings a little. Showed him some things. For the first time in his life, Jean was part of something. Thompson and Jolly let him smoke with them under the tree. And it worked. Maybe he didn't push drugs out of those seven schools, but he sure as hell pushed them out of the two in his neighborhood. Turning a blind eye to certain areas was hard to stomach, but Jean accepted the necessity of it. Thompson told him he could work with the inmates to control his cell block, or fight the world and suffer the prison crumbling around him. It made sense. Clicked. Jean sensed progress for the first time since he joined the force.

Even the first clean-up job felt right. Jolly called him one day to let him know some low-level dip shit called Papa Money had stopped playing well with others. Jean knew what that meant. Papa Money had stopped living up to his name. He no longer lined the right pockets. The morality of being a dirty cop never bothered Jean too much. He was in the loop, but not really. He got little payouts for taking care of things every now and then. And he had the steady promise of making influential friends in high places. But he didn't care about the money or the prospect of advancement. He enjoyed it. Human waste like Papa fucking Money needed their tickets punched. Jean couldn't give two shits about missing payments. He enjoyed being taken off his leash to rid the city of one more low-life.

Real justice was why he became a cop. He grew up in government housing, watching drug dealers and prostitutes and all the worst the world has to offer run rampant. Unchecked. Crawling under the floorboards of the city and spreading filth and disease. Crime disgusted him. Jail was a revolving door to these people. Putting them down was more effective. More humane. So dropping Papa Money into the spillway was like drowning a rat. Nothing about it made him feel sick or guilty or anything. He was doing his job.

Prostitutes were harder. No doubt. Something about a woman made the act more difficult. And always so up close and personal—choking, beating. Always in some seedy motel room. They were drug-addled filth, but sometimes they still looked like women when they cried. Those sensitivities made him hold back on the girl, Cary Trubody's friend. He pulled his punches because she looked so feminine in the end. They always do.

And to be honest, he carried as much disdain for the cops and politicians who used them and threw them away like garbage. It was always the same call: some senator or high-ranking officer got his dick sucked one too many times. The whore put things together and got smart. Jean was the guy they called in to end whatever blackmail scheme the girl cooked up. Sometimes she had some guy working with her, and Jean could put a bullet in his gut, let him die slow. While her pimp bled out, Jean usually convinced the girl to leave town and never look back.

One of those jobs was when he picked up his Walther P22. Thompson called him and gave him a name—fake name he stopped remembering months ago. The girl doled out blowjobs to a couple of state senators and the mayor at a campaign fundraiser. As it turned out, she was sixteen at the time. Jean was supposed to silence her slander before it became scandal. He tracked her to a shitty apartment complex—converted hotel from the fifties. He snuck into the girl's bedroom with a garotte in hand. She was fast asleep, which made everything so much easier. Jean never detected the lump of covers next to her move as he snapped the garotte tight around the girl's neck.

Before the girl stopped moving, the lump rose up and went for something in the bedside table. Jean acted fast. He jerked the girl up and around, tossing her out of bed and onto the floor. Her head whipped around and flopped limp like a ball on a string. The body looked like when he was a kid in Louisiana and his grandmother would wring the necks of chickens. The guy in bed with her was naked, and he swung up with something he pulled from a drawer. Jean took a lamp and clocked him across and eyebrow. When the naked guy raised up again, he was struggling to focus through the blood squirting out of the cut on his head.

Squinting to see so he could aim.

Jean brought both hands down hard and buried the gun into the bunched up covers on the bed. He lunged forward and cracked the guy's nose with his own forehead. It was disorienting enough to send the naked man wobbling back toward the wall. Jean advanced to him and pinned him against the window frame. Taking hold of his ears, he rammed the guy's head into the thick wood frame until the body below stopped wiggling. Jean retrieved the garotte from the girl's neck and finished him off. But before he left, he went to the bed and found the gun.

The guy had a nice Walther P22, unregistered. Perfect throw away gun. A month later, he talked Jolly into finding a suppressor for it. Told him the little pistol would make clean-up a million times more efficient. And he was right. Jean was careful when to use his Walther. He didn't want to part ways with the gun by having to toss it into a body of water somewhere. But all love stories have endings. The Walther may had seen its last dance. Or, next to last. Jean shoved the gun down next to his driver's seat. Sooner or later, the last stragglers of this mess would come back to the house he was watching. And the Walther was going to clean them up.

Chapter 35

Dante "Do Right" Holliverse had lived in a sublet apartment behind an old rental house. It was a freestanding structure about twenty feet into the backyard. There were two apartments—one upstairs and one down. Dante rented the top floor from an old man who paid rent for the whole property to a wealthy property owner. The old man signed Dante's check straight over, and it covered his entire rent. It allowed the old man to live off the grid like he preferred.

Bright learned all this after a rather tedious search to find where Dante had lived. Her suspicions that Thompson and Jolly had traced these same steps was confirmed by the sight of a car camped out in front of the old man's rent house. And if she saw it, she figured Dante's siblings would see it too. She kept a wide berth and circled around to the back of sublet, looking for where Dante would have parked. An alley ran from street to street parallel to the street with the cop staked out on it. Down a couple of yards from a cluster of trash cans, there were a couple of carved-out ruts in the gravel and dirt.

Making the block, Bright noticed a vacant house backed up to the alley. The driveway ran all the way to a carport butted up against a back chain link fence. She pulled up and parked under the carport, in clear view of the back entrance to the sublet where she expected Dante's siblings to park. Bright slunk down in her seat and waited.

And it took everything in her to fight off the sickening feeling of déjà vu.

Bright's parents had both been writers. Writers who had took very different paths. They were children of the sixties, and they spent their teenage impressionable years traveling around in stereotypical vans and dropping acid. Her father grew up in cold country and longed to feel the sun on his face and meet people and write about it. Her mother fancied herself a poet since age four. She ran away from home at age thirteen and never looked back. Taken to calling herself only Sunny. Bright didn't know what her real name had once been. When Sunny ran across Carneades

"Carnie" Day she felt like it was fate's way of winking at her. The two fell in love as much as their free spirited ways would allow. About twelve years later they gave birth to Bright New Day, named at her mother's insistence. Carnie settled a bit. He latched onto the protests of the sixties and seventies and become a reporter. Sunny never conformed. She scribbled poetry on canvases and stared straight at the sun throughout all of Bright's life. She was still doing it as far as anyone knew. Her drug-addled mind landed her in a retirement home by age sixty, but Bright didn't think she'd ever die.

Carnie, however, was not long for this world. He threw himself headlong and on fire into his work. Since Sunny wasn't fit to feed a fish, he often took Bright with him, which is what he was doing the night he died.

Bright was nine. The Reagan Era had transitioned to the Bush Era in an attempt to hold steady with the decadence of the eighties. Carnie Day, on the other hand, had spent the better part of a decade trying to rip it down. The hippy in him was strong enough to want to blow up political corruption from the inside. He wormed his way into a story about politicians and drugs and prostitutes and police cover ups. Bright was too young for him to tell her everything, but she picked up enough.

The city had a very exclusive boys' club. And it included a list of names even a nine-year-old recognized. She had gone with her father to meet a few prostitutes. She hadn't understood what they were at the time, but she could look back and realize he took her to put them at ease. An overzealous reporter looked like he was trying to scoop a story. But a father of a little girl appeared to be out for the well-being of disenfranchised young ladies. The night he died, he was supposed to have an interview with a girl who could break the story wide open. She lived with a couple of roommates in an apartment semi-attached to a house. It looked remarkably like the one Bright was staring at. Carnie couldn't leave Bright at home because Sunny had been rolling through a spell of very un-motherly behavior involving an experimental dabbling with crack. But looking back, Bright also appreciated Carnie's willingness to bring her along because of the calming effect she had on young prostitutes.

Bright had been fast asleep when Carnie woke her. She remembered having a dream about a puppy her grandmother took her to play with when she was maybe six. The dream always stood out. So innocent and childlike. Carnie carried her to the car. He didn't even make her get dressed. She wore mismatched pajamas and a threadbare robe with matching slippers. She was carrying a stuffed elephant, for Christ's sake. When they arrived at the apartment, Carnie seemed to change his mind for a second. He looked around and wouldn't turn the car off. Bright unbuckled her seatbelt, but Carnie caught it and fastened it back. He smiled at her and squinted. "Stay in the car this time, sweetheart. I'll be right back," he told her. Bright shrugged, slumped against the car door, and drifted off to sleep.

Years later, she would try to work out how long she had been asleep. She tried to remember glancing at the dashboard clock or hearing something on the radio or anything. But it never came. All she remembered was falling asleep and waking up with a start. There had been a loud pop in her dream. And another when she was wide awake. When she looked up, a woman was standing at the corner of the house, smoking a cigarette and biting at a thumbnail. She looked like she had been standing there for several minutes—Bright remembered her finishing the cigarette within a minute after the second pop. And the noises startled her, but they didn't surprise her.

A few seconds after the second pop, a man walked out of the apartment. Young Bright almost jumped out of the car, thinking it was her dad. But this man looked different. Larger and dressed strangely, like a soldier. She couldn't make out his face. He walked past the woman and said something to her, patted her on the shoulder. The woman cringed at his touch, but she nodded in agreement to whatever he said. The man walked away, maybe toward a car out of view. She remembered him walking under a streetlight and she tried to pay attention to his appearance. But she couldn't distinguish any facial details. Only the clothes. The boxy shoulders and hat. And the gloves. He took them off and tossed them in a dumpster as he walked off. They were rubber gloves. Blue ones. Like police wear.

The woman walked over to a pay phone in the alley and made a call a minute or so later. After making the call, she disappeared. She didn't go in to pack or anything. She just walked away. Bright spent years trying to track down the woman, but her name wasn't on any lease and no one claimed to remember her. She pored over her dad's notes, but never connected a name to the woman.

Within minutes of the phone call, police rolled up. They found a frightened Bright in the car and drove her to the police station. After several failed attempts to reach her mom, a detective drove her home to find the Day home ablaze. Sunny stepped out to buy milk, she claimed. The fire was attributed to Sunny's carelessness, but Bright always suspected something more sinister. Something which would have killed her had she stayed in bed.

Carnie Day's murder was never solved. He took two shots to the back of the head and died instantly. The three inhabitants of the apartment supposedly lived there in a cash only arrangement—no lease—and they never turned up for questioning. For the rest of Bright's compromised childhood, her mother made ends meet by stretching out the insurance payout until Bright turned sixteen and could start picking up odd jobs. In college, Bright considered following her dad's footsteps into journalism, but news stories would never provide any vengeance. She didn't want to simply write about corrupt cops and dirty politicians. She wanted to face them down and lock them up.

So whatever feelings of déjà vu came gurgling up into her throat needed to get pushed back down. Because this was exactly the kind of case Bright had joined the force to catch. And she would be damned if she didn't see it through.

As she worked to steel her nerve, she heard tires crunching gravel in front of her. A little SUV with its lights off eased into Dante's old parking spot. Two people eased out of either side, and Bright flipped open a file folder on her passenger seat. She leafed through papers until she found photos—Marlowe Holliverse's DMV photo and Shelley Doyle's picture from the police yearbook. It was them. And if she spotted them, she figured the cop outside did too.

Chapter 36

Carlos Moya walked into the police station break room and fished through cabinets until he found a hot chocolate packet. He filled a Styrofoam cup with hot water and stirred in the powder. He filled another cup with coffee and loaded his pockets with creamers and sugar packets. The hallways were busy with steady traffic, which would clear out in ten minutes or so. Carlos eased back into the interrogation room where Cary sat looking haggard. He set the cups in front of her and grimaced.

"I wasn't sure what you like. I made a coffee and a hot chocolate. Oh," he fished the creamer and sugar out of his pockets, "and this." He closed his eyes and bit his lip. "Dammit. I forgot a stir stick."

Cary laughed softly. "It's okay. I take it black. Thank you."

Carlos smiled back and sat down across from her. He jerked a thumb over his shoulder. "It should clear out a little in a few minutes. As soon as it does, we'll get out of here. Promise."

Cary nodded.

Carlos let her sip her coffee in silence for a moment before adding, "We need to decide on where to go, Cary. Is there anywhere you might feel safe?"

Cary rolled her eyes up and shook her head. "A couple of days ago? Sure. Lots of places. Now?" She heaved a breathy laugh.

Carlos grinned and nodded. "Yeah. I'm sorry. We're going to figure all this out, Cary. Bright—Detective Hudson—she's the best there is. When she gets on something like this, she doesn't let up until she ties up every loose end. And she's got the whole Sherlock Holmes thing going on." He waggled his fingers. "She makes all the connections, you know?"

Cary tilted her head. "You don't seem like a cop."

He laughed.

Cary winced. "I'm sorry. I hope that's not offensive. I don't mean it to be."

Carlos shook his head. "No, no. None taken."

Cary shook her head. "I only mean I've run across a lot of cops here lately. And, granted, I haven't been exposed to the best examples. But still, you've got the grizzled vets, the cocky patrol cop, the moralistic young cop, the Sherlockian detective, and then you. I'm not sure what you are. And I mean that in a good way."

Carlos smiled and nodded. "Well, I was raised by my abuela. Which may not come across as an explanation of any kind, but to me, it explains everything. I think those of us raised by grandparents have a certain softness about us. We care about people. And we nurture. Protect." He shook a finger. "And I'm not talking about being soft. Don't confuse it. I'm talking about caring a little more. Empathy. I do this job with empathy. That's what's different about me."

Cary smiled and sipped her coffee. "I see what you mean." Her eyes got wide. "Grandmother! Johnna's grandmother. I can go there. Thompson already ransacked Johnna's room. He won't go back. He thinks she will call him if I show up, so he won't expect me to go back."

Carlos squinted. "Will she?"

Cary shook her head. "No. She made a mistake, but she won't do it again. She'll keep me safe."

Carlos sighed and nodded. "Might be all we've got." He stood up and went to the narrow window in the door, peering back and forth down the hallway. "Okay. It's pretty clear. Let's go."

He escorted Cary out of the station and to his replacement car without drawing any attention. He opened the passenger side door for her and rushed around to jump in and drive off before anyone noticed them.

On the drive, Cary studied Moya. "You believe me, right?"

Carlos laughed. "Cary, if we didn't believe you, we wouldn't be taking you out of the police station once we got you in custody."

Cary nodded. "Good point."

Carlos glanced at her. "Look, in confidence, Detective Hudson and I have been working with Internal Affairs on some cases involving possible police corruption for a while. We've been connecting dots. Those dots led us to you."

Cary shook her head. "How?"

Carlos paused, but conceded an answer. "Graffiti Creek."

Cary frowned. "The place they took me? Out in the woods."

Carlos nodded. "Yeah. A couple of leads we followed pointed to Graffiti Creek as a"—he swallowed—"a dump site, I guess you would say. We had witnesses who named the site as the rumored resting place of some missing people. We never found anything, but we flagged the location to get called if anything turned up. And, well, you know the rest, I guess."

A few minutes of heavy silence later, they turned onto Johnna's grandmother's street. Carlos slowed into the curve in front of the house and pulled to a stop at the mailbox. Cary pointed forward with her head. "Is that a cop car?"

Carlos had been unbuckling his seatbelt and starting to open his door but stopped and looked up. "Shit." She was right. About a block up the road, a patrol car sat with someone slouched over on the door rest watching the house. Carlos buckled his seatbelt back and spoke to Cary without looking at her. "Go inside. I'll take care of this, and I'll be back."

Cary hesitated, but relented. Carlos watched to make sure she made it in. Johnna's grandmother looked surprised but welcomed her with an embrace. Carlos took the cue to ease on toward the police cruiser. He pulled up close, almost nose to nose and popped his hood. He got out, holding his badge up to Officer Reynard, who was lazily climbing out of his own car. Carlos smiled broadly, "How's it going, officer? Think you could help me out a little?"

Reynard returned the smile. "I can try."

Carlos thumbed back to his car. "My car's messed up and they gave me a temp. But the battery is acting screwy. I tried to check the connectors, but I can't get the damn strap off the top of this battery. You got a Phillip's head screwdriver or something I can use?"

Reynard sucked at his teeth and stared at Carlos' trunk. "Yeah. I got a kit in the trunk. Help yourself." He strolled back to his driver's side door and popped the trunk.

Carlos sighed, "Thanks, buddy. You're a lifesaver." He started toward the trunk. "So what? You patrolling the neighborhood?"

Reynard lifted Carlos' hood and propped it with the built-in stick. "Yeah. They got me watching a house for this wanted girl. In fact, I think it's the house you came from. Where you dropped off a girl."

"No shit? Yeah, we got her. You didn't hear it on the radio? Detective"— Carlos snapped his fingers—"Thompson, I think his name is. He's got me sitting on her over here until he sorts a couple things out."

Reynard shot a look over his shoulder. "Thompson?"

Carlos pulled up the trunk and scanned for the tool kit. "Yeah. You know him?"

Reynard's voice sounded closer, like he had taken a few steps down the length of his car. "Yeah. A little."

Carlos found the toolkit open and scattered about. The Phillip's head was missing. He searched the trunk to make sure it hadn't fallen out. "Good guy. Knows the job, you know?"

Reynard sounded closer. "Yeah. I do know. What'd you say your name was?"

Carlos searched the whole trunk in a frenzy and came up empty. "Hey, buddy. Your Phillip's head is missing from your kit."

"Yeah, I must've misplaced it. Anything should pop this strap though, right?"

Carlos came away with a small crowbar and reached to close the trunk. "Sure, sure. Yeah, I got something." Before he closed the trunk, he noticed strange markings on the roof of the trunk's lid. He paused and stared. They were scratchings, crude and blocky, like letters. He deciphered a J and a blocky O. Carlos squinted. H. Two N's.

Soft footsteps padded behind him. Turning, he found Reynard standing a couple of feet away and holding a small gun, outstretched, its silencer coming within a foot of Carlos' chest. Carlos made a swift move for his sidearm, but it was too late. The first pop was loud, like a firecracker. But the next two were nothing more than whistling snaps. The force felt like he'd been hit with a baseball bat and sent him falling back into a crumpled seat on the edge of the trunk. Carlos struggled to draw in a breath and looked up as Reynard pushed him down and folded him up into the trunk. The darkness crept in and enveloped his eyes before Reynard even slammed shut the trunk.

Chapter 37

Neither Marlowe nor Shelley owned a key to Dante's apartment. Marlowe pestered his younger brother to give him one for emergencies, but Dante never got around to it. In their desperation, they discussed the thought of breaking in, but Shelley convinced Marlowe to try the landlord first. It was a plan which proved easier said than done.

Marlowe knew the old man's name—Yancy Tannehill. It was a little hard to forget. But every search they tried came up empty. Even Shelley was about ready to give up when Marlowe remembered one detail. Dante was always making fun of the reclusive old man. He used to talk about how he couldn't understand how Yancy stayed so stick skinny when all he ever did was sit. Even at his job. Dante had said the old guy sat all day in a booth at the public library, taking dollars and passing out parking stubs. It was their one shot at gaining lawful entry to their brother's apartment, so they spent the few extra minutes.

Marlowe drove them to the public library, which was virtually empty. Sure enough, a painfully skinny old man sat in the lonely parking attendant booth reading some paperback mystery novel. Marlowe eased up to the booth and rolled down his window. Yancy Tannehill barely looked away from his novel to say, "One dollar, one hour. Two dollars, two hours. Three dollars, all day."

Marlowe smiled and raised his eyebrows at the man. "Mr. Tannehill? My name is Marlowe Holliverse. My brother is"—Marlowe lost the smile—"was Dante Holliverse. Your tenant?"

Yancy looked up from his book and stared at Marlowe, looked past him to Shelley, and looked back at Marlowe.

Marlowe nodded. "That's mine and Dante's sister, Shelley. Mr. Tannehill, our brother, well, he passed, Mr. Tannehill. We were hoping you might could give us the key to his apartment so we could begin collecting his things. And if he needs to finish out any rent or anything, I'm sure we can help settle out his affairs with you."

Yancy nodded. He put an old parking stub into his book as a bookmark and set it down. He motioned toward the parking lot with his head and started climbing down from his stool and jingling keys in his pocket. "Pull around. I can get the keys for you."

Marlowe put his hands together in a gesture of gratitude. "Thank you so much, Mr. Tannehill." He looked up and waited for the parking bar to raise, which it never did. He looked back to Yancy.

Yancy had a hand stretched through the window. "One dollar, one hour."

Marlowe cocked his head and started something, but Shelley shot a hand holding a dollar past him for Yancy, adding, "Thank you again, Mr. Tannehill."

The bar raised and Marlowe pulled in, cursing as he drove around to the far side. When they pulled up, Yancy was examining his key chain, flipping through huge cluster of keys. He held one out to Marlowe. Marlowe took the key without coming to a complete stop, mumbling a thanks as he did so. Yancy's grunt made him stop the car after he almost passed by the window completely. Marlowe and Shelley both looked back. Yancy glanced up from the keys and gave them a sour expression. "Don't you want the other one?"

Marlowe shook his head. "What other one?"

Yancy went back to scrolling through keys. "Downstairs. Your brother had the apartment upstairs and the studio downstairs."

Marlowe and Shelley looked at each other and said simultaneously, "Studio?"

Yancy found the key he was hunting and handed it out to Marlowe. "Yep. Spent damn near all his time down there. Messing with his movies." Marlowe took the key and stared at it. Yancy added, weakly, "Sorry to hear about your brother."

Marlowe waved, equally weakly, and drove off.

Shelley grabbed the key out of his hand. "I take it you didn't know about this either?"

Marlowe shook his head. "No clue."

"So if you and I had no clue..."

He nodded. "Odds are those assholes didn't."

"Yep. Screw the sock drawer. We need in that studio."

Chapter 38

Trust is a funny thing. Mark Thompson always had trouble trusting people. When he was a kid he had two dogs. They both loved to bury things in the yard. But typically, only one would dig them back up. He would bury his whole head under the ground and unearth some bone or treat. And almost every time he would let the other dog—a girl—lick dirt off of his head when he came up for air. They would sit together, with the bone laid out in front of them, one dog giving the other a gentle cleansing. But every single time, the girl dog would end bath time by snapping at him and stealing the bone. As far as Mark was concerned, he never saw a better analogy of the human condition.

In fact, Mark could never think of a time when he let anyone get close enough to snap at him. Other than a handful of partners and even fewer women. The partners mostly held true. The women fared a little worse, but, to be fair, Mark didn't always bury his bone in his own yard either. He was sure of one thing, though. Doyle and her brother were not about to be added to his trust list. There was no doubt in Mark's mind they would screw him five minutes after they found what they were looking for. So Mark planned to be there in four.

He had no choice but to let them out of his sight. They were both getting antsy, and he couldn't imagine Doyle tipping her hand. But Jolly taught him the best way to follow someone was to stay in front of them. Didn't always work, but if you had a general idea of where a suspect was headed and were well enough acquainted with the streets, you could pull it off. In this case, there were only a few possibilities. He had Reynard sitting on one. So Mark made his way to the other.

Thompson knew where Dante lived. He and Jolly tossed his apartment right after they got rid of Do Right, himself. They combed it pretty thoroughly, but family might know something they didn't. Dante's place was a sublet—top floor of a two story building behind the rented house of a cranky old man. Thompson and Jolly braced the old man, but he was one tough bastard. He valued his privacy and the privacy of his tenants. So they only learned what they had already learned: Dante Holliverse rented the upstairs apartment. They let themselves in and wrecked the place. If the copy was in Dante's apartment, it was next to the Holy Grail and Bigfoot. But Mark had no doubt this would be their first stop. It was his and Jolly's. Doyle would think the same way. So he parked up the road a bit to spy them coming and going through the old man's carport.

The cover of being in a beat-up Celica lulled him into relaxing, and Mark couldn't help but nod off a bit. He dozed on and off for almost an hour before slapping himself around. He searched the car until he found an unopened bag of trail mix to keep himself awake. Stakeouts were a young man's game. He used to be able to red eye it for hours on end. But now, he could fall asleep standing in a car wash.

He was up and alert for maybe a couple of minutes when he saw a detective's car roll by. The woman driving didn't appear to have made him. She completed a circle of the place and then appeared to move on to her next stop. So they had pieced Dante together with all this, then. Mark snapped a peanut into his mouth and gnawed at it. This changed things. If somebody was working this, and they had put Dante into it? Then his timeline got a whole lot shorter.

If the video Dante shot got out, Mark would be worrying about more than his pension. Sure, the pension would be gone. He and Jolly were on camera beating the shit out of a handcuffed man. Jolly's reputation would be tarnished. Thompson and Reynard would get shit canned. But Reynard would carry on with his dickless life. Thompson? He would swing. Because it wouldn't take Columbo to track down who they had in those cuffs. And once they figured out, it wouldn't be long before they started connecting dots. Thompson and Jolly, and Reynard, for that matter, got paid handsomely to protect those dots. And plenty of other assholes like Thompson and Jolly patrolled this town. If Dante's video leaked, Thompson had no doubt he would be getting a visit from one of them.

Before he made it through all the possible, and equally horrible, scenarios in his head, Mark spotted Marlowe pull up in an SUV behind the house. Dante had a make-shift parking spot in a dirt road alleyway behind his apartment. Marlowe pulled into it and he and Doyle hopped out. They both trotted toward the apartment, which meant Mark lost sight of them for a moment. He kept the stairs to the top level in his line of sight, though, so he waited for them to emerge on their way to Dante's apartment. But they never did.

They disappeared somewhere at the base of the stairs. Almost, Mark thought, like they went into… "Son of a bitch," he mumbled to himself.

Mark checked his gun, creaked open the old door of the Celica, and climbed up and out. He scurried to the side of the street shared by the old man's house, keeping close to the line of bushes next to the sidewalk. At the carport, he pulled his gun, holding it at his hip. Positioning himself to peer into the downstairs apartment, he noticed a light come on through the window in the door. "Son of a bitch," he mumbled again.

He and Jolly searched every fiber of Dante's apartment, but they didn't know about the one downstairs. The old man never mentioned it, and nothing showed up in any official records. Mark kicked himself at the thought, but the inhabitant of the downstairs apartment never crossed his mind. He assumed it was empty—maybe the old man used the extra space for storage or something.

The only memory Mark had of even thinking about the bottom apartment was when they first approached. Jolly checked a window, but it was too dark to reveal anything. He said the place looked empty. Mark stayed low and worked his way around to the back where he remembered the window being. Light glowed from the bottom floor now, so he eased up to catch a peek through the back window. He reared up and took hold of one of the bars on the outside, craning his neck to glance in. "Son of a bitch," he mumbled one more time. He didn't see Marlowe or Doyle, but he could immediately tell why Dante wanted both apartments.

The place was set up like an obvious studio. Computers and recording equipment lined the room. Thompson and Jolly wondered where the budding filmmaker did his editing. They never found the kid's computer. And this was why. He had a whole goddamn studio.

Mark gripped his gun tighter and started toward the door. This was it. This had to be it. The copy was in there. And so were two of the only three people who knew what any of this was about. He paused at the thought, his hand hovering at the door knob. Jolly had been right. His partner said from day one this required a "scorched earth" campaign. Thompson tried a lighter hand. Clean everything up with a broom and a dust mop. Jolly called for the blow torch. And he would prove right in the end.

Mark backed away from the door and moved around to the carport. The old man was not home. Mark found a storage room attached to the house and planted his foot next to the doorjamb three good times until the door popped open with a splintering crack. He rummaged around until he found a gas can next to a lawn mower. It was at least half full. Mark holstered his gun and picked up the gas can along with a long metal pipe from a clutter of trash in the corner. He hurried back around to the apartment door and slid the pipe under the bars of the storm door, blocking it from being opened from the inside.

He huffed up the stairs with the gas can while fishing around in his pocket for Dante's key Jolly had lifted from the kid's body. Mark opened the door and started spreading gasoline all over the scattered papers and clothes. After he emptied the gas can, he fished out his cigarette lighter and groaned over to pick up a handful of loose papers. In a frenzy, Mark lit the papers and waved them over curtains and furniture and clothes until the blaze was licking at his arms.

Mark backed out, slapping at the embers leaping onto his sports coat. He scrambled down the stairs and almost fell back into the carport. In a sprint, he started back for his car when he heard, "Freeze!"

The voice rang out and echoed across the roof of the carport. If it had been coupled with anything other than the distinctive sound of a round being loaded into the chamber of a Glock 22, he would have kept right on running. But he stopped, raised his hands above his head, and turned around.

The female detective who cruised by him earlier eyed him down from about fifteen feet away. He didn't doubt her ability to put a couple in his fat ass from the distance. Mark nodded. "Detective," he raised his eyebrows to finish the question.

The woman panted, whipping her head back and forth from Thompson to the flames licking out of the upstairs apartment. "Hudson," she gasped.

Mark watched her. He grinned at her concern. His only hope of getting back to his car might be her big ass hero heart.

Hudson stuttered. "I—I—I need you to lie down and place your hands behind your back."

Mark started to say something, but Hudson cut him off with a bellowed "Now!"

Mark nodded. "I hear you detective. I do. But here's the thing. I don't think you're going to shoot me. And I don't think you're going to let those two young people burn up either. So here's how this is going to go. I am about to turn around and walk to my car. And you—well, you have a choice to make. You can shoot me in the back. You can chase me, wrestle me to the ground, and arrest me. Or, you can save a couple of people from a burning building."

Hudson listened, swiveling her head back and forth in a panic. She blurted out a few meaningless phrases: "Down on the ground!" and "Don't you move!" Things of the sort. But she knew he was right. And so did Mark.

He turned. Slowly. And he walked with his hands in his pockets toward his car. He visualized Hudson freezing in a moment of indecision behind him before she resigned herself to holster her gun and run for the door.

Mark smiled and picked up the pace for the car. He felt pretty certain Detective Hudson wouldn't be able to pull those two dip shits out of the inferno the clapboard apartments were about to become. So on the plus side, he had taken care of the siblings and, quite assuredly, the copy of the video. But there was still Cary to take care of. And, now, Detective Hudson.

Chapter 39

Marlowe and Shelley pulled up and parked in Dante's old spot in the alley behind his apartment. They had both visited Dante there multiple times, only ever going to the upstairs apartment. They both assumed the bottom floor was available for rent, or maybe the landlord used it to store junk. Neither of them ever gave any real thought to it. This time, instead of turning to head up the exterior stairs, they used the key to let themselves into Dante's secret studio.

Marlowe laughed and shut the door behind them. He looked around at the computers and sound equipment. "Sneaky little bastard."

Shelley sighed. "I hate to admit it, but I'm less impressed now. I always thought he was editing those films on his phone or some shit. He had a damn studio?"

Marlowe nodded. "I know, right? I wish I'd known. I would've given his lazy ass hell for not making more movies."

Shelley pointed at a row of three computers. "You check those. See if you can get them turned on and log in. I'm going to check the other rooms for any kind of library of footage or anything. He's got to have some sort of organization system."

Marlowe wrinkled his brow. "This is Dante we're talking about." But he still did as directed, working his way down and punching the power buttons on each computer. They were password protected, but, as he expected, "MarsBlackmon" worked on all three. He called out to Shelley in the other room, "You gotta love how consistent our brother was."

Shelley combed through drawers and cabinets, checking labels on any DVD or flash drive she came across. She called back, "Everything in here seems old. They have dates and nothing is recent."

Marlowe answered, "Same on this first computer. Every file is dated and nothing is in the last few months."

Shelley stepped back in. "It has to be new, right? Whatever set them off was triggered very recently."

Marlowe started to reply, but froze. He cocked his head and pointed toward the ceiling. He mouthed, "Footsteps."

Shelley cocked her head and listened. He was right. Heavy footsteps plodding around in Dante's apartment. She motioned for Marlowe to follow her and backed into a sound room Dante had set up in a pantry—the only room without a window. They listened as the noises continued. Heavy footsteps and items being dropped or kicked over. Then, running on the stairs. Shelley pulled her gun and worked around until she could watch the door.

After a moment or two of frozen silence, with Shelley gripping her gun and staring intently at the door, Marlowe glanced into the next room. He slid around Shelley and walked toward the vent in the ceiling. He pointed up. "Hey, Shelley. Is that smoke?"

Chapter 40

Bright watched Mark Thompson walk away. He had the smug confidence of a man who knew no one would stop him. And he was right. For now. Bright holstered her gun and ran for the door to the apartment. Smoke billowed down from the top floor in cascades of silvery gray. The smell of gas fumes stung her nose before they were swallowed up by the smoldering burn of wood. She yelled out to Marlowe and Shelley, using their full names, but got nothing in return. The bar Thompson jammed into the door stuck at both sides. Bright grabbed one end with both hands and put a foot against the doorjamb to pull.

She fell back onto her ass, coughing and spitting and rubbing at her eyes. Whatever Thompson did to wedge the bar in the door, it worked. She looked up to the second floor. Smoke crept out of crevices in the wood siding, pooling at the windows of the first floor. Bright took out her gun and shot out windows upstairs and put one through the upper corner of a downstairs window to release some smoke and pressure.

She put her gun back in its holster and reached for her phone. She dialed 911 and rattled off her name and badge number to get the dispatcher's attention. She gave Dante's address and reported the fire with civilians trapped inside. Ignoring further questions, she hung up and returned to the door.

Chapter 41

Shelley whipped around and ran toward Marlowe. "Shit. We gotta leave. Now." She led the way for the door. Three shots rang out, one rattling through a window in front of them and punching a hole in the ceiling. Smoke snaked through the hole like a ribbon, with glowing embers drifting in behind the silvery flumes. Shelley and Marlowe dropped to a crouch, covering their heads and waiting for more gunfire.

Bright pulled on the bar again, but it was still wedged in tight. She took out her gun and used the butt to bang on the metal bars of the door, calling out, "Shelley Doyle! Marlowe Holliverse!" over and over again.

Marlowe grabbed Shelley's gun hand and lowered it to the ground. "You hear that? It's a woman." Shelley shook her head, but Marlowe stood up anyway. He approached the door, starting to hack and cough. "Here! We're here!"

Bright leaned into the door and stuttered. "Y—yes! Yes, I hear you! The door is blocked! Is there another way out?"

Marlowe looked back at Shelley, who shook her head. He turned back to the door and hung his head. "No!"

Bright closed her eyes and swallowed the taste of smoke. She looked at the edges of the door. "I'm going to shoot the hinges! Stand back!"

Marlowe did as asked and heard five loud cracks and could see damage breaking through the storm door and into the house.

Bright put her gun away and shielded her eyes from smoke with the crook of her arm. She shouted, "Okay! Try it!"

Marlowe jerked open the interior door and looked at the splintered wood of the door frame where the heavy storm door attached. He gave it three hard kicks about midway up before the connected edge of the door separated from the wall and leaned over enough for them to fit. He waved Shelley over first, and Bright helped pull her out. He followed, falling into a roll and coughing. They all ran blindly toward the alley. Smoke was beginning to spread out toward Marlowe's borrowed car. Bright tugged at his arm and pointed to the house backed up to the edge of the alley. A car was parked pointed toward them. Bright motioned to it and tried to yell through coughing fits, "My car! Go to my car!"

Chapter 42

Sameer assumed if Do Right went missing around the same time as Seamus, going to his apartment was pointless. An ex-girlfriend, however, might be willing to offer some insight into where he could have gone. Although Booker seemed pessimistic about the situation, he did make it sound like Seamus and Do Right could be on the run from someone. After a reverse search of the address Booker had given him and a little online research, Sameer discovered Do Right had stopped at the home of a Brenda Langley. She was single, in her late sixties, and had no work affiliations online. She had a minimalistic Facebook profile, which included one photo of her with a young blonde girl, tagged in as Johnna Kitteridge. Sameer found the Kitteridge girl connected to Do Right's address, but also listed as a possible relative of Brenda Langley. Sameer guessed he was parking in the driveway of a grandmother, whose granddaughter had dated Do Right some time back.

He checked himself in the rearview mirror, smoothing his hair and taking deep, thought-collecting breaths. He marched up to the door and rang the bell. Ms. Langley answered within seconds. She pulled the door open with both an impressive and dangerous level of trust and goodwill.

Sameer smiled, keeping his hands clasped in front of him and practically bowing. "Ms. Langley? My name is Sameer Zardari. I hate to impose on you, but I was wondering if I could ask you a few questions."

Ms. Langley frowned at him, but nodded. "What about, dear?"

Sameer nodded along with her. "Yes, thank you. I'm looking for my husband. His name is Seamus Fitzgerald. I believe you know a friend of his."

The old woman glanced up, like she was trying to look at her own forehead. "Fitzgerald. Yes. Yes. Writes for *The Pitch*?"

Sameer grew wide-eyed. "Yes. Yes, he does. You've met him?"

Ms. Langley tilted her head. "Oh, well, no. Sweetie, I'm sorry. I didn't mean to—" She shook her head. "No, I've read his work. I like his articles. I'm sorry. I didn't mean to get your hopes up. Come in. Please. I'll fix you a coffee or some tea."

Sameer followed her in and agreed to a cup of whatever she was having. He waited on her tiny floral love seat as she made a pot of tea. When she returned, she had the tea on a wooden tray with some cookies and a bowl of sugar. She looked like such a typical grandmother Sameer's smile almost grew into a warm-hearted laugh. Ms. Langley sat next to him on the sofa and placed the tea on a table at their knees. She patted Sameer's back and gestured for him to take his tea, which he did. "Now, your husband, you can't find him?"

Sameer nodded. "Yes. He has been missing for several days now."

Ms. Langley closed her eyes and shook her head. "I'm so sorry."

Sameer took a sip of tea. "Thank you. I was hoping you might could help me, actually."

Ms. Langley frowned. "How, dear?"

Sameer turned toward her. "A man visited your house recently. He goes by the nickname of Do Right. I believe he dates your granddaughter."

Ms. Langley frowned and nodded. "Yes. Dante. Dante Holliverse. He stopped by two," she thought back, "maybe three days ago. Maybe more. My days are all mixed up."

Sameer wrote the name down on a notecard. "Not a problem. I was hoping I could speak with your granddaughter to find out what Dante wanted."

Ms. Langley's eyes welled with tears. She struggled to speak. "I'm afraid my Johnna passed."

Sameer's lips parted, but he couldn't speak. He shook his head and looked down, managing, "I'm so, so sorry."

The old woman hung her head and let herself cry softly into her chest. "It's okay, dear. You didn't know. I only just found out myself. Can't even bury her until the police sort it all out."

Sameer shook his head and placed a hand at her back. "What happened?"

"She was killed. No idea why. She was a sweet girl." Ms. Langley smiled. "Let me show you something. Do you mind?"

Sameer returned the smile. "Of course I don't mind."

Ms. Langley left for a moment and returned with a pair of photo albums. She proceeded to flip through them with Sameer, showing him photos of Johnna at every stage of life. For every photo, there was a story: Johnna getting harassed by a goat at the petting zoo. The time Johnna had three birthday cakes. Johnna refusing to stay home from the homecoming dance when she was sick as a dog. Sameer drank three cups of tea and laughed along with each story. He added the requisite comments about how beautiful Johnna had been and how energetic her eyes were. He tapped on one photo. "She had a wonderful sense of humor. I can tell."

Ms. Langley laughed and nodded. "Too wonderful, some would say. She was a bit of a smart ass." She ran her fingers across the picture.

Sameer laughed. "Oh, I know about smart asses."

Ms. Langley's face drooped. "Oh, sweetie. Look at me. Your husband. Of course. Do you have a photo of him? I don't think I ever saw what he looks like."

Sameer took out the wedding photo and handed it to her.

Ms. Langley smiled at the picture. "Such handsome boys. You look so happy."

Sameer smiled. "Was"—he swallowed—"was Johnna here when Dante came by?"

She shook her head. "No. I'm not sure where she was at the time."

"What did he need with her? Did he say?"

She nodded. "Yes. He sat and spoke with me for a moment. We always got along so well, even after they split. And then he asked if he could go in her room. He had loaned her a movie and he needed it back for a class he was taking. He said he hated asking, but it was a bit of an emergency. I was so proud he was taking some classes again. I told him to go ahead. I trusted him, and I'm sure Johnna would, too. They were still on pretty good terms."

Sameer frowned. "A movie? What movie?"

She shook her head. "I'm not sure. He kept it in his jacket pocket, I guess. He said he found it, though. He left soon after."

Sameer started to ask another question, but he was interrupted by the doorbell. Ms. Langley excused herself to go to the door. When she returned, a woman was with her. The woman was about Sameer's age, somewhere on either side of thirty. She was pale-skinned and dark-haired, attractive, but the slouchy police department sweatsuit she was wearing did little to flatter her figure. And her hair and makeup were both frazzled. She looked to be a little bit of a mess, in all honesty. Sameer stood to greet them as they entered the room and had to put in some effort to avoid staring.

Ms. Langley held a hand out between them. "Cary, this is Sameer Zardari. He's asking about Dante." She turned to Sameer. "Cary knows Dante. She was friends with Johnna."

Sameer noticed Cary's eyes bug out when Dante was mentioned. He and Ms. Langley returned to their seats, but Cary remained standing, frowning down at Sameer. "Why are you asking about Dante?"

Sameer held his hands out in a non-threatening gesture. "I'm only looking for my husband." He handed her the photo. "Seamus Fitzgerald. He was working with Dante on a film when they both went missing."

Cary shook her head at the picture, dismissing it, and handed it back. "Well, he wouldn't come here."

Sameer looked at Ms. Langley, who fluttered. "Oh, he did, dear. A few days ago."

Cary shot a look at Ms. Langley. "What? Dante came here? Why?"

Ms. Langley shared the same story with Cary about the movie. Cary nodded. "Must have been why the police searched Johnna's room."

Ms. Langley frowned. "The police never searched Johnna's room. What's going on, sweetie?"

Cary looked up and squinted at Ms. Langley. "Wait, what? The police didn't search her room?"

Ms. Langley shook her head. "No."

Cary ran her hands through her hair. "Then who was the last person in Johnna's room? Before me?"

Ms. Langley thought. "Well, it would've been Dante, I guess."

Cary took off for the stairs, ignoring Ms. Langley's questions. Sameer stood and put a hand on Ms. Langley's shoulder, pointing toward Cary and upstairs. "Ms. Langley, do you mind?"

Ms. Langley waved him to follow her. "No, no. Go."

Sameer caught up with Cary in Johnna's room. She was beginning to rummage through drawers and a closet. Sameer stepped into the room. "May I ask what it is you're looking for?"

Cary whipped around and looked at him. She shook her head. "I'm not sure."

Sameer nodded. "I don't mind helping you. If it's connected to Dante, then it's connected to Seamus. But I need to know what I am helping to looking for."

Cary nodded. "Yeah. Well, Dante's—" she paused and hung her head. She looked back up at him and softened her eyes. "Dante is dead. I don't know your husband. I have no idea about him. He could be fine. But Dante—he's—he's not."

Sameer forced a lump down his throat and stared at the ceiling. He nodded and looked back at her. "Okay. Go on."

Cary continued, "Before he died, he sent me a text. A blank text. And then my life exploded. I have people after me, trying to kill me. The thing is, Dante and I hadn't been friends for a while. It didn't make any sense. But there has to be a reason. There has to be something. You said…what?" She frowned. "A movie? Your husband and Dante were doing a movie together?"

Sameer nodded. "Yes. A documentary. Seamus is a journalist. He and Dante were working on a film. About police corruption."

Cary raised her eyebrows. "Makes sense. Was it called *Everybody Kill Cary*?"

Sameer chuckled. "No." He thought back. "It was called *Chicken Little*, I believe."

Cary's eyes widened. She ran over to a bookshelf and got down on her hands and knees. She started rifling through a huge stack of DVDs on the bottom shelf.

Sameer stepped over and stood behind her. "What is it?"

Cary kept flipping through DVDs. "I can never remember seeing Dante quite as mad as he was one year when he took me and Johnna to a film festival. We gave him the slip and skipped out on some artsy film he had been talking about. We went to see a James Bond movie instead. He was so pissed at us. None of us ever forgot it."

Sameer frowned. "Which James Bond movie?"

Cary spun around, holding up a DVD. She smiled. "*Skyfall*."

Sameer nodded and smiled back. "Chicken Little."

Cary opened the case and popped out the disc. A homemade, unlabeled disc was sitting on top of the copy of *Skyfall*. Cary showed Sameer. "Do we watch it?"

Sameer shook his head. "I think we need to contact the authorities. Do you have anyone we can trust?"

Cary cocked her head. "Well, funny you should ask…" She stood and started for the door.

Sameer held a hand out. "Would you like me to keep it in a pocket? You don't appear to have any in your"—he eyed her up and down—"tracksuit."

Cary stared at the disc and looked up at Sameer with a wince. "I think I'll hold onto it. No offense."

Sameer shrugged. "None taken. You seem to be working through a rough time. Full of experiences which might challenge your trust."

Cary laughed. "You could say so, yeah."

Sameer followed Cary down the stairs. "So who is this person you do trust?" He pointed toward the front of the house. "Who's out there?"

Cary shook her head. "A cop. And I don't trust him. Not completely. But I'm out of options."

Ms. Langley stood as they came into the living room. "Is everything okay, Cary? What is that?" She grew visibly upset. "What's going on?"

Cary walked over to Ms. Langley and took her by the shoulders. "Ms. Langley, I promise you I will tell you everything. Please, trust that I am doing everything in my power to make sure the people who hurt Johnna get what they deserve."

Ms. Langley pursed her lips and nodded. "I know you are, dear. I"—she rolled her head around—"I wish I knew how to help."

Cary smiled. "You are, Ms. Langley." She held up the disc. "I'm going to take this outside and give it to a police officer. And then you're going to give me a safe place to stay while this all gets sorted out. At least, I hope you will."

Ms. Langley sighed and returned the smile. "Of course I will, dear." She turned away and busied herself with the tray of tea. She held the tray of kettle and cups up and motioned toward it with her head. "I may not be much use, but I can at least offer hospitality." She laughed on her way to the kitchen. "In fact, tell those police officers to come in and drink a cup of coffee if they want."

Cary laughed along and offered, "Thank you, Ms. Langley. It means a lot to me." She started for the door, with Sameer in tow, but stopped short. She half turned and frowned, calling toward the kitchen. "Ms. Langley? Why did you say police officers?"

Ms. Langley stuck her head around the corner and raised her eyebrows. "I said for you to offer them a cup of coffee."

Cary shook her head and took a step toward her. "No. Why plural?"

Ms. Langley frowned. "Because there are two of them."

"Two of them? What do you mean 'two of them?'"

Ms. Langley pointed toward a window at the front of the house. "I looked out to see how you had gotten here while you were upstairs."

Cary turned in horror. Sameer ran to the window and peeked out. He turned back to Cary. "I only see one."

Ms. Langley shook her head. "No, no. There were two. A detective in a suit and a policeman in a uniform. They were talking."

Sameer glanced back and shook his head. "No. Only the uniformed officer."

Cary ran a hand across her eyes and into her hair. She stepped over to the window, easing toward it in slow shuffling steps. She leaned over to look, swallowing hard before prying the blinds apart. The blinds snapped shut and Cary collapsed against a wall in a cursing mumble.

Sameer closed his eyes and sighed. "Not the officer you hoped, I take it."

Cary shook her head. "No. Not at all." She looked at Sameer and held out the disc.

Sameer glanced down at it and back up at Cary. He tilted his head. "Out of options again?"

Cary nodded. "Yeah. I need this to find its way to someone who can do something with it. Tell me, Sameer, in your search for your husband, has the name Bright Hudson come up?"

Sameer nodded. "Yes. It has."

Cary squinted. "Can she be trusted?"

Sameer shrugged. "Maybe. I found no reason not to trust her. In fact, I suspect she may be Seamus' contact inside the police."

Cary nodded. "Yeah. Okay. Good enough. Take this to her. Put it in her hands yourself."

Sameer took the disc and put it in an inside jacket pocket. "And you?"

Cary jerked a thumb over her shoulder. "I'll handle him. He's here for me. I doubt he knows anything about you. I can keep him distracted while you go out the back. Work your way through the backyard. It connects to a neighbor's yard and you can work your way to the street and keep going."

Sameer looked from Cary to the back of the house. "What about my car?"

Cary shook her head. "In the driveway?" She laughed. "No. You can come back for it. For now, make do. Find a way. Trust me. You'd be surprised how many ways you can find to move around the city if you try hard enough."

Sameer nodded and patted at the disc in his pocket. "I will make sure it reaches the proper hands."

Cary smiled. "I hope you find your husband."

Sameer glanced at the front window. "I hope you do not die."

They shared a laugh and went their separate ways. Cary walked straight for the front door, took one big breath, and opened it. Reynard vaulted out of the driver's side of his car and started strolling casually toward the house. He smiled broadly at Cary. "Hey there, Cary Trubody. Long time, no see."

Cary smacked her lips like she was trying to remove a bad taste from her mouth. "Officer Reynard. How's life treating you?"

Reynard shrugged. "Can't complain. You?"

Cary chuckled. "Kinda shitty, to be honest." She looked around. "You haven't seen Officer Moya around, have you?"

Reynard followed her gaze, swiveling his head with a comical frown. "Moya? I don't think so. Was he here?" He clapped his hands. "Tell you what, Cary." He pointed back to his police cruiser. "Why don't you hop in the car?" He swirled a finger around. "You and me—we'll do a little ride around and look for him."

Cary nodded. "Okay. Do I get to ride up front? Or do I need to stuff myself in the trunk?"

Reynard laughed. "Well, the trunk, see, it's a little full right now. So you can ride in the front seat." He licked his lips. "With me."

Cary shook her head. "I'll save you the trouble of telling me how I don't have too much of a choice."

Reynard sighed and grinned in appreciation. "Thank you, Cary."

They both walked toward the car. Reynard watched to make sure Cary got in on the passenger side before starting around to his own side. Cary looked over in disgust at his huge smile as he flipped open his car door.

The noise seemed to explode in her ears before her brain could register what she was seeing. A crashing of metal and breaking glass. A heavy grunt and a thud. Reynard was gone. He was standing there smiling one second and gone the next. The figure of Reynard had been replaced by the front end of a very familiar red Ford Fusion.

Haley was freaking out, waving her hands in front of her face and starting to cry. Grayson had her window down waving Cary to come on. Haley cried out, "Oh my god, oh my god, oh my god. Is he dead? Did I kill him?"

Grayson leaned back over her own shoulder. "Shut up. Probably not. Which means he is about to come up shooting." She looked back at Cary. "Which means, get in the car!"

Cary scrambled to get out and ran around to the driver's side of the Fusion, since the passenger side was pinned up against a cop car. She jumped in the back to find Sameer curled up into the seat and shaking. He looked up and forced a grin. "These young ladies claim to be your best friends."

Cary nodded. "Oh yeah. We go way back."

Sameer cut his eyes toward Haley. "For the record, I did offer to drive."

Haley backed up and took off out of the neighborhood, slowing to a normal speed on the first major road she came to. She was still shaking and crying. Grayson, on the other hand, was leaning over into the backseat and smacking her gum. "We were just getting home when we saw that cop Haley ran over shoot this other cop and shove him in his trunk. I said to Haley, 'Betcha twenty bucks this has something to do with Cary.' And what do you know?" She eyed Haley, who was still borderline hyperventilating. "You owe me twenty bucks, by the way." Grayson turned back to Cary and slapped her leg. "But enough about us. What've'ya been up to, Cary? Where you need us to take you this time?"

Cary shook her head. "I need somewhere with lots of cops. I can't be isolated anymore."

Grayson closed one eye. "Yeah, because that worked so well for you the first time."

Sameer glanced over at Cary. "First time?"

Cary rolled her eyes. "Long story. Look, I need uniformed, normal ass cops. They can't all be bent."

Haley squeaked. "The movies."

Grayson pointed and nodded. "Yep. It's getting close to prime time. That place is always crawling with cops."

Cary leaned forward and softened her voice. "Take us to the movies, Haley. It's going to be okay. I promise." She turned to Sameer. "Bright Hudson. How can we get her there?"

Sameer raised one eyebrow and pulled a card out of his pocket. "I could call her."

Chapter 43

Mark Thompson climbed into his stolen Corolla and drove off, catching sight of the first puffs of smoke from Dante's apartment in his rearview. After a minute of driving, a report came through on his radio about a fire being called in by a Detective Hudson. He radioed in, claiming to be on the scene and with Detective Hudson. "Fire on Roderick Drive is a false alarm, dispatch. No fire. I repeat, false alarm. No fire." He listened long enough to hear fire and rescue being called off and switched off his radio.

Mark pulled over into an alley several blocks away and lit a cigarette with the car lighter. He slouched into the seat, taking long, deep drags. His hands were shaking. This was Jolly's area of expertise. Things had gotten tangled before. Mark simply never had to untangle them by himself. Jolly had always been there to step across that line.

He thought back to a time when he and Jolly were beat cops. They had barely started down the path they'd end up on. It was all girls then. Nothing more or less than keeping a few of the working girls' storefronts open and connecting them with some high-profile clients. Mark had no clue how deep the racquet ran back then. By the time he and Jolly were calling any shots, it was like inheriting your dad's general store. You never looked around to see what sat on the shelves until you started selling the products yourself. And by then, who's going to stop?

But once during those early days, one of the girls hooked up with some reporter and got a little loose with the pillow talk. Somebody up the chain from Thompson and Jolly got wind she was set to start listing some names. Mark had a way with the girls back then—still did to some extent. But back then, he could charm them into killing their mothers if he wanted to. Mark had the girl ready to button up and bus out to Omaha or Toledo or somewhere. Jolly, though, he didn't think chasing the girl off was enough. He got ambitious. Saw an opportunity to punch their ticket to middle management. Jolly had a killer's eyes. Mark had known he'd done some time in the service. Jolly wouldn't talk about it, but from the vibe Mark got, he earned those eyes. This reporter, however, was the first time Jolly acknowledged his darkness to Mark. They asked the girl to wait a bit before she jumped on a bus, and they set up watching her apartment. When the reporter showed up, Jolly looked at Mark and said, "Stay in the car. You don't have to cross that line yet." When Mark half-heartedly objected, Jolly told him, "I've been living on the other side of the line all my life, partner. I can do the things we need to do so you don't ever need to. Just keep the car running."

It had been so many years ago. And he was right. Jolly kept blood off Mark's hands for thirty years. Mark looked at his shaking hand as his cigarette sprinkled ashes all over his lap. Jolly wasn't around anymore. It was high time Mark get a little blood on his hands.

His phone rang and he answered with a grunted, "Yeah."

The voice on the other end sounded strained and weak. "Thompson. I had her. Turn on your radio."

Mark frowned. "Reynard? Is that you? What the hell's wrong with you?"

"I'm okay. But Cary Trubody. She was at the grandmother's. She got something, I think."

Mark gritted his teeth. "Where is she now?"

"Red Ford Fusion. Maybe a 2010 or so. Young white girl driving. Two or three passengers. One of them is Cary. I put out a BOLO. Listen to your radio."

Mark nodded and hung up. He switched on the radio and almost immediately heard the BOLO being repeated. Flicking his cigarette butt out the window, Mark started driving aimlessly with the radio practically pressed to his ear. He made his way toward the part of town where Johnna's grandmother lived, working his way across town in looping zigzags. After fifteen or twenty minutes of nothing, a voice called out, "I have eyes on a red Ford Fusion. White female driver. Two white females and one male, possibly Hispanic, passengers. I'm at Tinseltown Movies in the Berrywood area."

Chapter 44

Bright pulled out of the carport and into the street. She, Marlowe, and Shelley were all three hacking and coughing from the smoke. Bright struggled to drive, pulling down a couple of quiet side streets until she had put distance between them and the fire.

Marlowe leaned against the passenger side door and tried to catch his breath. "What the hell happened?"

Bright parked on the side of a residential street and rubbed at her eyes. "Mark Thompson happened. He tried to block the exit and set the apartment on fire."

Shelley coughed out, "Motherfucker."

Bright turned. "I take it you know him?"

Marlowe nodded. "He and his partner killed our brother."

Bright looked back and forth between them. "Dante."

They both nodded. Shelley said, "Dante had some kind of film they wanted. They think he gave a copy to Cary Trubody. We think he may have hidden it somewhere." She pointed back toward the fire. "Maybe in there."

Bright hung her head. "Any idea what's on the film?"

Marlowe and Shelley shook their heads.

Bright frowned. "Why Cary?"

Marlowe shrugged. "We're not sure. Cary was dating Dante's ex-girlfriend. They used to all be friends. But Dante hadn't talked to either one of them in a while. Not that I know of."

Bright laughed. "I'd imagine not."

Shelley sat up in the backseat. "Why kill us before we found the copy he was looking for?"

Bright shook her head. "I don't know. I think he's cleaning up loose ends. Once Jolly died, he seemed to start spiraling."

Marlowe hung his head. "Cary. Do you know where she is?"

Bright nodded. "She's safe. She's with my partner."

As if on cue, Bright's phone rang. When she answered it, the voice on the other end was unfamiliar, vaguely foreign, with a slight, almost imperceptible accent. He said, "Detective Hudson? My name is Sameer Zardari. I believe you know my husband."

Bright frowned. "Okay, Sameer. I'll bite. Who is your husband?"

"Seamus Fitzgerald."

Bright swallowed and switched ears with her phone. "Yeah. Yeah, I know Seamus. Is he with you?"

"No. He's missing. But Cary Trubody is with me. And she and I found something we would like to give you."

Bright looked up at Marlowe and Shelley's puzzled faces. She switched to speakerphone. "Cary Trubody is with you?"

"Yes. Right now."

"Can you put her on the phone, please?"

After a moment, the phone on the other end clicked to the echo of speakerphone, itself. Cary said, "Detective Hudson? I'm here. I'm okay."

"Where is Detective Moya?"

Cary hesitated. "I don't know. Reynard showed up. He tried to take me, but Sameer and a couple of friends helped me get away. We think we found the copy of this film everybody's looking for. We have it."

Marlowe and Shelley leaned toward the phone. Bright motioned for them to stay quiet. "Where are you, Cary? I'll come to you."

Sameer said, "We are pulling into a movie theater."

A new female voice called out between smacks of gum, "Tinseltown. In Berrywood. Meet us there." And the phone disconnected.

Chapter 45

Haley pulled into the Tinseltown parking lot, drove right up to the long row of ticket booths out front, and put two wheels on the curb. She drew the attention of at least three police officers monitoring the growing crowds. One of them stared hard and started talking into a radio strapped to his shoulder. Cary leaned forward over into the front seat. She got right next to Haley's ear. "As soon as we get out, you go. Drive slow and park this car in a friend's garage or something for at least a week."

Grayson ruffled. "No way. That dude was going to kill you. We don't need to hide out."

Cary turned to her. "Yes. You do. This could still go south on us. And if it gets back around to you, which it probably will, you say I held a gun to your heads. You say you had no choice."

Sameer sat forward. "You say I carjacked you. I was driving."

Cary looked back at him and nodded. She spun to Haley. "You got it? Sameer was driving. Understood?"

Haley nodded. Cary looked to Grayson, who reluctantly shrugged and nodded. Cary put a hand on each of their shoulders. "Thank you, girls."

Sameer was looking out the window. "Cary, one of the officers is coming toward us."

Cary leaned back and looked. "Well, then let's go introduce ourselves."

Cary and Sameer hopped out of the car and approached the officer, both of them keeping their hands in plain sight and moving deliberately.

The cop frowned at them. "Let me have a word with you two." He turned to his radio, "Red Ford Fusion is in the parking lot. Two suspects exited the car. They're in custody."

Cary held her hands up. "My name is Cary Trubody. I believe you're looking for me."

Sameer cut his eyes at her. "You are very well versed in surrendering."

Cary shrugged. "It's not my first time."

The cop raised his eyebrows and laughed. "You're Cary Trubody, huh?"

Sameer nodded. "Yes, she is." He glanced at her. "As far as I know." He looked back to the officer. "We need to speak with Detective Bright Hudson."

Cary and Sameer were still several feet away from him. The cop smirked and nodded. "Oh, that's what you need, do you?" He laughed and leaned into the radio again. "I have a female suspect claiming to be Cary Trubody."

A voice barked out over the radio. It sounded frantic. Almost panicked. "Detective Thompson responding. I'm in route. Officer, detain the suspect until I arrive."

Cary and Sameer stopped walking and exchanged a look. Cary's eyes got wide and she shook her head subtly. Sameer pursed his lips and nodded. He looked past Cary at a huge group of teenagers approaching from a bus. Cary turned and looked. They appeared to be a female track team from a high school. They were all wearing sweatsuits similar to the one Cary was wearing. Sameer took the disc out of his inside jacket pocket and handed it to Cary.

As soon as Sameer's hand went in his pocket, the cop started calling out to him—not yelling, more advising him to keep his hand out of his pocket. The sight of the disc gave the cop pause and he took his hand off his sidearm. As soon as the track team got close, Sameer turned and walked swiftly, almost in a run toward the officer. The cop responded with, "Hey, hey, hey! Stop! Stop!" He fumbled his hand back toward his gun, but before he could reach it Sameer had reached him in a full embrace.

Sameer hugged the police officer and blubbered, in fake tears, "Thank you, sir! Thank you! I am so happy to have found you! You can help me! Thank you!"

The officer didn't know what to do with the emotions. He gave Sameer a half hug and a pat and tossed out a half-hearted, "Okay, buddy. That's enough." He started scanning past Sameer for Cary, but she had become lost in the crowd of girls. The cop pushed Sameer off and ran forward to the back of the crowd, searching.

Using the momentary lapse, Sameer backed away toward an exit door. A small crowd was coming out of a movie, and Sameer let himself move upstream through the crowd and into the parted doors. On his way he snatched a ticket stub from a lady who was starting to throw it away. She looked at him in shock and gasped, to which he gave a slight bow and offered an apology as they both continued moving in opposite directions.

Chapter 46

Mark Thompson dropped his police radio into the passenger seat, and the walkie rolled onto the floorboard as he took a sharp corner. He was maxing out his little stolen Corolla trying to make it to Tinseltown. By the time he pulled into a handicapped space near the front, he was unfastening his seatbelt and even opening the door. He killed the engine but tossed the keys into the floorboard along with the police radio.

Scanning the crowd for uniformed officers, Mark barreled past people, shouldering them out of the way while flashing his badge. The first officer he came to didn't speak—only nodded and pointed Mark on toward the ticket booths.

A dejected-looking cop flagged him down, and Mark put the badge away and sidled up next to him. The cop shook his head. "She gave me the slip."

Mark hung his head and rubbed at his eyes.

"She was with a Middle Eastern guy. He distracted me and she shot off into a crowd." He pointed toward the theater. "She's in there, though. They both are, I think. He's about five nine, thin, some facial hair, wearing a denim jacket and green T-shirt. She's maybe five four; a little full-figured—"

Mark waved him off. "I know what she looks like."

The cop shrugged. "Yes, sir. She's wearing a sweatsuit. I think it was a police issue."

Mark had started away, but he stopped and spun around. "What?"

The cop shrugged again. "Looked like it, yeah."

Mark made a sour face and shook his head, starting back for the door.

The cop called out, "Oh yeah! She had a disc. The guy gave it to her before they split up."

Mark stopped and turned back, squinting. "What kind of disc?"

The cop shook his head. "I didn't get a good look. But that's what it looked like. Like a DVD. Colorful, commercial packaging. But I didn't make it out."

Mark took several deep breaths. "Yeah. Yeah, it's okay." He swallowed. "Tell you what, why don't you go around back? Check the emergency exits. Make sure they don't slip out." He jerked a thumb toward the officer who had guided him earlier. "Ask your partner over there to watch the front."

The cop nodded once. "Yes, sir."

Mark loosened his tie and clutched his chest as he watched the officer spring into action, eager to make up for his mistake. He closed his eyes and breathed. Counted by threes the way his girlfriend had encouraged him to do when he started to have a panic attack. Mark turned, flashing his badge to the movie staff at the door, and headed in.

Chapter 47

As Bright drove, Shelley listened to the police radio, hearing and relaying the chatter between a Tinseltown cop and Mark Thompson. The news made Bright speed even more than she had been. Marlowe gripped the door handle and placed his other hand on the dashboard. "We ain't gonna help her if you get us killed on the way."

Bright weaved through traffic, passing someone on the on-ramp to the interstate. "It's not my first time behind the wheel. Close your eyes if you're going to be a delicate flower about it."

A moment later, they heard the Tinseltown cop report having lost sight of Cary going into the theater. But Detective Thompson was in pursuit.

Bright winced. "Shit." She glanced back at Shelley. "Do you have your badge?"

Shelley sighed. "No. I didn't bring it."

Bright nodded. "Did you bring cash?"

Marlowe checked his pockets and came out with two twenties. Bright grabbed one and handed it to Shelley. "Each of you buy a ticket and go in the front. I'll drive around back and try to use my badge to access some employee entrance or something. How big is Tinseltown?"

Marlowe cocked an eyebrow. "Huge. Multi-level. Maybe twenty screens."

Bright chuckled. "Great. Okay, so split up." She fished her phone out and handed it back to Shelley. "Load our numbers in. We call if we spot anyone—Cary, Thompson, or even Sameer."

Shelley used Bright's phone to call hers and Marlowe's, typing in contacts as she did. "Goes for you, too, you know?"

Bright nodded into the rearview mirror. "I know." She pointed a finger into Marlowe's face. "But get one thing straight. Your sister and I? We're police. No macho bullshit. If this shit goes sideways, you stand down and let the professionals do their job. Understood?"

Marlowe smiled. "Have you met my sister? I been standing down since she was eight."

Bright whipped into the Tinseltown lot and pulled up to the ticket booths. Marlowe and Shelley jumped out, both checking their guns were tucked under their shirts and clutching wrinkled twenty-dollar bills. Bright didn't wait to see them off. She surged off and drove around to the back of the building.

Chapter 48

Cary kept her head down and wedged herself between a couple of cliques of girls who were too busy laughing and talking to notice her. A teenage boy with bad complexion and a Tinseltown vest was standing at the door counting heads. As they passed through, another boy in a matching vest handed each of them a ticket to some inspirational sports-themed movie.

Once inside, the crowd of girls thinned out as some went for the concession counter and others broke off toward the restrooms. Cary lingered in the rear of the restroom pack. As soon as they had rounded the corner, she veered off to one side and started up the escalator, taking two steps at a time to speed it along.

The second floor was, for the most part, a carbon copy of the first. A concessions counter stretched around in sort of an octagon in the center lobby area. At each corner of the octagon, a hallway led off to numbered theater doors. Cary looked for exits to the outside. If Bright Hudson was on her way, Cary's best chance of flagging her down before Thompson caught up with either of them was to be outside. But the second floor didn't appear to have any.

A security guard over by a popcorn station caught Cary's eye. He was staring at her. Too much. She worked her way around the concession counter until she was at a popcorn station across from him, as far away as she could get. The guard tapped fingers on a gun holster at his hip and listened to a radio he had been speaking into a moment earlier. Cary cursed under her breath and turned her back to the guard. A young girl was next to her putting oily butter all over her little brother's popcorn. The girl's own popcorn was sitting precariously on the edge of the counter. Cary pretended to reach for a napkin and elbowed the container of popcorn so it went flying out into the floor. The girl's mother started into a chorus of "It's okay. Don't worry about it," before Cary could offer any apology. Tinseltown employees flocked over to offer the little girl more popcorn, and Cary used the cover to slip down a hallway.

She ducked into an alcove with a bottled water vending machine. Within seconds, a manager hurried to a supply closet and used his keys to retrieve a broom and dust pan, leaving the door cracked open. Cary trotted over to the closet and stepped in and around to one side. She had made pointed eye contact with the security guard as she slid into the closet. He would be walking through the door and into the tiny room within ten seconds. Cary pawed around on the shelves until she found an industrial sized jug of hand soap. She tugged the bottle down and held it against her body with one arm, using her hand not clutching the disc to wrench off its cap. She tipped it up and poured soap all over the entrance to the supply closet and leaned back into one corner.

On cue, the guard took one bumbling step into the closet and his foot shot out from under him. He grabbed at the doorjamb, but overcorrected and ended up going face first into a series of three shelves straight in front of him. Ending up on his back in an awkward position, he looked up at Cary and tried to shake a flood of cobwebs from the corners of his eyes. Cary gingerly knelt and, making sure to avoid the soap, slid his gun from his belt. The guard reached for her feebly, but his head was fuzzy from the fall and his feet were still slipping around and throwing off his feeble balance. Cary cocked her head at him and offered, "I'm so sorry." She hopped over the patch of soap and pushed the door shut behind her, hurrying off down the hallway of theaters before anyone noticed what had happened.

Chapter 49

Sameer emerged from the crowd feeling like he sprung up from underwater. He took a breath and found a girl in a Tinseltown vest and a security guard talking right in front of him. They both froze and glowered at him. Sameer flashed the ticket stub and asked sheepishly, "May I go look for my phone? I believe I left it."

The girl smiled and stepped aside. The security guard nodded and said, "Let me know if you need a flashlight."

Sameer passed them with nods to both and a thank you to the guard. He glanced back to ensure they returned to their conversation. Working his way down the curved hallway, he passed multiple theaters, but couldn't find a way to get across to the lobby. Each time, he would peek in to see if a movie was in process. Almost every time, there was, which meant he ducked back out to avoid drawing attention. The one time no movie was playing, a crew was cleaning and he pretended to search for and find his phone.

His limited sense of direction told him he had made his way around to the back of the entire complex. This was reinforced by the cluster of four exit doors marked with large red signs declaring, "Employee Only. Reentry by Key Code Only."

This stretch of hallway was deserted, so he stopped to call Detective Hudson. He had to warn her about Detective Thompson, even though he was not entirely sure what it was about Detective Thompson which required forewarning. He dialed the number and she answered on the first ring.

"Detective Hudson. It is Sameer. We apparently have a problem."

Chapter 50

When Mark Thompson flashed his badge at the door, one pock-marked kid had the nerve to step in front of him and try to examine it more closely. Mark rolled his eyes and shouldered pat the kid. Once inside he trotted toward a group of girls wearing navy sweatsuits. He grabbed a couple of brunettes by the shoulder, spinning them around before feebly apologizing. After the third girl, a middle-aged Latina woman stepped between Mark and the girls and held a hand into his chest. "Excuse me. What do you think you're doing?"

Mark flashed his badge and looked past her into the crowd.

The woman craned herself up into his line of sight. "I don't care if you're the FBI. It doesn't give you the right to put your hands on my girls."

Mark snapped back to the moment and flashed a grin in place of the badge. "I'm so sorry. I got carried away. Let me start this over. Do you mind?"

The woman squinted at him and crossed her arms.

Mark placed one hand on his chest. "I'm Detective Mark Thompson. I am pursuing a very dangerous woman who is dressed in a similar fashion to your girls. I'm afraid she may have used the similarity to sneak into the theater. And I would like to find her before she hurts anyone."

The woman lowered her arms and looked around nervously.

Mark nodded. "It's okay. Just tell me where all your girls may have gone."

She glanced around. "Most are here. Getting snacks. A few split off to go to the restroom."

Mark pointed in each direction while raising his eyebrows at her. She pointed to her right, his left. Mark turned and started that way, looking back at her. "Do you mind accompanying me to make sure it's only your girls in the restroom?"

"Of course," she replied, hurrying after him.

As the woman stepped into the bathroom, calling out to her girls, Mark heard a commotion from above him. Behind him was an escalator, so he hurried over and rode up. As he neared the top, a Tinseltown manager came running toward him. "Are you a cop? You look like a cop. Are you?"

Mark stepped off the escalator nodding. "Yeah. I'm a cop. What happened?"

The manager motioned toward a security guard who was being helped over to a bench by two men. "Some girl knocked him out. She took his gun. She has a gun. Do I need to evacuate the theater?"

Mark walked past him and called back. "No. You need to tell me which way she went."

Chapter 51

Shelley and Marlowe each hurriedly bought tickets and found each other on the other side of the entrance. Shelley pointed toward an escalator over to their right. "Take the second level. Work your way east. I'll scan this level and come up on the east side and meet you."

Marlowe nodded and started away before stopping and looking back. "East is—"

Shelley rolled her eyes and pointed left. "That way. Yes."

Marlowe shrugged and nodded. "I'm just calibrating. Like, getting synchronized, you know."

They took off in their respective directions. Marlowe hurried up the escalator, slipping past several people who called after him with a choice word or two. Upstairs, the concession area bustled with the aftermath of some sort of accident. Marlowe eased his way toward the center of the action and found a security guard being helped out of a supply closet. He couldn't worm his way close enough to pick up everything, but he did overhear something about a girl and ciphered some pointing down a hallway. Marlowe smiled and shook his head, mumbling, "Cary," under his breath.

The ruckus had drawn most of the employees from down the hallway, so Marlowe was able to step into each theater and do a quick scan. The crowds were sparse. Each movie on this hallway was a classic—lots of black and white, some film noir, a western or two, a couple of Hitchcock.

About the seventh theater down, when Marlowe stepped back out, Mark Thompson bounded down the hallway toward him. Marlowe ducked back into the theater and scrambled up toward the empty balcony seats. Only a handful of people populated the theater at all, but no one sat in the balcony. He slid down between a row of seats and pulled out his phone. Shelley's number was the easiest to hit quickly, so he dialed it and waited while peering up over a seat at the entrance to the theater.

Shelley answered out of breath. Marlowe watched Mark Thompson step up the entrance ramp and start looking up and down rows. He breathed into the phone in a muted whisper, "I think I'm in a theater. I'm not sure which one. Somewhere between number ten and number fourteen. It's *Butch Cassidy and the Sundance Kid.* Detective Thompson followed me in. I need you to get here fast."

Shelley's voice grew shaky from running. "On my way. Stay out of sight. I'll be right there."

Thompson worked his way into the balcony. Marlowe slid back in a crouch. Looking behind him, he found a dead end. Without going over seats, he was trapped. Thompson rounded the edge of Marlowe's aisle and smiled. Thompson nodded and pulled out his gun. Marlowe went ahead and stood up, holding his hands out in a calming gesture.

Marlowe and Thompson both glanced down at the handful of oblivious moviegoers. They looked back at each other. There was no way he could shoot him here. But Thompson glanced over at the screen and smiled back at Marlowe. Marlowe frowned and looked over. Robert Redford and Paul Newman readied themselves for the final shootout. In a matter of seconds, the whole theater would erupt in the sound of gunfire.

Chapter 52

When Bright pulled around behind the theater, the back parking lot was deserted except for one cop who appeared to be walking the perimeter. She pulled up next to him and rolled down her window, flashing her badge. "Did you call it in?"

He squinted at the ID next to her badge. "Yeah. Detective Hudson? You're the one they asked for."

Bright nodded and threw her car into park right where it sat. She jumped out and motioned for the cop to hurry. "Can you get me in from back here?"

He pointed up ahead. "This cluster of doors in an employee entrance. I can't open it, but I can call for somebody to let you in."

Bright ran ahead while the cop fumbled with his radio. As she got to the doors, her phone rang. She jerked the phone to her ear and the voice on the other end said, "Detective Hudson. It is Sameer. We apparently have a problem."

Bright stopped. "Sameer. Where are you?"

"A Detective Thompson is here now."

Bright walked a little farther, stopping at the set of doors. "I know, Sameer. Where are you?"

"Cary is afraid of him. I think he is bad."

Bright sighed. "Yes, Sameer. He is. Where are you?"

"I am at a set of four doors. An employee entrance at the back of the theater."

Bright shook her head and knocked on the doors.

"Wait. Someone is knocking on the doors." Sameer pushed a door open.

Bright waggled her phone and stepped inside.

Sameer hung his head and put his phone away. "I promise I am usually quicker than this."

Bright looked back with a patronizing smile. "Don't worry. I have that effect on people." As Bright hit end on her call with Sameer, the phone rang again. Bright looked down and saw Shelley's name on the screen. "Shelley? What's wrong?"

Shelley was out of breath, panting and shaking the phone while running. "Thompson. He's in a theater with Marlowe."

Bright tugged Sameer by the arm and started moving. "Where?"

"He's not sure. It's somewhere between ten and fourteen."

Bright barked, "I'll take fourteen. You take ten. Work our way together." And they both hung up.

An employee came rounding a corner and jumped as Bright shoved her badge in his face and yelled, "Get me to theater fourteen now!"

Chapter 53

Cary kept running down the hallway, hoping for some way to go down. She felt like one of those women in a horror movie who keeps going upstairs when she should be two blocks away. As she came to the end of the hallway, she had nowhere left to go. She looked over to her right and found a young man in a Tinseltown vest using an employee keycard to open an elevator.

She hurried over and jumped on with him just ahead of the doors. His face went from startled to bored and he said, "This elevator is for employees only. You'll need to use the escalators in the main lobby."

Cary pulled the gun out and grinned. "I'm sorry. But I need to use the elevator right now."

The man jumped back, dropping the box of Raisinets he was eating. "Okay. Okay. You don't have to do that."

Cary pointed at the buttons with the gun. There were only three. She said, "First floor." But before the man could hit the button, Cary did a double take. "Wait. What's on the third floor?"

His voice shook. "The projection booth."

Cary frowned and glanced at the disc in her hand. "Do you know how to work it?"

The man nodded.

Cary shook the gun at him. "Floor three. Go."

The projection booth was empty. It was an expansive room, whirring with projectors connected to huge black towers full of blinking lights and touch screens. Cary waved the disc in the man's face. "Can you make them play this?"

The man came out of his fright long enough to roll his eyes. "These are seventy-five-thousand-dollar, state-of-the-art digital projectors. It's not a Blu-ray player. They have 4K capabilities and—"

Cary leveled the gun toward his face. "Can you make them play this?"

The man gulped. "You must really like James Bond."

"Can you?"

He nodded. "There's a computer override. I can use it to link in and convince the projectors to perform a test of the emergency notification system we built in after—"

Cary shook the gun.

He recoiled. "Which one?"

Cary looked around at the multiple projectors. "All of them."

Chapter 54

Sameer ran after Bright as an employee led both of them up a dark set of stairs to the second floor. They came out in a hallway leading to numbered doors. The employee pointed to the first door on their left with the glowing number fourteen hanging above it. Bright took off for the door while Sameer mumbled a thanks to the man.

The theater was showing *The Big Sleep*. The seats held a smattering of ten or twelve people. Bright came running out after doing a quick scan. Sameer shook his head. "I don't know who we're looking for."

Bright looked past him, causing Sameer to turn around. A woman ran toward them with a gun drawn, held close to her body to keep it somewhat concealed. Bright pointed. "Her brother."

The woman nodded to them and ducked into theater number ten.

Sameer looked at Bright. "What do we do?"

Bright shook her head. "This is too slow. You ever yelled 'Fire' in a theater before?"

Sameer cocked his head. "Once. I had turned seven a few days earlier. And my mother had taken me to see to see *Jumanji*. I can't remember her ever spanking me as hard as she did—" He nodded once. "And we can share the story later. I'll take twelve, you take thirteen."

* * *

Mark held his gun with both hands. The people below were locked in on the screen in front of them. Marlowe's hands twitched and he glanced back and forth, looking for a nonexistent escape route. Mark snuck glances at the screen. Robert Redford steadily loaded his gun. Paul Newman crouched, ready to run.

Finally, Redford snapped, "Go!" And the theater's lifelike speakers blasted gunfire.

Mark fired off one shot as Marlowe hurled himself forward over two rows of seats. He twisted around and found Marlowe scrambling to his feet. Before trying again, Mark looked down into the theater. The distraction worked. His shot got lost in the riotous gunfire of the film.

But the screen had gone quiet. Paul Newman was easing up toward some horses and Robert Redford was quietly readying for another round. Mark and Marlowe eyed each other in the silence, waiting. Marlowe inched down the aisle toward the exit. Mark waited and bit down on his lip to keep from shooting too soon.

Again, gunfire sounded from all sides of them. Mark bore down on his aim, waiting to track Marlowe's move. Marlowe went down and to the right. As Mark followed him, he saw a flash out of the corner of his eye. Something hit him in the side and spun him around. He caught himself on the seat in front of him and looked up to find Shelley standing at the entrance ramp, gun drawn.

Mark started to raise his gun, but the theater suddenly went silent. Everything stopped. Mark, Marlowe, and Shelley all three turned to look at the screen. What had been *Butch Cassidy* seconds ago was now replaced with shaky homemade footage from the city. The film looked like it had been taken by a cell phone. Maybe by someone trying to hide as they recorded.

* * *

Bright ducked into theater thirteen as Sameer took off for theater twelve. She could hear him screaming "Fire" and the commotion beginning. She stepped in with her badge and gun both out. "I need everyone to quietly and calmly exit the theater! We have a report of an emergency!"

Although confused, the crowd started working their way to the exits with only a murmur. Bright turned to start out when the screen flashed and changed. It had been *The Wild Bunch*, she thought, but suddenly it was a shot of an underpass in town.

Everyone stopped and stared. Bright recognized the two standing figures on the giant screen. Thompson and Jolly stood looming over a man in handcuffs. She recognized him, too.

Bright ran out of the theater and sprinted toward theater twelve. She was shouting, "Sameer! Sameer, don't watch! Don't look, Sameer!"

* * *

Cary could see the footage starting through the squares of dark glass looking into the theaters. She surprised herself by how little she cared about what was on the disc. She simply wanted it known. Whatever they wanted to hide, she wanted to expose. Once certain the video was playing, she grabbed the man's employee keycard and ran for the elevator. As soon as Thompson saw the film playing, he would be coming for her in the projection booth. She didn't plan on being there when he arrived.

* * *

As soon as he yelled out, Sameer ducked into a crevice with a trash can to let people run past him. They were almost all cleared out when the screen changed. He started out but stopped suddenly when the sound disappeared and was replaced by frightened breathing. Sameer turned around. Behind him, Detective Hudson shouted his name. But on the screen. On the screen was his Seamus. Seamus. On his knees. Handcuffed. Scared. The video was shot from too far off to comprehend what he said, but he was clearly begging. Begging for his life. Two men stood over him. They laughed. Talked to him. They wore cheap suits and they stood with sad, defeated postures. The postures of broken men who can only find it in themselves to break others so they aren't alone. One was fat. The other tall and thin. The tall one stepped forward and shot Seamus. One shot. A quick spray of blood and then he slumped to the ground. The camera shook violently and the person filming started to run before everything went dark.

Detective Hudson stood at his back. She placed a hand on his shoulder and said, softly, "You shouldn't have had to see that. I'm sorry."

Sameer turned and fell into her and he sobbed and shook.

* * *

Mark struggled to stand. He had taken the shot from Shelley in the shoulder, it felt like. He started walking out before the screen showed Jolly shooting the reporter. He didn't want to see that again. Shelley turned to watch, so she let him walk right past her. He stepped into the hallway and stood for a moment. Let himself bleed. He looked down at his gun, glanced over at a trash can, and tossed the gun. It landed with a *thunk*. Mark took out a cigarette and fumbled for a lighter which wasn't there.

He looked up and found Cary creeping toward him with a gun held level with his chest. Mark smiled. "Hey, Cary."

Shelley stepped up behind him, her gun drawn and pointed at his back.

Bright Hudson walked out of a theater helping a man who was crying on her shoulder. When she spotted Mark she started up with her own gun, but Mark waved his hands and smiled around the unlit cigarette clutched between his teeth. "Enough already. I get it, I get it. I just want a light."

Shelley stepped past him and took Cary's gun as Bright began to recite Mark Thompson's rights.

Chapter 55

A few weeks later, Cary was in the front seat of a car with Shelley Doyle, who was driving them out to Graffiti Creek. Shelley balanced a bouquet of flowers in the backseat between the fold down console and a box of charred things from Dante's apartment. She brought the flowers to remember Dante, even though he hated flowers. The whole scene had been roped off for days after Mark Thompson got arrested. Bright Hudson worked him down—got him to show roughly where he remembered Dante being buried. It ended up being not far from where they found Johnna.

Cary and Shelley hung out a few times after it all ended. They went to Seamus Fitzgerald's funeral together. Forced Sameer to let them take him out for dinner a few nights later. Once with Shelley and once alone, Cary went to sit with Carlos Moya in the hospital. He'd taken quite a few hard hits to the chest, cracking ribs and collapsing a lung. And one shot had missed the vest and messed up his gut a bit, but he'd be okay. He had showed Cary a card from Bright Hudson that read, "Thanks for being pudgy." It made reference to working some things out to put him on the path toward becoming a police sketch artist, so Cary brought him a sketch pad and some charcoal pencils.

They even met Bright for drinks one night. She couldn't tell them everything, but she confided in them a few bits and pieces. Reynard took a quick attempted murder plea for shooting Moya in exchange for his cooperation. Thompson was being charged as an accessory to four murders—Seamus, Dante, Johnna, and Karen Webster. The evidence on Seamus was ironclad, so he was likely to die in prison. The district attorney's office was not currently pursuing anything on Bright's father. But she filled Cary and Shelley in on the cold case and swore she wasn't letting it drop.

Shelley and Marlowe went back to life as normal for the most part. So much so they carried a little guilt over it. They had both gotten to where Dante was a rare occurrence in their lives. Life without him became way too normal way too quickly. They both had to work to keep his memory fresh. Marlowe set up an account to work toward offering a film school scholarship in his brother's name. Shelley visited the bridge every couple of days. She claimed it felt more alive with Dante than some tombstone.

Cary refused to go with her the first few times after it was cleared. But she finally gave in. Cary had been staying with Johnna's grandmother. Although they cleared her of everything—including the death of Detective Jolly—the fallout still cost her a graphic design job she genuinely enjoyed. But Sameer got her an interview with his company for a similar job, and she did well enough to get a second interview lined up. If it worked out, she could afford to find her own place within a month or two. In the meantime, Ms. Langley enjoyed the company, and Cary liked the neighbors—it was like having little sisters again.

Shelley parked with her car angled to face the side of the bridge with the bulk of the graffiti. She reached back into the backseat and snagged the flowers. "Do Right hated flowers. I don't know why the hell I keep bringing them."

Cary laughed. "Because nobody knows what to do with death. You know how many casseroles Ms. Langley has gotten?"

Shelley smiled. "Too many?"

Cary shook her head. "Lord, no. I love casseroles. But it is an odd thing to bring in response to a death. So are flowers. It all is. Nothing makes sense."

Shelley got out and started toward the bridge. She brushed the flowers she had left days ago off into the stream below and placed the new bouquet. "Maybe that's the point."

Cary stood several feet back, allowing her a moment. "What?"

Shelley turned around. "Not making sense. Maybe that's the whole point. Maybe it's our way, as a society, of saying 'this didn't make any sense, and I'm sorry it happened.' So we show up with flowers and food and all this stuff. Not making a damn bit of sense. Because neither did the death."

Cary nodded and shrugged. "Maybe you're right. Or maybe it's to remind the people still here that we're still alive. You know? You still have to eat. You still can see and smell and taste."

Shelley walked over and took Cary in an embrace. They stood, holding each other, for several minutes. They each listened to the other's sniffles and pretended not to notice. Cary broke the silence by reaching into her purse. "You know what does make sense though?"

Shelley smirked. "What?"

Cary came out with a can of orange spray paint. She pushed her purse toward Shelley and started shaking the can. "Hold this."

Cary trotted over to the spot where Mark Thompson had spray painted, "I love you, Johnny. I'm so sorry. CAT." She glanced back at Shelley and flipped the cap off the paint. Working over the *y*, Cary managed to turn *Johnny* into *Johnna*. She stood back and admired her work. Shelley walked up to her smiling and put an arm around her shoulder. Cary held the can over toward her. "What do you say?"

Shelley laughed and grabbed the can. "Hell yes."

The End

Acknowledgments

I tend to shy away from politics in my writing. I enjoy writing mystery and comedy and sometimes I mix the two together. This book deals with some social issues which were weighing heavily on my mind during the few months I frenziedly wrote it. I made every attempt to avoid being too "on the nose" about those issues. And for good reason. I have no place inserting myself into the dialogue. So this book is a crime novel. Plain and simple. My hope is that it's a fun read and a decent mystery, with a couple of twists and turns which were fun to take along with the characters. I am, however, a writer, which makes me an empathizer. So it was also that. It was an exercise in empathy. As those issues weighed heavily on me, I tried to listen to those who do have the right to insert themselves into the dialogue. And I tried my damnedest to empathize with the many victims for whom I felt such deep sorrow. When I write, I try to further empathize through creating characters I love. There are a lot of characters I love in this book.

With that said, I would like to thank my family—my parents and my sister—who taught me how to be an empathetic human. I would like to thank my daughters, who helped me care about the world around me. I would like to thank my Pandamoon family (especially my editors, Zara, Jessica, Forrest, and Rachel) and Matt Lyle, who have always pushed me to become a better writer. And I'd like to thank Sam. Not only did you tell me the story that this all grew from, but you're also just you. Thanks for that.

About the Author

Matt Coleman's first pieces of writing were about his great-grandmother's homemade beer and his own childhood trips into the backwoods of southern Arkansas to search for Bigfoot. Since then, both his writing and his life haven't strayed too far from his Arkansan roots. He lives in Texarkana, Arkansas, where he is a single father to two daughters.

Matt graduated from Texas A&M University-Texarkana with an M.A. in English. While finishing his degree, he worked with the East Texas Writing Project. After college, he spent five years teaching seventh grade English in a rural East Texas town. He then returned to Texarkana to teach for another four years at the high school where he graduated, while also teaching night classes in writing and literature at a local college. His career in education has also included work in adult learning with teachers of all levels. This work in adult learning has led to an expertise in teacher training and leadership development. For the past several years, he has served as a director of school improvement, dealing primarily with teacher development, strategic planning, and leadership.

As a writer, Matt has long been inspired by crime writers such as Dashiell Hammett and Walter Mosley and southern writers like Flannery O'Connor. Matt's second novel, *Graffiti Creek*, is a crime thriller following Cary Trubody through a nightmare of mistaken identity and police corruption. His debut novel, *Juggling Kittens*, drew from his experiences as a first-year teacher through the fictionalized account of Ellis Mazer and his search for a missing student through the wastelands of a small Arkansas town. He also spent three years as a writer for the comedy podcast, *The City Life Supplement*, and was able to return to his love of comedy writing by co-writing (with Matt Lyle) the upcoming play *Raptured: A Sex Farce at the End of the World* (coming Spring 2019 from Theater Three in Dallas).

Thank you for purchasing this copy of **Graffiti Creek** by Matt Coleman. If you enjoyed this book, please let Matt know by posting a review.

Read More Books from Pandamoon Publishing

Visit www.pandamoonpublishing.com to learn more about other works by our talented authors.

Mystery/Thriller/Suspense

- *122 Rules* by Deek Rhew
- *A Flash of Red* by Sarah K. Stephens
- *Fate's Past* by Jason Huebinger
- *Graffiti Creek* by Matt Coleman
- *Juggling Kittens* by Matt Coleman
- *Killer Secrets* by Sherrie Orvik
- *Knights of the Shield* by Jeff Messick
- *Kricket* by Penni Jones
- *Looking into the Sun* by Todd Tavolazzi
- *On the Bricks Series Book 1: On the Bricks* by Penni Jones
- *Rogue Saga Series Book 1: Rogue Alliance* by Michelle Bellon
- *Southbound* by Jason Beem
- *The Juliet* by Laura Ellen Scott
- *The Last Detective* by Brian Cohn
- *The Moses Winter Mysteries Book 1: Made Safe* by Francis Sparks
- *The New Royal Mysteries Book 1: The Mean Bone in Her Body* by Laura Ellen Scott
- *The New Royal Mysteries Book 2: Crybaby Lane* by Laura Ellen Scott
- *The Ramadan Drummer* by Randolph Splitter
- *The Teratologist* by Ward Parker
- *The Unraveling of Brendan Meeks* by Brian Cohn
- *The Zeke Adams Series Book 1: Pariah* by Ward Parker
- *This Darkness Got to Give* by Dave Housley

Science Fiction/Fantasy

- *Becoming Thuperman* by Elgon Williams
- *Chimera Catalyst* by Susan Kuchinskas
- *Dybbuk Scrolls Trilogy Book 1: The Song of Hadariah* by Alisse Lee Goldenberg
- *Dybbuk Scrolls Trilogy Book 2: The Song of Vengeance* by Alisse Lee Goldenberg
- *Dybbuk Scrolls Trilogy Book 3: The Song of War* by Alisse Lee Goldenberg
- *Everly Series Book 1: Everly* by Meg Bonney
- *.EXE Chronicles Book 1: Hello World* by Alexandra Tauber and Tiffany Rose
- *Fried Windows (In a Light White Sauce)* by Elgon Williams
- *Revengers Series Book 1: Revengers* by David Valdes Greenwood
- *The Bath Salts Journals: Volume One* by Alisse Lee Goldenberg and An Tran
- *The Children of Colondona Book 1: The Wizard's Apprentice* by Alisse Lee Goldenberg
- *The Children of Colondona Book 2: The Island of Mystics* by Alisse Lee Goldenberg
- *The Crimson Chronicles Book 1: Crimson Forest* by Christine Gabriel
- *The Crimson Chronicles Book 2: Crimson Moon* by Christine Gabriel
- *The Phaethon Series Book 1: Phaethon* by Rachel Sharp
- *The Sitnalta Series Book 1: Sitnalta* by Alisse Lee Goldenberg
- *The Sitnalta Series Book 2: The Kingdom Thief* by Alisse Lee Goldenberg
- *The Sitnalta Series Book 3: The City of Arches* by Alisse Lee Goldenberg
- *The Sitnalta Series Book 4: The Hedgewitch's Charm* by Alisse Lee Goldenberg
- *The Sitnalta Series Book 5: The False Princess* by Alisse Lee Goldenberg
- *The Wolfcat Chronicles Book 1: Wolfcat 1* by Elgon Williams

Women's Fiction

- *Beautiful Secret* by Dana Faletti
- *The Long Way Home* by Regina West
- *The Mason Siblings Series Book 1: Love's Misadventure* by Cheri Champagne
- *The Mason Siblings Series Book 2: The Trouble with Love* by Cheri Champagne
- *The Mason Siblings Series Book 3: Love and Deceit* by Cheri Champagne
- *The Mason Siblings Series Book 4: Final Battle for Love* by Cheri Champagne
- *The Seductive Spies Series Book 1: The Thespian Spy* by Cheri Champagne
- *The Shape of the Atmosphere* by Jessica Dainty
- *The To-Hell-And-Back Club Book 1: The To-Hell-And-Back Club* by Jill Hannah Anderson
- *The To-Hell-And-Back Club Book 2: Crazy Little Town Called Love* by Jill Hannah Anderson

Made in the USA
Columbia, SC
13 August 2018